OFFICERS AND GENTLEMEN

For duty, for honour, for love

Bound by honour and family ties, three brave men fought for their lives in France…

Now, back in the drawing rooms of England, they face a new battle as three beautiful women lay siege to their scarred hearts!

COURTED BY THE CAPTAIN

PROTECTED BY THE MAJOR

DRAWN TO LORD RAVENSCAR

AUTHOR NOTE

This is the first of a new Regency trilogy: *Officers and Gentlemen*. The story of Jenny and Adam is charged with drama when Adam's cousin is murdered and the cousins, who have formed a lasting friendship, set out to discover the culprit. Adam also has the added problem of trying to rescue his grandfather's debt-laden estates without marrying an heiress. Jenny seems a brave and beautiful young woman, for whom he immediately feels a deep attraction, but if he is to rescue his grandfather it seems he needs a rich bride. Jenny is nursing a secret of her own, which she dares not reveal... though perhaps it might solve Adam's problem.

I hope my readers will enjoy this Regency love story, which has a good sprinkling of intrigue and adventure, and will look forward to the stories of Hallam and Paul Ravenscar. I always like to hear what my readers think—you can e-mail me through my website: www.lindasole.co.uk

COURTED BY THE CAPTAIN

Anne Herries

LARGE PRINT

MILLS
BOON®

First published in Great Britain 2013
by Mills & Boon, an imprint of Harlequin (UK) Limited,
Large Print edition 2014
Harlequin (UK) Limited, Eton House, 18-24 Paradise Road,
Richmond, Surrey TW9 1SR

ISBN: 978 0 263 23960 7

Harlequin (UK) Limited's policy is to use papers that are natural, renewable and recyclable products and made from wood grown in sustainable forests. The logging and manufacturing processes conform to the legal environmental regulations of the country of origin.

Printed and bound in Great Britain
by CPI Antony Rowe, Chippenham, Wiltshire

Anne Herries lives in Cambridgeshire, where she is fond of watching wildlife and spoils the birds and squirrels that are frequent visitors to her garden. Anne loves to write about the beauty of nature, and sometimes puts a little into her books, although they are mostly about love and romance. She writes for her own enjoyment, and to give pleasure to her readers. Anne is a winner of the Romantic Novelists' Association Romance Prize. She invites readers to contact her on her website: www.lindasole.co.uk

Prologue

'**B**y God, we did it!' The four cousins looked at each other in triumph. The news had just arrived that Napoleon was in retreat. After days of bitter fighting, when it had seemed that Wellington's troops must suffer defeat, even a rout, their astute general had turned the tide. 'We've suffered terrible losses, but we've done it.'

Each of the four men had been wounded. Mark Ravenscar, the eldest, had but a scratch on his cheek and some slight damage to his sword-hand. Since he was generally considered to be a lucky so-and-so, handsome, rich and favoured by the gods, that was, in the opinion of his friends, hardly to be wondered at. His younger brother Paul had wounds to his head, right arm and left thigh, but was still amongst the walking wounded. Hallam Ravenscar, their eldest cousin, also had a head wound and another to his left arm, and Adam Miller, their cousin through the female line, was severely wounded in his right shoulder. However, they had all been patched up by the surgeon and none of them were considered in danger of their lives. Indeed, their wounds had merely made them first in line for transport home to England.

'Boney is done for,' Hallam said. 'Old Hookey won't let him off so easily this time. He escaped from Elba to cause chaos once more, but he wasn't the same man. Even so, he can't be allowed to run riot again. They will have to make sure he's confined securely.'

'Well, we've survived and that's what matters,' Mark said and smiled at his cousins. 'At last I can marry Lucy.'

'You lucky dog.' Adam grinned as he clapped him on the shoulder. 'Lucy Dawlish is the most beautiful girl I've ever seen. You have it all, my friend—a wonderful life waiting for you in England.'

Mark's eyes reflected concern as he nodded. 'Almost too perfect,' he said. 'You'll come about, Adam. Your grandfather has the title of earl and a large estate…'

'Most of which is mortgaged,' Adam said

gloomily. 'The earl feels it to be my duty to marry an heiress. This little sortie was my escape from being thrust into a marriage I could not stomach.'

'He can't force you to marry to save his skin,' Hallam said. 'You have your father's small estate––don't let the earl bring pressure to bear.'

'He says it's my duty to the Benedict name.' Adam sighed. 'The trouble is, I know he's right. I ought to do my duty by the family—but I'm not ready to marry just yet.'

'Stick to your guns,' Mark told him. 'You were not the one who wasted the Benedict fortune. Your grandfather gambled recklessly. He should have known better at his age.'

'He claims he was cheated,' Adam said. 'If he would give me the name of the rogue who fleeced him, I would call the devil out.'

'That's why the earl won't tell you,' Paul added. 'He would rather have his only grandson alive than recover his losses. I dare say you'll find a way to pull through. Besides, you may find an heiress you like.' He smiled fondly at Adam. 'We'll all look round and find you one—a girl who is neither ugly nor stupid, but as rich as Croseus.'

'An impossible task,' Adam said, laughing. 'I am lucky to have such good friends. I trust you will remain my friends if I'm reduced to marrying the daughter of a wealthy Cit?'

'Through thick and thin,' Hallam said. 'We'll all stand by each other. We came through this war by watching each other's backs—we shall remain friends for life.'

'Hear, hear,' the others echoed.

'If any one of us is in trouble, the others will back him up.'

'In life and in death.'

Each of the men repeated the solemn promise they had made a few days previously when they'd been facing death together. Now they had only to face the future, and for four gentlemen of varying degrees of fortune, the future looked far brighter than it had only days ago.

'In life and death…'

They clasped hands, one upon the other, and grinned at each other. Adam's troubles were nothing that good fortune and a determined mind could not overcome.

Chapter One

Miss Jenny Hastings glanced round the crowded ballroom and knew she had to make an instant escape. If the marquis saw her he would find a way to corner her, and she was determined he should not catch her in his trap. If there was one man she truly could not bear, it was Fontleroy. The way his eyes followed her was enough to send cold shivers down her spine. His was a calculating gaze, as if he thought her vulnerable and at his mercy—which, since the death of her beloved father, she was in danger of becoming.

'Oh, Papa,' she murmured beneath her breath. 'Why did you have to leave me alone so soon?'

She was not of course entirely alone, but her Aunt Martha and Uncle Rex were all but useless at protecting her. Her aunt believed anyone above the rank of lord must be conveying a favour on her niece by seeking her hand, and her uncle spent most of his life shut up in his library, unwilling to bother his head about his pretty niece.

In a hurry to quit the ballroom, Jenny almost bumped into one of the most beautiful girls she'd ever seen. She smiled and apologised, instantly recognising Miss Lucy Dawlish.

'Forgive me,' she said. 'I wanted to avoid someone—did I tread on your foot?'

'No, not at all,' Lucy said and smiled. 'Jenny— it is you. I thought I caught a glimpse of you earlier, but it is such a crush, isn't it?'

'Awful,' Jenny agreed. 'Which means the evening is a huge success. I came with my aunt and her friend Mrs Broxbourne. They have been talking all night and I was dancing quite happily until *he* turned up.'

Jenny moved her head to indicate the man watching them from the far side of the room. Lucy frowned and looked at her curiously.

'I do not think I've met the gentleman. He is not unattractive.'

'His soul is as black as pitch,' Jenny said. 'I can't prove it, but I think he had something to do with Papa's accident. He lost a considerable sum to the marquis that night…'

'Oh, Jenny—are you in trouble?'

Jenny considered, then inclined her head, her cheeks a little warm. 'Papa lost a great deal of money, Lucy—and my aunt seems to imagine I should be glad of the marquis's interest. But I would rather die than be forced to marry such a man.'

'Then you shall not,' Lucy replied instantly. 'Although only my close friends know it, my engagement is to be announced quite soon and we shall be going home to the country to prepare. Do say you will come and stay, Jenny. Mama was only saying yesterday that she did not know how she would part with me when I marry. I shall not be far away, but she would be delighted to have you as her companion. She has always thought you a sensible girl with beautiful manners and I know you would be doing her a kindness if you would make your home at Dawlish Court.'

'How kind you are,' Jenny said, looking doubtful. 'Are you certain your mama would welcome a long-staying guest?'

'She would love it of all things. I am her only daughter and neither of my brothers has yet obliged her by marrying. They spend all their time in London or Newmarket. Mama would adore to have you—if you can persuade your aunt to allow it.'

'Oh, I think I might.' Jenny breathed a sigh of relief as the marquis walked away, heading, she imagined, for the card room.

'Then it's all arranged. We shall take you up next week when we leave town. You must bring plenty of clothes for you will need them.'

'Thank you.' Jenny smiled at her. 'I think that gentleman is coming to ask you to dance. I shall go and speak to my aunt at once.'

Leaving Lucy to dance with the extremely handsome man who had come to claim her, Jenny began to make her way through the crowded ball-room. It was difficult to reach the other side of the room, where the dowagers sat, and she was forced to wait until the press of people allowed her to move on.

'Where is this paragon you promised me?' A man's voice charged with amusement claimed her attention. 'An heiress, pretty if not beautiful, not stupid and available. Now did you or did you not promise me such a rare item?'

'It is not as easy as that,' a second young man answered in kind.

'You are too particular, Adam. We have already

shown you two perfectly suitable young ladies and neither was to your taste.'

'One of them giggled at everything I said and the other one had bad breath,' the first gentleman said. 'God save me from simpering heiresses. I've had them paraded in front of me ever since I rose from my convalescence bed and I despair of ever finding one I should wish to marry.'

The second gentleman laughed. 'If the young lady has a fortune, you immediately find some fault in her. I think the woman you would marry has yet to be born.'

Adam laughed and shook his head. 'I dare say you are right. I am a sight too particular—but the whole notion of it fills me with disgust. Why should I marry simply for the sake of a fortune?'

Jenny glanced over her shoulder at the young men who were so deep in their amusing conversation that they were completely unaware she'd heard every word. The coxcomb! The young man who was so hard to please was indeed handsome, but not above ordinary height. His hair was dark, almost black, and his eyes bright blue. He must have a high opinion of himself if none of the young ladies here this evening could please him. Jenny knew of six young women present that evening who were considerable heiresses and each of them had something to recommend them.

Miss Maddingly was blonde and extremely pretty in a delicate way. Miss Rowbottom was as dark as her friend was fair with rather striking eyebrows. Miss Saunders was a redhead and much admired. Miss Headingly-Jones was another blonde, with large blue eyes; Miss Hatton was not as beautiful as the others, but still attractive, and Miss Pearce was unfortunately a little squint-eyed, but her twenty thousand pounds should make her acceptable to most. What did the particular young man want in his future wife? Was he above being pleased?

His eyes seemed to rest on her for a moment and then passed on. Jenny frowned and moved further into the crush.

It was several minutes before she reached her aunt, who looked up and smiled vaguely at her.

'Fontleroy was looking for you earlier, my love. I think he meant to ask you to dance, but could not get near you for the crush.'

'It is exceedingly warm in here this evening, Aunt,' Jenny said. 'I met Lucy Dawlish. They go home next week and I have been invited to stay for some weeks—until after her wedding.'

'Indeed?' Mrs Martha Hastings frowned for a moment. 'I was not aware her engagement had been announced. Well, I dare say it will be good company for you, Jenny. Lady Dawlish entertains only the best people and you must be flattered to be asked. I dare say you may meet a suitable gentleman in her company—and the marquis may post down to visit you if he chooses.'

'Lucy's engagement is not yet announced, but her friends know she is to marry Mark Ravenscar. I've met him only once, but he seems pleasant.'

'If you would but consider Fontleroy, you might be engaged yourself.'

Jenny sighed. She had tried on several occasions to make her aunt understand that she would never consider marriage to Fontleroy. Had she not a penny to her name she would prefer to work for her living as a governess or a companion. Being a paid companion could not be worse than living with Mrs Hastings.

'I have a little headache, Aunt. Do you think we could leave soon?'

'Well, it is very warm this evening,' her aunt

agreed. 'Go and put on your pelisse, my love. We shall leave as soon as the carriage may be sent for.'

Jenny did not need to be told twice. She decided that it was easier to quit the room by keeping to the perimeter rather than trying to cross it. As she reached the door that led to the hall, which led up to the room provided for ladies to change, she caught sight of the gentlemen who had been discussing the heiresses earlier. One of them was dancing with a very pretty young woman, but the other—the particular gentleman—was standing frowning at the company as if nothing and no one pleased him. What a disagreeable young man he must be.

For a moment their eyes met across the room and his narrowed. Seeing a flicker of something in those relentless eyes, Jenny put her head in the air and turned her back. She had no wish to be the object of his interest even for a moment!

Adam's eyes moved about the room, picking out the various young ladies who had been recommended to him. They were all very well in their way—to dance with any one of them would be a pleasure—but the very idea of having to court a young lady for her fortune made his stomach turn. It was quite unfair of the earl to expect it of him. That it was expected had become ever more plain since Adam's return from the war.

'So you managed to escape death or crippling injury this time, Adam,' the earl had said in a voice of displeasure. 'Do I need to remind you of what might have happened had you been killed? It is time you set up your nursery, my boy. Unless you give me heirs the title will pass into oblivion—and that prospect causes me pain. We have been earls since the time of the Conqueror. To lose the title or the estate would be equally painful to me. Do you mean to oblige me by marrying an heiress or not?'

'I do not wish to disoblige you, Grandfather,' Adam said, 'yet I would crave your indulgence a little longer. I would at least marry a young woman I can admire if nothing more.'

'Well, well,' the earl said tolerantly. 'There is time enough yet, but I do not have many years left to me. I should like to know the estate and the succession were safe.'

Adam had left his grandfather's estate and journeyed to London. It was his first appearance in the drawing rooms of society for a while. He had been away for some years, like many young men now returned from the wars. Adam knew that several of his friends were seeking young women of fortune. His was not the only estate to be encumbered with mortgages and in danger of sinking into extinction.

Had he seen a young lady who caught his attention he would have done his best to court her, even though the whole idea filled him with repugnance. To be seeking a wife for her fortune was not what Adam would have wished for given his choice. Indeed, he had not yet made up his mind to it. He had been invited to stay at Ravenscar for Mark's wedding and would do so, but before that he hoped to have some sport. There was an important meeting at Newmarket the following week and it was Adam's intention to attend.

A wry smile touched his mouth. If he could but place a lucky bet and win the stake he needed to improve his grandfather's fortunes, it would save the need for a distasteful decision. He was about to leave the ballroom when he saw a young woman regarding him from the far end of the room. Her expression was one of extreme disapproval. For a moment he wondered what he could have done to upset her—to his certain knowledge he had never met the young lady.

He had time to notice that she had particularly fine eyes and a soft mouth before she turned away and left the room. She was not one of the notable heiresses pointed out to him that evening by his obliging friends. By the plain look of her attire and her lack of ostentatious jewellery, he doubted that she was one of those rare females. However, her reddish-brown hair and delicate complexion was out of the ordinary. She certainly had the beauty he'd jokingly demanded that his heiress ought to have and there had been intelligence in those eyes—but she probably did not have a fortune.

So much the better, if Adam had his way, but he had promised his grandfather that he would at least attempt to attach an heiress. Glancing at the least displeasing of the young ladies he knew to be on the catch for a title, Adam breathed deeply and began to swathe a path through the crush of people.

The least he could do was to ask Miss Maddingly to dance…

'You cannot leave before Lady Braxton's dance,' Mrs Hastings said firmly. 'Your friends can certainly spare you a few days longer. You will oblige

me in this, Jenny. Your uncle will send you down
to Dawlish in his own carriage at the end of the
week.'

'But, Aunt, if I leave tomorrow I may travel with
Lucy and save my uncle the expense.'

'You speak as if your uncle would grudge the
expense,' her aunt said and shook her head. 'I
know you cannot be so very ungrateful as to refuse me this request, Jenny. Neither your uncle
or I have asked anything of you before this—and
I really think you must attend the dance, for my
word was given.'

Jenny gave up the argument. She knew Aunt
Martha would end in a fit of vexation if she refused to accept her wish upon the matter. Much
as she would have liked to travel with her friend,
she could not insist on it—though her uncle's lum-
bering travelling coach was not at all comfortable. It would have been far better to travel post,
but the cost was exorbitant and her uncle would
never approve when he had what he considered a
perfectly good coach.

Mr Keith Hastings's own coach had been sold
along with many of his personal possessions.
Jenny had tried to protest that such stringent
economy was unnecessary. Papa might have lost

money, but there was surely still more than sufficient for Jenny's needs? However, Uncle Rex liked
to practise economy and could not be brought to
accept that there was no need to pinch pennies.
It was a matter over which Jenny's father had always been at odds with his brother.

'Your uncle is a good man, Jenny love,' he'd
once told her. 'But he is a regular nip-farthing
and will not spend a penny if a ha'penny will do.'

Jenny had laughed. Papa had perhaps been
a little over-generous with his money and that
might be why her uncle was determined to make
economies. She was not perfectly certain of how
Papa had left things, for she'd been content to
leave business to her uncle—though it was perhaps time that she had a word with Mr Nodgrass.
Papa's lawyer could tell her where she stood fi-
nancially and what had happened to Mama's jewels. Had they been sold to pay debts? Her uncle
had mumbled on about something of the kind,
leaving Jenny with the idea that she had very little to call her own—which made her all the more
indebted to her uncle for taking her in.

However, she had only a string of seed pearls
of her own and if any of Mama's jewels remained
she was determined to lay claim to them. Jenny

was almost nineteen and Papa had been dead for a year. It was certainly time that she discovered exactly where she stood.

Her mind made up, she decided to call at her lawyer's office the very next day.

'Come in, come in, Miss Hastings,' Mr Nodgrass greeted her kindly, but with some surprise the next morning. 'There was no need to put yourself to so much trouble, for had you asked I should have been pleased to call on you at your uncle's house.'

'I hoped to see you alone, sir,' Jenny said as she was ushered into his private office. 'My uncle was unclear about the state of Papa's affairs. I wished to know if any of Mama's jewels were still available to me?'

His thick eyebrows climbed. 'Certainly Mrs Hastings's jewellery is available. It sits in my vault awaiting your instructions, Miss Jenny—if I may call you that?'

'Yes, sir, of course. I had no idea the jewellery was here. Why have I not been informed?'

'Your aunt considered that you were too young to wear any of the more expensive pieces and your uncle thought them safer in my vault. However, I know there are several small pieces suitable for a young lady and I wondered why you did not avail yourself of them.'

'I should certainly like to do so. I am going to stay with friends soon and would like something pretty to wear at a wedding. If I might see what there is, sir?'

'Of course.' Mr Nodgrass pulled a bell-rope and gave the instructions to an underling. 'You may take everything with you—or as much as you consider suitable to your present way of life.'

'Thank you, sir. Perhaps while I am here you would acquaint me with my circumstances. I know that Papa lost a considerable sum of money at the tables just before he died in that driving accident—but do I have any money of my own?'

Jenny was thoughtful as she left the lawyer's office an hour later. In her reticule there were six items of pretty but not particularly valuable jewellery—things that her aunt might easily have secured for her use before this had she been bothered. Distressed by her beloved father's death, Jenny had not thought about the jewels or her situation for some time. Mr Nodgrass had not been able to give her full details, for the accounts had been placed in a safe and the clerk had mislaid the keys. However, he had told her that her situation was far from desperate, and he could make her a small quarterly allowance if she wished for it, though much of her inheritance was invested either in property or shares.

'I cannot tell you the exact amount of your inheritance until I find those accounts,' he told her regretfully. 'However, I think you need not worry too much, my dear. I will send a copy to you once they have been transcribed and you may peruse them at your will and let me know if you wish to make changes to your portfolio.'

Mr Nodgrass was as honest and well meaning as any man she'd met—it was the behaviour of her uncle and aunt that shocked her. Why had they not considered it necessary to tell Jenny her true position in life—and why were they trying to push her into marriage with a man she disliked?

Lost in her thoughts, Jenny was not aware that the object of her thoughts was making his way towards her until he waylaid her path.

'What a pleasant surprise, Miss Hastings,' the marquis said. 'I was hoping we might meet tomorrow evening, but this is both unexpected and delightful.'

'I beg you will excuse me, sir,' Jenny said and looked at her maid. 'Come along, Meg. We must be getting home.'

'Allow me to take you both up in my carriage…'

'I thank you, no, sir,' Jenny said. 'I see some friends I have arranged to meet—excuse me. I must join them…'

Ignoring his look of displeasure, she walked past and hurried up to Mrs Broxbourne, whom she'd just noticed emerging from a milliner's shop further up the road.

'Jenny, my love,' the woman said. 'Have you been shopping?'

'I had a little business, but it is done. Do you go home now, ma'am? Could I prevail on you to take me up as far as my uncle's house?'

'Certainly, my love.' The lady's gaze travelled as far as the marquis and her brow crinkled. 'Yes, I see. I have told Martha I do not approve of that creature. I have no idea why she imagines the match would be a good one for you, Jenny.'

'It will never happen, ma'am. I dislike that gentleman excessively.'

'Well, I suppose your aunt hopes for a good marriage for you—and there is a title and some fortune.'

'But no liking on my part. I am very grateful to you for taking me up in your carriage, ma'am. I should otherwise have had to summon a cab.'

'Your uncle should make his chaise available to you in town. You may always call on me should you wish. I should be happy to make mine available when it is not in use.'

'I thank you for your good offices,' Jenny said and smiled inwardly. 'However, it will not be necessary since I am to leave town very shortly and I do not intend to return for some months. Lady Dawlish has asked me to live with them for a time and I shall certainly take advantage of her kindness.'

'Lady Dawlish is everything she ought to be,' Mrs Broxbourne said. 'I shall be glad to think of you with kind friends, Jenny. I am not completely sure how you are situated, but if you should ever need a friend you may apply to me.'

'How good of you, ma'am,' Jenny said. 'Should I be in need I shall not forget your offer—but I believe I am perfectly situated for the moment.'

She was smiling as she slid into the comfortable carriage, hugging her secret to herself. She had no intention of challenging her uncle or aunt or of demanding an explanation of their conduct.

It was enough to know that she was independent of their charity and could make her own way in the world. For although she had no idea how much had been left to her, she did know that she had some money and could probably afford to set up her own modest establishment if she chose.

Jenny wished that her uncle had not thought it wise to sell her old home without consulting her. She had accepted his decision, believing she had no choice, but this might not have been the case at all, she now realised.

She would not know the extent of her inheritance until the copy of Mr Nodgrass's accounts reached her, and by then she would be staying in the country with Lucy Dawlish.

Chapter Two

'Have you noticed that when Lady Luck decides to desert one she does so with a vengeance?' Adam asked and twirled his wine glass so that the rich ruby liquid swirled enticingly in the delicate bowl. 'That damned horse might have won for me. Had it done so I should have been beforehand with the world for a month. As it is I must go into the country.'

'My own pockets are sadly to let or I should offer to frank you.' Captain John Marshall joined him in the sad perusal of their joint fate, having both put down too much of their blunt on a sure thing. 'No, no, don't poker up, Adam. Only meant pay our shot at the inn. You'd do the same for me.'

'I can manage that,' Adam replied ruefully. 'Kept enough back for it, but I'd thought to return to London for a few weeks. However, my allowance for the month is shot and I refuse to borrow—so the country it must be.'

'I shall avail myself of my uncle's hospitality,' John said. 'He has been asking me to stay this age. Bores one to death with his stories, but he's got a good heart. He'll leave me a fortune one day, I dare say.'

'Had I such a relative I should be delighted to stay with him.' Adam laughed. 'The cure for my dilemma is in my own hands, but I can't seem to make up my mind to it.'

'Know where you're coming from.' His friend tapped the side of his nose. 'Heiresses are the very devil. If they're ugly, it makes one want to run a mile—and if they're beautiful, they look through one as if there was a bad smell under their pretty noses.'

Adam was forced into laughter. He sipped his wine, feeling the cloud of gloom lift slightly. The future looked exceedingly dark, but at the moment he was still free to enjoy his life as he would.

'I've been invited to Mark Ravenscar's wedding. I think I shall go down and stay. I've decided I shall give him one of my breeding mares as a gift. He has been after buying her for an age and I could hardly think of anything better—though

I must give Lucy something for herself. A piece of my late mother's jewellery, perhaps.'

'Ladies can never have too many trinkets.' John nodded wisely. 'I plan to send them a silver tea-and-coffee service myself—we have about twenty of them at home.'

'It's what all the uncles and aunts give,' Adam smiled in amusement. 'Which is why I settled on the mare.' He finished his wine and stood up. 'Think I'll go up. If I don't see you in the morning, you'll be at Mark's wedding?'

'Wouldn't miss it for the world. There wasn't one of us in the regiment that didn't envy him Lucy Dawlish—a regular golden goddess fit for one beloved of the gods.'

'Yes, Mark always has been a lucky devil,' Adam replied with an odd smile. 'Good night, old fellow.'

Leaving his friend to finish the bottle, Adam exited the private parlour and walked upstairs to his room. He lay down on the bed and closed his eyes, still fully clothed. Dashed tired and dispirited, but he'd enjoyed meeting an old comrade. Now that his wounds had healed, Adam was considering whether he might do better to return to an army life. He would be an officer on half-pay during peace time, however, which meant he would find it difficult to manage. Perhaps it would be better to try to set his own small estate in order. He was unlikely to inherit anything but an ancient pile of stones and huge debts from his grandfather—debts that he could never pay unless he married a considerable heiress.

Back to the same old problem, he closed his eyes and was soon snoring gently as his mind drifted away and in his dreams he saw a woman's look of disdain.

'Well, Jenny, I'm sure I do not know why you wish to leave us,' Mrs Hastings said as her niece came down dressed in a smart but plain green travelling gown. She sniffed her disapproval. 'I think we've done our best to make you comfortable.'

'Yes, Aunt Martha. You've both been kind—but I wished for a change. I am not certain what I would like to do with my life, but I intend to make up my own mind.'

'I still cannot see why you dislike the marquis so much. You would have a prestigious title and he would settle money on you…'

'I think I can manage for myself on what I have,

Aunt. Papa may have lost some money, but I am not a pauper. I am not reduced to earning my living as a governess.'

'No one would employ a girl as pretty as you for their governess.' Mrs Hastings sniffed again. 'Your uncle was only trying to protect you from the wrong kind of suitor.'

Jenny smiled and shook her head. 'I must not keep the coachman waiting,' she said. Although it would have been perfectly possible for her to travel by post-chaise, she had been unable to get out of using her uncle's antiquated carriage. He was annoyed with her for visiting the lawyer without reference to him and Jenny had had to endure a homily from him on the ingratitude of younger folk today.

'I did what I thought right in the circumstances, Jenny. Your father left me the task of guarding you and your funds until you are either one and twenty—or married. You had no need of a larger allowance whilst you lived under our roof.'

'You are one of the trustees,' Jenny gently reminded him. 'Mr Nodgrass is the other and he saw fit to give me the monthly sum I requested.'

'Yes, well, since you are removing yourself from my house I suppose you will need more. But you should learn economy, Jenny. Even had you a huge fortune, which to my mind, you have not, you may easily run through it if you spend too freely.'

Jenny had not answered. From what Mr Nodgrass had told her she had funds enough for her needs and she saw no point in the stringent economy her uncle thought right. However, her aunt and uncle had been kind enough in their way and she had no wish to quarrel with them.

A sigh of relief left her lips as she climbed into the carriage and the groom put up the steps. Her maid Megan was already sitting quietly in one corner, waiting for her. She smiled at her, feeling as if a heavy weight had been lifted. Her uncle and aunt were good people in their way, but they had made her feel beholden to them for all these months and there was no need for it, no need at all. Jenny could have remained in her father's house had her uncle not sold the property together with so many other things that Jenny would have preferred to keep. Thankfully, Mr Nodgrass had refused to give up her mother's jewels, keeping them safe for her in his strongroom.

Jenny had decided to leave the more valuable diamonds and rubies with him, because in that much her aunt was right. Such ostentation would

not become a girl of her age and should be kept
for marriage or some years in the future. Papa had
bought the finest he could for his beloved wife,
but Jenny loved best the trinkets she'd chosen for
her own use, which had also been her mother's
favourites and worn more often than either the
diamonds or the rubies.

'Are you looking forward to your visit, miss?'

Jenny glanced at her maid and a little gurgle of
laughter broke from her. 'So much! It should be
the greatest good fun—lots of dances, dinners
and picnics. We have the summer before us and
with the wedding next month everything will be
so exciting. You'll enjoy yourself in the country,
Meg. You can make friends and go out for walks
when I don't need you.'

'I was a country girl until your papa employed
me to look after you,' Meg replied. 'We make
our own fun in the country. I always loved the
haymaking as a girl—and gathering in the May
blossom.'

'Tell me about your childhood,' Jenny said.
'We've never talked like this before and I should
so much like to know all about your family and
what you did as a young girl...'

* * *

His thumping head had almost cleared now. The fresh air was doing him a power of good and he was glad he'd decided to drive himself down in his phaeton. Alas, his favourite high-perch phaeton with the bright yellow wheels and the matched blacks he'd prized so much had had to be sold to pay his immediate debts. He now had more than five hundred guineas in his account, which meant he could stop worrying—at least for the time being.

Adam's goal of having one of the best breeding stables in the country might have suffered a little from the loss of his blacks, but he still had the greys and the chestnuts, both teams excellent horseflesh. He'd always been a good judge of horses and gentlemen wishing to improve their stables often sought his advice. Had he wished he could have begun to put his land in order by selling more of his stable, but then his dream would vanish into thin air. However, the perch phaeton was a luxury and the more mundane vehicle he was driving now served him just as well.

It would be good to see his cousins again. Since they were forever pressing him to stay he would not feel that he was in any way impinging on their hospitality. Mark had spoken of wishing to buy some good bloodstock in order to set up his stables and, with the addition of the mare Adam had decided to give him as a wedding gift, it could easily be done. They might ride out to a few sales in the neighbourhood and discover whether there was anything worth purchasing.

Seeing the carriage blocking the road ahead, Adam brought his horses to a gentle halt and threw the reins to his tiger as he got down to investigate. It was obvious that the coach was old and something had broken—the leading pole by the looks of things. It had lurched sideways, only prevented from overturning by some skilled handling of the horses by the coachman. As Adam went to investigate, he saw two young women sitting on a blanket at the side of the road. One was obviously a maid, the other was a young lady of gentle birth dressed plainly in an elegant, but serviceable rather than fashionable, gown.

'I am sorry to find you in trouble, ladies,' he said and swept off his hat. 'Is there anything I may do to help you?'

'My uncle's groom has gone to fetch a blacksmith,' the young lady in green said. 'I think it will need several men to get this wretched coach off the road—and I am informed that the nearest inn is more than a mile away.'

'Yes, I believe there is an inn of sorts—but not at all suitable for ladies.' Adam hesitated, then, 'Where are you headed?'

'The Dawlish estate. I am going to stay with Lucy and her family.'

'Yes, I know the Dawlish family,' Adam said. 'I am going down to stay with Lucy's bridegroom's family—my cousins. The estates are not far apart. I could take you both up in my phaeton. However, your coachman must make arrangements to send on your baggage for I cannot accommodate it.'

'Most of my things were sent ahead by wagon,' Jenny said. 'Coachman shall do as you suggest—if I may bring my box with me?'

Adam saw the small trunk lying on the grass beside them and guessed it held her personal items and valuables.

'Yes, of course. Your companion may hold it on her lap.' He approached and offered his hand, 'Allow me, Miss…'

'Hastings—Jenny Hastings.' Adam noticed the faint blush in her cheeks and the way her hand trembled in his, as he helped her to rise. It was only as he was handing her into his phaeton that he realised she was the lady he'd noticed at the last ball he'd attended in London. She'd looked at him with decided disapproval that night, though as far as he knew they'd never met before today. 'I knew Lucy at school. My father is dead and they have kindly offered me a home.'

Her slight embarrassment and the plainness of her gown and pelisse made Adam think that she was reduced to accepting kindness from her friends. It would seem that her father's demise had left her in difficult circumstances and she was to be some kind of a companion, though treated as a friend rather than a paid servant. It was a situation that many young ladies of good birth found themselves in when a death in the family left them with too little fortune to manage for themselves.

She was wearing a pretty silver-and-enamelled brooch pinned to her pelisse. Of little value, it was exactly the kind of ornament a girl in her position would prize. He wondered that she had told him so much of her situation for she need not, and yet perhaps she felt her come down keenly and did not wish him to think her a privileged guest. He smiled at her kindly, because now he understood the expression she'd worn that evening in London. She had not been disapproving of him in particular, but was at odds with the world itself for leaving her in her present circumstances.

Adam could sympathise, for his own circumstances were not too far different. Miss Hastings would not have the avenue of marriage to a rich heiress open to her. Being a man, and heir to a title, he had a distinct advantage, as his problems might have been solved had he a little less pride. For a young woman like this there were few options open to her other than to seek paid employment or live as a dependent in the home of a friend—unless she was fortunate enough to be asked for in marriage. If she were prepared to accept an older man or a widower with a family, she might be fortunate enough to find a comfortable match—although was there any comfort to be had in a loveless marriage?

Having settled Miss Hastings in the carriage, he helped the young maid to sit behind and took up the reins from his tiger. By driving with great care, he managed to pass the stricken coach and mount the grass verge, negotiating a tricky passage with ease.

'You drive very well,' Miss Hastings observed and Adam smiled. He was considered a notable whip, but had no intention of puffing off his consequence. 'Papa was a whip—indeed, I shall never understand how he came to overset his chaise at such speed that he was thrown to the ground and killed.'

'Accidents will happen even to the best of us,' Adam said in a sympathetic tone. 'I am sorry for your loss, Miss Hastings.'

'It was almost a year ago now, which is why I've left off my blacks. My aunt was anxious for me to wear colours again—but I shall continue to wear grey and lilac for a little longer.'

'Your gown today is a very pretty green, however.'

'A present from my aunt. I felt obliged to wear it since she had gone to so much trouble to have it made up for me.'

'Ah, I see…' Adam concentrated on his driving. 'It will be late afternoon by the time we arrive at Ravenscar. If we dine there, I can send word to Lady Dawlish. She may have you fetched—or I can drive you there after we've eaten. To arrive after dark without explanation might cause some adverse comment…'

'You think Lady Dawlish might consider it improper in me to allow you to take us up?'

'I would not wish to have anyone form the wrong conclusion.'

'But surely…I have my maid…'

'Yes, but I…well, I have been known to support a pretty…mistress in the past and I would not wish anyone to receive the wrong impression.'

'Oh…' A sideways glance told him that her cheeks flamed. 'I had not thought…only how kind it was…' She floundered and Adam took pity on her.

'You are quite safe with me. I do not seduce innocent young ladies, even if I have the reputation of being a rake—which is not truly deserved, though I say it myself.'

'You are very thoughtful for my sake.'

'A young woman in your delicate position cannot be too careful.'

'In my…' She swallowed hard, a startled look in her eyes. She could not have realised how revealing her words had been and he was sorry to have embarrassed her. 'Yes, I see. You fear that it might cause Lady Dawlish to rescind her kind offer?'

'Great ladies can sometimes be a little severe in matters of propriety,' Adam said. 'Safer to reach my cousin's house and then send word that we took you in when your coach met with an accident.'

'Yes…thank you. You are very considerate.' Adam risked another glance at her. Her cheeks were rather pink and she seemed in some sort of difficulty. He was not sure whether her foremost emotion was embarrassment or…was that a gasp of despair or could it possibly be laughter?

'You may think me impertinent, perhaps? Yet I should not wish you to lose your home because of a misunderstanding.'

'No, certainly not, that would be unfortunate.' She had herself in hand now and smiled at him. 'I assure you I do not find you in the least impertinent, sir. Indeed, I am grateful for your care of my reputation.'

Adam made no immediate reply. She was obviously much affected by her change in situation. He could only suppose that she had been brought up to expect the best from life and her new circumstances were distressing her.

'I should never wish to be the cause of harm to a young lady, especially when you find yourself in difficulties,' he assured her and heard a little gasp from the maidservant. 'Now tell me, are you looking forward to Lucy's wedding?'

'Yes, very much indeed,' the reply came easily now. 'The summer holds many treats ahead, I think, for Lady Dawlish is a generous hostess and will not permit herself to show me any lessening of regard because of my reduced circumstances.'

She had brought herself to speak of it and Adam was respectfully silent. He knew how much it must have cost her to speak of such things and was determined to be as generous and kind as he could.

For the next half an hour he regaled her with stories of his and his cousins' exploits on the field of battle, describing the fierce fighting and their feelings of despair when at first forced to retreat. Also, the true comradeship and care for one another their experiences had forged.

'When Old Hookey gave the orders to advance I was never more delighted in my life. What might have been a rout ended in a brilliant victory—and it was due to his strategy and the bravery of men who would cheerfully have died for him.'

'I fear too many died,' Jenny said. 'I recall my uncle speaking of it—but he did not say much for he knew any talk of such things would distress me.'

'Yes, indeed, it is not the subject for a lady's parlour,' Adam admitted. 'I believe Wellington is now in Vienna. I fear he will find making the peace more difficult than he found the campaign. It is always so, for politics is a dirty business and men who would not know how to command a fly have a deal too much to say about how things shall be settled.'

'My uncle was of the opinion that Napoleon should be tried and executed, but I dare say that will not happen.'

'I think too many voices would be raised against it. He must certainly be contained for we cannot allow him to wreak further havoc in Europe—but he is a fine general and an execution might be a hard way to end such a life.'

'You sound as though you almost admire him?'

'Yes, in a way, I suppose I do. He was a worthy opponent. At one time the most brilliant general that ever lived, barring Wellington himself— though at the end he made mistakes he would not have made when he was younger. Like many others before him he grew too big for his boots. Power went to his head. Had he known when to stop, he might still have been emperor.'

'Yes, perhaps. I had heard some speak of him in

romantic terms, but thought them foolish girls—
but if you admire him, the case is proven.'

Adam chuckled for such forthright speech was
not often met with in a young lady and he found
her views refreshing. Glancing at her sideways,
he wondered what other pearls of wisdom might
drop from those sweet lips given the chance.

Jenny glanced round at her maid. 'Are you comfortable, Meg?'

'Oh, yes, miss. Much more comfortable now.'

'My uncle's coach rattled us almost to death,'
she said and laughed. 'Casting a wheel was better fortune than we knew.'

The sound of her laughter warmed Adam. He
was suddenly aware of her sitting close to him,
her femininity, and her subtle perfume that he
thought was her own rather than from a bottle.
She was quite lovely—though no cold beauty. He
thought of some of the proud London ladies he'd
seen dressed in their rich gowns. In her simple
travelling gown this young woman cast them all
into shade. He felt something stir in his loins—a
feeling he did not often associate with innocent
young ladies.

Adam's taste was normally for older women,
opera singers or dancers, or the occasional widow

who needed a friend's support to keep the wolf from the door after the death of her loved one. Over the years he'd taken his lovers lightly: a Spanish tavern wench, a French actress, several English ladies who had been married, some more than once. To feel the heat of desire curl through him because of a proper young lady sitting beside him was a new experience. Though it made him smile inwardly, he ruthlessly crushed all thought of what her lips might taste of or how the softness of her skin might feel pressed against his.

Miss Jenny Hastings was out of bounds. She had no fortune and neither did he so marriage was not a viable proposition had either of them had the inclination, which it was much too soon even to consider—and anything else was out of the question, even if this feeling happened to be more than fleeting lust. He could offer her friendship and he would—but his honour forbade him to take advantage of her vulnerability. No, he must conquer the sudden and ridiculous desire to stop the carriage and catch her up in his arms. It was quite ridiculous. They were complete strangers and knew nothing of one another. He really did not know what had got into him! And yet when he'd caught her eye in that London ballroom he'd felt drawn to her somehow.

'Are we very far now?' she asked after he had lapsed into silence for some twenty minutes or more.

'Are you hungry or tired?' he asked and glanced at his watch. 'I suppose we might have stopped, but I thought it unwise to eat at an inn. We should be at Ravenscar Court in a few minutes.'

'Oh, good,' Jenny said. 'My aunt's cook put up a hamper for us, but in the distress of the accident it went rolling into the ditch and was lost.'

'And you are hungry.' He heard a sound that could only be her stomach growling and became aware of his own hunger—not the sexual hunger he'd felt earlier, but a natural desire for food. 'I promise you it will not be long. My cousins will provide us with refreshments as soon as we arrive."

Adam pulled his chaise to a halt at the front of a large, imposing country residence some fifteen minutes later. His tiger jumped down and went to hold the horses' heads, while he helped first Miss Hastings and then her maid to alight.

'Well, here we are,' he said. 'I am expected so someone should be here at any—'

The sound of shots being fired startled him. He looked about him in search of their source, thinking that they must have come from somewhere at the rear. It was even as he was deciding what to do for the best that a man came from the front porch and stumbled towards him. Adam saw the blood and gave a cry of distress and shock, rushing towards his cousin. He was in time to catch Mark before he collapsed. Holding him in his arms, he knelt on the gravel, looking down at the face of the man he had always believed the most favoured of the gods and practically invincible.

'Mark, dear fellow,' he said, for he saw that the wound was fatal and his cousin had but a short time to live. 'What happened—who did this to you?'

'Father…Paul…tell Father to watch out for him…'

The words were so faint that Adam scarcely heard them. His head was in a whirl, his mind suspended in disbelief. How could this be happening? Mark had sailed through all the campaigns on the Peninsula and in France. How could he be lying in Adam's arms dying of a shotgun wound now when he was at his own home in peaceful Huntingdonshire?

'What is happening?' Paul's voice cried. He came running from the side of the house, a shotgun broken for safety and lying over his arm. As he approached, he dropped the gun and flung himself down by his brother's side. 'No—oh God, no,' he cried and tears started to his eyes. 'Did you see what happened? Who could have done this? I heard shots almost at the same moment as I shot a rat in the walled garden. Did anyone come this way?'

'No one but Mark,' Adam said. He stood up as servants started to converge on them from all sides. 'Some of you make a thorough search of the grounds. One of you must go for the doctor. I think it is hopeless, but the attempt must be made. If you see a stranger or intruder, apprehend them—I want justice for my cousin.'

Pandemonium broke loose. Men were shouting at each other, feet flying as they divided into groups to search for the murderer. Adam lifted Mark off the ground, carrying him into the house. Then, remembering his passengers, he turned to look at them. Both young women looked stunned.

'As you see, my cousin has been shot,' Adam

said. 'Forgive me. I had not expected to bring you to such a reception.'

'You must not think of us,' Jenny said and dabbed at her cheeks with a lace kerchief.

'Mrs Mountfitchet,' Adam addressed a woman dressed all in black, who hovered nearby. 'These young ladies were in distress for their carriage has broken down—send word to Lady Dawlish, for they are meant to be her guests, and please feed them. They are hungry.'

'Do not worry for them, sir,' the housekeeper said. 'Come along, my dears. I'll find you a comfortable parlour to sit in and you shall have some bread and butter, cold meats and pickles—and a pot of tea.'

'Thank you…so kind…' Jenny said, then, in a louder voice. 'Please, I would know how your cousin goes on, sir.'

Adam made no answer for he was hurrying away and up the stairs, the younger man hard on his heels.

'I can't believe it,' the housekeeper said. 'That such a thing should happen to the young master here in his own home. It's scandalous, that's what it is, and no mistake.'

'It was such a shock,' Jenny said and dabbed

at her eyes again. 'I am so very sorry. I wish we were not here to cause you more trouble.'

'Now don't you be worrying about that, miss. It has given me a proper shock, but as for looking after you, well, I'd rather have something to do. His lordship's man will do all that is needed upstairs. Are you related to Miss Dawlish, miss— the poor young lady? What she'll do now I dread to think.'

'It is terrible for both families. Everyone was so happy, looking forward to the wedding…' Jenny's throat caught. She had come down for Lucy's wedding and now her husband-to-be was dying. 'I cannot believe such a wicked thing could happen here.'

'There's a good many wicked things go on,' the housekeeper said in dire tones. 'But not at Ravenscar. What his lordship will say to it all I do not know…'

Chapter Three

'How can it have happened?' Lord Ravenscar asked, staring at Adam in disbelief. 'You say that you heard shots just as you arrived?'

'We had just got down from the phaeton,' Adam confirmed. 'I had brought a young lady I found in distress, her coach having broken down, and was about to take her into the house when it happened. The shots seemed to come from the back of the building'

'And my son?'

'Mark is dying, sir,' Adam replied. There was no way of softening the blow. 'He was conscious only for a moment or two after he fell into my arms. I carried him to his room and the doctor was summoned, but he thinks as I do that it is only a matter of time. The wound is fatal. I have seen such wounds before and Mark cannot survive more than an hour or so.'

'My God!' The elderly man covered his face with shaking hands. 'It beggars belief that he should come through so many battles with hardly a scratch only to die of gunshot wounds here in his own home.'

'Whoever shot him did so at close range. He would have had little chance to defend himself,' Adam said grimly. 'I am sorry, sir. I wish I could give you better news, but there is no point in giving you false hope.'

'Has the assassin been apprehended?'

'Not to my knowledge. I have scarcely left Mark's side until now. I hoped we might do something to save him, but all the doctor was able to do was to give him something that would ease his pain should he come to himself.'

'If only I had been here when it happened...'

'How could it have altered things?' Adam looked at him with compassion. 'Paul and I were here and there was nothing either of us could do.'

'Has Hallam been sent for? Those two have always been close—as you know, Adam.'

'Yes, sir. All of us loved Mark. He was like a golden god to the men he commanded. They would have followed him anywhere and he was universally loved by his fellow officers.'

'Someone did not love him,' Mark's father said, his features harsh with grief. 'I would have sworn he did not have an enemy in the world—but this was murder. Someone must have done this wicked thing deliberately—come here on purpose to kill Mark. Have you any idea of who might have done it?'

Adam shook his head. He could not forget his cousin's last words, but how could he raise doubts in the grieving father's mind? Mark might have been accusing his brother or he might have been warning them to watch out that the same fate did not happen to Paul. The fact that Paul had appeared carrying a shotgun that had been fired at about the time of the fatal shooting was damning—and yet it might be coincidental. Adam would not cast the first stone until he'd had time to investigate—even if it were the truth he would find it difficult to believe.

'I believe I shall sit with my son now,' Lord Ravenscar said, his face showing the extent of his shock and grief. 'If you will excuse me...'

'Of course.' Adam watched him walk up the stairs and then turned towards the sound of voices coming from the large front parlour. There was the sound of crying and a babble of voices. If he were not mistaken, Lucy Dawlish had arrived.

He hesitated outside the parlour and then walked in on a touching scene. Lucy was in floods of tears at the news, as one would expect. Miss Jenny Hastings had her arms about her and was attempting to comfort her—and both Paul and Hallam were watching with varying degrees of distress and horror.

'Oh, Adam,' Lucy cried as he entered the parlour. 'Tell me it isn't true, I beg you. Please tell me Mark will recover and this is all a bad dream.'

'I wish that I might do so,' Adam said. Lucy's grief was a piteous thing. He noticed that she threw a look almost of accusation at Paul, almost as if she blamed him for being hale when his brother lay dying. 'However, the doctor told me that it is a matter of hours. He does not expect that Mark will recover consciousness.'

'It cannot be.' Lucy fell into a renewed fit of wild sobbing. 'We were to be married…how can this have happened here? He promised he would come home safe from the war and we should marry. Now…' She shook her head and broke from Jenny's protective arms. 'May I see him? I must say goodbye to him…' She looked so fragile, so close to breaking that Adam was wrenched with pity for her.

'His father asked for a little time alone with his son—but I am sure he will send for you as soon as he has made his own farewells.'

'Adam…' Hallam drew him to one side away from the others. 'This is a bad business. Has the culprit been found?'

'No, I have not been told of anything. We set men to searching immediately, but I am sure the rogue would have fled as soon as he'd worked his wicked plan.'

'Does anyone have any idea who might have done this?'

'My uncle asked me the same question. I have no answers and to my knowledge Paul has no more idea than I. I would have sworn that Mark did not have an enemy in the world. You know how much his men adored him. Even in society he was admired and liked—no one seemed to grudge him his good fortune. We all felt that he deserved it. He was a hero, generous and loved. Why should anyone want him dead?'

Hallam's eyes flicked towards Paul for a moment, but then he gave a slight shake of his head, as though dismissing his thoughts.

'I have no idea—but I shall discover the name of this devil if it takes me the rest of my life. I shall see that he pays the price of his evil deed.'

Paul had moved closer, listening to their conversation. 'I intend to track the fellow down,' he said and glanced at Lucy. 'This has caused pain and grief to us all—and I shall never rest until the culprit is caught and brought to trial.' He frowned as his cousins remained silent. 'You can't think I…? I shot a rat and I heard shots from the back parlour almost at the same moment.'

'I think we should begin our investigation there,' Adam said. 'If the murder happened in the parlour, we should find evidence of it there.'

'Yes, I'll make a search at once,' Hallam said. 'Excuse me, I will leave you to comfort the ladies as best you can.'

Adam nodded, watching as his cousin walked away. He glanced at Paul. 'You have not remembered anything? You did not see anyone? Did Mark have an enemy that you know of?'

'I've already told you.' Paul glared at him. 'Just because I had a shotgun—for God's sake, Adam, you know I would have given my life for his.

He saved mine in France. I adored him. He was always my idol—the brother I admired and followed since I was in short breeches.'

Adam glanced towards Lucy, who had been approached by the housekeeper and was about to visit her dying fiancé.

'No, no, Adam, do not think it,' Paul said fiercely. 'Whatever my feelings may be in that direction, she was Mark's. I would not…you cannot imagine that I…' He gave a snort of disgust and walked swiftly from the room, leaving Adam alone with Jenny.

'I must apologise for bringing you here,' he said. 'I did not dream that we should find such a distressing situation.'

'You could not have known,' Jenny replied and dabbed at her cheeks. In trying to comfort Lucy, she had shed tears of her own. 'It was a terrible, terrible thing to happen. I am sorry to be causing you some bother. I should not be here.'

'I am glad you are,' Adam said. 'Lucy will have much to bear in the next few days and weeks. She will need a good friend. You came to share her happiness. Instead, you find yourself her comforter. It is not a pleasant situation but I believe you will rise to the occasion. Had you not been here I think she would have given way completely.'

'She would have been at home when she received the news and her mama would have comforted her,' Jenny said in a practical tone. 'She came to collect me, of course—but at least it may give her the comfort of seeing him still alive. I understand that tomorrow might have been too late?'

'I am certain it would. I do not imagine he will last the night. I do not know if that will comfort her at all—I can only pray it will once her first terrible grief has abated.'

'You must all be grieving,' Jenny said. 'You held him and he was conscious for a moment—did he say anything of importance?'

'A message for his father only. Had he given me a name I should have sought the villain out at once—'

A terrible cry from Lucy broke into their conversation. They looked at one another. Lucy's wild sobbing from upstairs must mean only one thing.

'Your cousin…should you go up to them?'

'Yes, please excuse me. Forgive me, this is a terrible experience for all of us.'

Jenny nodded. 'I beg you do not think of us—go to your family. If Lucy needs me, I shall be here in the parlour.'

Adam had already said his farewells to his cousin, but it was obvious that Lucy was in great distress, as was his uncle. He sent for the house-keeper, who tried to persuade Lucy to go to bed, but she could not be persuaded for more than half an hour, flinging herself on the bed and holding Mark's hand as if she would never let go. Eventually she was persuaded to leave her fiancé's body, led away by the housekeeper to a bedroom where she could weep in grief and given a hot tisane to calm her nerves.

Mark's father sat pale and still looking ill and Adam persuaded him, too, to seek his bed while the housekeeper did what was needful for his cousin. He looked down at Mark, a mixture of regret, pity and anger in his handsome face.

'Forgive me that I could do nothing,' he said with the ring of emotion in his voice. 'You saved my life, Cousin, but I could not save yours. One thing I promise you—I shall not rest until your murderer is brought to justice.

Leaving his cousin's room, he went downstairs

to the parlour. Jenny looked at him, grief and pity in her face.

'Lucy is distraught, of course, as your uncle and cousin—and you, of course—must be—' She broke off as Hallam returned to the front parlour.

'I have found our evidence,' Hallam said a look of grim determination of his face. 'Some shots broke a Chinese vase before entering the wall in the back parlour, the garden entrance to which is just beyond the entrance to the walled garden, where Paul was shooting a rat. The culprit could not have entered from the walled garden or left that way. Anyone making an escape from the Chinese parlour would have had to leave by running across the open courtyard that leads to the stables.'

'Then one of the grooms may have seen something,' Adam said. 'Shall I speak to them—or shall you?'

'I shall question them,' Hallam said and frowned. 'I must say I am relieved to find the evidence. There is only a locked gate from the walled garden to the courtyard and anyone there would not have seen the murderer escape that way. Anyone in the walled garden would have had to go through the house if he came from there…unless he had a key to the gate?'

'Paul came from the side of the house and must therefore have the key. If he were in the walled garden in the first place…'

'You doubt it?' Hallam's brows arched. 'I know your thoughts, Adam—but I cannot think…' He glanced at Jenny. 'We shall discuss this another time. Please excuse me.'

Adam glanced at Jenny again. 'I fear this is most uncomfortable for you, Miss Hastings. Did the housekeeper bring you some tea?'

'Thank you, she did. You must not be anxious for me, sir. I know you wish to be with your cousin. You have important business. I shall sit here quietly by myself while you do what you must. When Lucy is ready we shall return to her house.'

'You are a sensible young woman,' Adam said. 'I can only repeat that I am glad you were here for Lucy's sake—though I wish you had both been spared such a terrible tragedy.'

'We must all wish that, sir.'

He inclined his head to her and then hurriedly left the room in his cousin's wake. Jenny sat down again and let her eyes travel round the elegant parlour. It was a beautiful house and Mark would have inherited it in due course—and Lucy was to have been his wife.

Could his brother have killed him in the hope of stealing his birthright and his fiancée? His cousins had clearly considered it, to judge from their odd looks at him and each other. To Jenny's impartial eyes the answer seemed clear. Paul Ravenscar had been shocked and distressed to see his brother bleeding and wounded in Mr Miller's arms. Yet she sensed that both the cousins had half-suspected him, though reluctantly. Paul Ravenscar might covet his brother's future wife, but Jenny was as certain as she could be that he had not murdered Mark to gain his heart's desire and she felt sympathy for him. In the unfortunate circumstances there was bound to be some doubt, however.

As no one was likely to ask her for her opinion she could not give it. She was a bystander in all this and must make herself as unobtrusive as possible. Only when she was alone with Lucy and able to offer comfort might she speak her mind—should her friend wish to discuss the identity of the rogue who had killed the man she loved.

* * *

'Why do you suspect Paul?' Hallam demanded as the two men met on the way to the stables. 'I know he had a gun—but he is devoted to Mark. You know it as well as I that he would have done anything for him…'

'It was something Mark said as he fell into my arms—a warning that may be taken two ways.' Hallam frowned as Adam repeated Mark's cryptic words. 'He may have meant that his father should protect Paul—or something else.'

'Yes, I see. Now I understand why you have doubts, but I feel that Mark meant to warn you that his brother's life could also be in danger.'

'I shall interpret it that way for the moment, but I must keep an open mind. I care for them both and this is more painful than I can express.'

'As much for Paul as for us,' Hallam said. 'To be suspected of harming his brother is terrible, especially as he is torn apart by his grief.'

'Yes, I know. I could see it in his face, therefore I must accept that the warning was in order to protect Paul from this enemy—but who is the rogue and why would he wish Mark dead?'

'If we knew that we might have some hope of discovering his identity. One of the grooms recalls seeing a man run past the stables and disappear into the orchard, where he must have left his horse. His impression was that the man was in his thirties, dark-haired and a gentleman by his clothes—and that is all he can recall. He was grooming one of the mares and did not bother to look more closely.'

'That description might fit anyone,' Adam said and ran his frustrated fingers through his hair. 'What do we do next, Hal?'

'I imagine we must make a search of Mark's rooms. If there is a clue, it may tell us something.'

'Then we must wait until after the funeral,' Adam said. 'We cannot search his rooms while he lies there—or until he has been interred in the family crypt.'

'I see no help for it but to wait. I know you are impatient to begin your search, as I am—but it cannot be. We could make enquiries in the village as to whether a stranger has been seen. Someone may know more of this man Paul's groom saw.'

'It was Paul's groom that saw the stranger running away?'

'Yes, why?' Hallam frowned. 'No, no, that is too much, Adam. The man is as honest as the day and I would swear he had no thought of lying to protect Paul. You do him and Paul a disservice.'

'Yes, I am not being fair,' Adam admitted. 'I shall accept that the murderer was a gentleman of sorts and that he came here to murder Mark—what we need to discover is why.'

'I shall ride to the village to discover what I can.'

'I think I should escort Lucy and Jenny to Dawlish Hall. I should not care for them to go alone with a murderer on the loose for we do not know if my cousin was killed because of his coming nuptials.'

'By someone who wants Lucy for himself?' Hallam nodded. 'There are several men who might covet her for her beauty and her fortune. I believe her maternal grandfather left her more than twenty thousand pounds in trust, which may be broken on her marriage.'

'I suppose that would be as good a motive as any for some men,' Adam said and frowned. 'Yet I have a suspicion that the mystery may go much deeper.'

'Whatever, it will not do to have the ladies return to Dawlish alone. You must certainly escort them.'

* * *

'Lucy does not wish to leave this evening. I shall sit with her and together we shall keep a vigil,' Lord Ravenscar told Adam later that evening. 'I have instructed Mrs Mountfitchet to provide rooms for the young ladies so that Lucy may retire when she feels able. The ladies wish to be together and it is the least we can do. I have sent word to Lady Dawlish. I asked Miss Hastings if she would wish for an escort to the Dawlish house, for it must be awkward for her here, but she says she shall not desert Lucy.'

'I would not expect her to say anything else,' Adam said. 'You need not worry for her too much, sir. I shall take it upon myself to keep the young lady company. When the funeral is over I shall search his rooms for evidence—there may be something in his papers that will help us discover the truth of this terrible business.'

'Yes, well, I shall leave it all to you and Hallam,' Lord Ravenscar said. 'Paul is in dark despair at the moment, but I think he will wish to help as soon as he is able.'

'Yes, of course. We shall all do our utmost to bring this evil monster to justice, Uncle. I give you my word that if it is possible he will hang for his crimes.'

'I know I can rely on you all. Now, if you will excuse me, I think I shall sit with Mark again for a while. Lucy ought to rest, but she cannot be brought to leave his side. Perhaps it is the best way for her to grieve, poor lass, but I shall persuade her to her bed as soon as I can.'

'In the circumstances it is hardly to be expected that she would not be deeply affected. She would have been his wife next month.'

Lord Ravenscar passed a shaking hand over his brow and went away. Adam turned towards the parlour where he knew Miss Hastings to be sitting. Although it had been a warm day the evening had turned chilly and a fire had been lit in the parlour. Pausing on the threshold, Adam was struck by the quiet beauty of the young woman's face as she sat staring into the flames. A glass of wine and a plate of almond comfits had been placed on a small wine table beside her and she had a book in her hand, but it was clear she had been unable to concentrate. She looked up as he entered the room, inquiry in her steady grey eyes.

'Mr Miller—is there any news?'

'I fear not and it may be some time before we

can track him down, but I promised my cousin I would do it and I shall,' he told her. He went forwards to warm himself by the fire as she sat down again. 'You find us at a very sad time for all concerned, Miss Hastings.'

'Do please call me Jenny,' she said. 'We have gone beyond formality, I think. I feel a part of this family for I grieve sincerely for your loss.'

'How kind of you.' Adam inclined his head. 'How could it be different for at such times we are drawn together in grief. It is all the worse because we had such hopes for the future.'

'Lucy is distraught,' Jenny said. 'I do not know how she can bear it, to be so close to happiness and have it snatched away so cruelly. I am determined to be here when she needs me. I know her mother is close at hand and I dare say she may come—but sometimes it is easier to talk to one's friends, do you not think so?'

'Yes, I agree entirely. This terrible tragedy will not change your plans?'

'Oh, no. I shall stay for Lucy's sake—and in truth for my own. I should not wish to return to my uncle's house.'

'Was he unkind to you?'

'Not exactly—but he did not treat me just as he

ought and I prefer to live at Dawlish for the moment. The family will be in mourning and perhaps there are ways in which I can help.'

'Lucy will need a companion she can talk to. I dare say she may weep on your shoulder a deal of times.'

'Then we shall weep together for I find this very sad.'

'Indeed. I think my grief may ease a little in pursuit of my cousin's killer. I can do nothing for the moment, but I intend to search him out—whoever he may be.'

'Do you have a clue?'

'One of the grooms saw a man running away— a gentleman by his clothes, dark hair and perhaps thirty-something in years.'

'So many men fit that description. You will need more if you are to find him.'

'Yes, I fear that is the case. We shall not give up until we catch him. There are ways to draw the devil out, I dare say.'

'I wish you good fortune,' Jenny said, and then as they heard voices in the hall she stood up once more and turned towards the door. 'I believe that is Lady Dawlish…'

She was right for the lady in question surged

into the room and opened her arms to Jenny, who went into a perfumed and tearful embrace with every evidence of warmth and affection.

'Where is my poor darling girl?' the lady said, sniffing into a handkerchief heavily doused in lavender water. 'I do not know how she will bear this terrible blow.'

'She is sitting with Mark,' Jenny said. 'I fear she is suffering greatly, ma'am, but we shall help her to bear her grief.'

'He has gone then…' Shock was in the lady's face and she made the sign of the cross over her breast. 'How terrible for Lord Ravenscar—and my poor child. She was so happy…'

'Yes, I know. This has been a terrible blow—to lose the man she would have married, her child-hood hero…it is devastating.'

'You will not leave us,' Lady Dawlish said. 'My poor child will need you to support her in this her hour of need. I know it will be hard for you and not what was promised.'

'Do not fear, ma'am. I shall not desert her. Lucy is as dear to me as the sister I never had. You may rely on me to be there for her whenever she needs me.'

'I was certain I might.' Lady Dawlish blew her

nose. 'My sensibilities are almost overset. I do not know how I could have borne to see my child in such affliction, but you will be my strength, Jenny. You will help us to face what must be.'

Adam saw that Jenny was well able to cope with the lady's slightly histrionic behaviour and felt it a good thing that Lucy would not have to rely solely on her mama for support.

He rang the bell and asked for tea to give the distressed ladies some temporary relief and left them to comfort each other. Having remembered that Mark kept some of his belongings in the boot room, he decided to go through the pockets of his greatcoats. There might just be a letter or a note of some kind that would give him a starting point.

Watching Lady Dawlish's distress and seeing the reflection of it in Jenny's eyes had affected him deeply. Anger and grief mixed in him, sweeping through him in a great tide.

When he discovered who had murdered his cousin in cold blood he would thrash him to within an inch of his life.

Chapter Four

'Paul…' Adam cried as he saw his cousin in the boot room removing the muddy boots he'd worn for riding. 'Thank God you're back safe. I was beginning to think you might have come to harm. There is a murderer out there and he might not have finished with this family.'

Paul turned his head to look at him, a glare of resentment in his deep-blue eyes. 'You've changed your tune. Earlier today you thought I'd killed Mark. Do not deny it, for I saw it in your eyes.'

'You had the shotgun and…' Adam shook his head. 'I'm sorry if I doubted you. I know you loved him.'

'So you damned well should,' Paul muttered furiously. 'Yes, I love Lucy and if she'd ever looked at me I should have asked her to marry me—but it was always going to be Mark. I would never have harmed him. You must know it, Adam?'

'It was just something Mark said.'

'Explain,' Paul demanded and Adam told him word for word. He nodded. 'I see why you might have thought—but I swear it was not me.'

'Then you must be careful. I came here to go through the stuff Mark keeps here. I cannot search his rooms yet, but I need to be doing something. I want that devil caught, Paul. When I get him I'll teach him a lesson he'll not forget before I hand him over to the law.'

'He won't live long enough for the law to deal with him if I find him first,' Paul said and cursed. 'Mark didn't deserve this, Adam. It makes me so angry…and it hurts like hell.'

'Yes, it must. I know. We shall all miss him like the devil.'

'It's as if a light has gone out,' Paul said and dashed a hand across his cheek.

'We'll find him,' Adam promised. 'We shall search until we find him whoever he is. He will not escape justice.'

'I shall not rest until he is found.'

'Nor I.' Adam had begun to go through the pockets of Mark's coats. He found an assortment of string, bits of wood and a receipt for two hundred guineas for a new chaise. 'There is nothing here—unless he fell out with someone over this?'

'The chaise he bought from Parker? No, nothing wrong there—they were both quite happy with the deal.'

'Well, we must wait until after the funeral...'

'Don't!' Paul said and struck the wall with his fist. 'I can't bear to think of him lying dead in his room.'

'There is nothing you can do for him except help to find his killer.' Adam placed a hand on his shoulder, but Paul shrugged it off and strode from the room, leaving him alone. He swore beneath his breath. 'Damn it...damn it all to hell...'

'Miss...Jenny,' Adam called as he saw her at the bottom of the stairs, clearly preparing to retire for the night. Her air of quiet composure struck him once more. What a remarkable woman she was—an oasis in a desert of despair. 'Are you all right? Is there anything I can do for you—or Lady Dawlish?'

'Lady Dawlish is with Lucy for the moment. I am going to the room, which I shall share with Lucy. Her mama is trying to persuade her to rest for a while. She looks so drained.'

'Yes, she must be. I am relieved that she has you to turn to, Jenny. You have behaved with great restraint and yet so much sympathy. Many young ladies would have needed comforting themselves after what you saw.'

'My feelings have been affected, but to give way at such a time when others had so much more right to be distressed would have caused unnecessary suffering. I did only what I considered proper, sir.'

'No, no, you must call me Adam.' He smiled at her. 'You must know that your conduct has given me the greatest respect for your character. I think we were fortunate that you were here.'

Jenny flushed delicately. 'You make too much of my part. Lucy is my friend and I thought only of her feelings—and your family.'

'Yes, precisely. But I am keeping you when I am certain you must need some privacy and a place to rest. Goodnight, Jenny.' He took her hand and touched it briefly to his lips.

'Goodnight…Adam.'

She blushed prettily before turning away. Adam watched her mount the stairs. He noticed that she had a way of walking that was quite delightful.

Her presence had lightened the load he might otherwise have found unbearable.

A swathe of grief rushed through him, but he fought it down ruthlessly. He would not give way to the arrows of grief that pierced him; anger should sustain him—anger and his admiration for a quiet young woman who had problems of her own to combat, but had unselfishly thought only of her friends.

Jenny closed the bedroom door. It had been a difficult evening and at times she'd felt close to giving way to a fit of weeping. However, she'd sensed that Lucy was on the verge of hysteria so she'd controlled her own nerves and done all she could to ease her friend's terrible grief. And then Lady Dawlish, a kind but sensitive lady who seemed almost as overset by the tragedy as her daughter.

However, Mr Adam Miller's kind words and the look in his eyes had lifted Jenny's spirits. She was astonished at the change in his character, for at the ball in London he'd seemed proud and arrogant—but in times of stress and tragedy one discovered the truth about the people around one. She had gone from feeling wary when he offered to take her up in his phaeton, to being amused and now her feelings were far warmer than was sensible for a man she hardly knew.

Jenny had realised shortly after she was taken up in Mr Miller's phaeton that he thought her in the position of an unpaid companion—perhaps some kind of poor relation. Her uncle's antiquated carriage, the plainness of her gown, which her aunt had purchased in a spirit of generosity, but according to her own notions of economy, and something Jenny had said had made him think her if not penniless, then close to it.

Mr Miller—or Adam, as he'd invited her to call him—had taken pity on her because of her situation. What would he think if he knew that her father had left her comfortably situated? He might despise her, think her a liar or that she had deliberately deceived him. Yet there was no need for him to know. None of her friends knew the truth. Most must have assumed that her father had lost much of his money—why else would her uncle have disposed of his house, horses and carriages? Jenny thought it nonsensical for had she still been able she might have lived in her own home and paid a companion. Yet she was content to live with her friends. She liked pretty clothes and trinkets, but would not have bought an extensive wardrobe even had she been consulted. However, her aunt's taste for very severe ensembles was not precisely what Jenny liked and, as soon as she received the allowance Mr Nodgrass had agreed to, she would indulge herself with some prettier gowns. For the moment grey or dark colours would be more suitable, because Lucy and her family would undoubtedly wear mourning for a time.

Taking the pins from her hair, Jenny let it fall on her shoulders. Dark and springy with red tones, it was apt to tangle and she had to attack it with her brush to make it settle into acceptable waves and curls. Her eyes were a soft grey, her mouth inclined to curve at the corners most of the time and her nose short with a sprinkling of freckles. She knew that she was considered attractive, though she thought her nose too short for beauty. Had Papa and Mama lived she would have been having her Season this year—or perhaps she might already have been married. Her father's tragic death had led to her living in seclusion for months at her uncle's house. The prospect of Lucy's wedding had been enticing for she was due some gaiety and a relief from mourning, but that was no longer to be.

Her heart was too tender to feel resentment. For the moment all that mattered was to be of comfort to Lucy and her family. However, she could not help thinking that Adam Miller was one of the most attractive men she'd ever met. When he'd kissed her hand a tingle had gone down her spine and she'd been aware of an urgent desire to be taken into his arms and be kissed on the lips— and that thought was too disgraceful!

How could she think of such a thing at a time like this? Was she shameless?

Her thoughts were nonsensical. Besides, he had made his feelings about heiresses plain in London. Adam might need to marry one, but he did not like them. If he discovered that she was not the poor companion he thought her, he would probably imagine she'd lied on purpose to entrap him.

Shaking her head, Jenny hid her smile of amusement as the door opened and Lucy entered. She looked pale, but her tears had dried and when Jenny held out her hands she took them.

'I have left him with his family,' she said. A little sob escaped her. 'Do you think he knows that I sat with him, told him I loved him? There is so much I wished to say and now it is too late.'

'I am sure he knew you loved him…'

Lucy shook her head and turned away to unpin her hair. She slipped off her dress, but did not remove her petticoats. 'I feel so guilty,' she said. 'Oh, Jenny. If only I could bring him back…if I could explain…'

'Explain what, dearest?'

'Nothing. I cannot speak of it now,' Lucy said and dashed away her tears. 'I must try to sleep if I can.'

'We shall be quiet, but I am here if you want to talk.'

'I need to talk, but I cannot yet,' Lucy said, an oddly defensive expression in her eyes. 'Perhaps in a few days—but you must not condemn me when I tell you and you must promise not to leave me. I do not think I could bear Mama's smothering if you were not here.'

Jenny pulled back the sheets for her. 'Come to bed, Lucy.'

Lucy smiled gratefully. 'I think that perhaps I could sleep now.'

'Yes, we shall both sleep if we can.'

Jenny lay listening to the sound of Lucy's laboured breathing as she tried to smother her tears. Her body trembled as the grief poured out of her, but after a while she quietened and then fell asleep. Jenny was too thoughtful and uncertain to sleep herself for some time and the reason for her restlessness was a pair of dark eyes and a face that was almost too handsome.

'Mark slipped away quietly with all his family about him,' Adam said to the vicar when he called the next day. 'I am certain Lord Ravenscar will want to talk to you about the arrangements, perhaps later this afternoon. He is resting for the moment.'

'Yes, of course. I am entirely at his disposal. I shall return later.'

Adam nodded. Lord Ravenscar had already arranged for his son's body to lie in state in the chapel for three days before the funeral.

'The tenants and workers will want to pay their respects,' he'd told Adam earlier. 'He would have been their lord when I depart this earth and it is only fitting that they should have the chance to say goodbye.'

Adam had agreed. It also meant that he could now make a search of his cousin's rooms, which he needed to do as soon as possible. Hallam had remained at the house through the night and he, Paul and Adam were to meet shortly to begin their search. Lucy and her mother were at that moment enclosed with Lord Ravenscar, but would be leaving for home later that morning. So if he were to make his search before escorting them, he must begin now.

After taking leave of the vicar, Adam went up to Mark's room. Hallam and Paul were already there and had begun the search in Mark's sitting room. Paul had the top drawer of the desk open and was looking through some papers he'd discovered.

'I thought I'd take the dressing room,' Hallam said. 'Adam—would you do the bedchamber, please?'

'Yes, of course.'

Adam walked into his cousin's room. The bed had been stripped down to the mattress and left open, the maids having been told to leave it that way for the time being. All the bloodstained sheets and covers had been taken away to be burned. A shiver of ice ran down Adam's spine as he approached the bedside cabinet. Pictures of his cousin lying in the bed made it feel wrong to be searching this room, which was why Paul and Hallam had decided against the task.

In normal circumstances the room would

have been left for weeks or months before being touched, but they did not have that luxury. Painful as it was, it must be done now. Gritting his teeth, Adam pulled open the drawers of the chest at the right-hand side one by one. Mark's trinkets had been thrown carelessly into them and there was an assortment of fobs, shirt pins, buttons, a silver penknife, a small pistol with a pearl handle, a pair of grape scissors and some gloves—a woman's by the look of them. Also a scented handkerchief that smelled of roses, also a lady's, almost certainly Lucy's. There was besides a bundle of letters tied with pink ribbon.

Extracting the top one, Adam discovered that they were from a lady, but not Lucy—instead, her name was Maria. After dipping into the first, Adam formed the opinion that the lady had been Mark's mistress for a time. She seemed to have accepted that their liaison must end when he married, but asked that they meet one last time—and she thanked him for a ruby bracelet, which he'd given her as a parting gift. He replaced the remaining letters unread.

In another drawer, Adam discovered a jeweller's receipt for the ruby bracelet and also two more for a set of pearls and an emerald-and-diamond ring, also a gold wedding band. He searched all the drawers in the expectation of perhaps finding the jewels, but they were not to be found. He would have to ask if Paul knew anything of them and if they might be in Lord Ravenscar's strongroom.

His search extended to a handsome mahogany tallboy, which contained Mark's shirts, handkerchiefs, gloves, silk stockings and smalls. It was when he came to the very last drawer that he found a black velvet purse hidden under a pile of cravats and waistcoats. Drawing it out, he tipped the contents into his hand and gasped as he saw the diamond necklace. It lay sparkling on the palm of his hand, the stones pure white and large, an extremely expensive trinket—and not one that he'd seen an invoice for.

'Found anything?' Hallam's voice asked from the doorway. Adam held up the necklace. 'What is that? Good grief! That must have cost a fortune!'

'Yes, I should imagine so. I found a receipt for some pearls and an emerald-and-diamond ring, but a bill for the diamonds was not amongst the receipts. This was in the tallboy, but no receipt.'

'Mark bought pearls and a ring for Lucy,' Hallam said. 'I know because Ravenscar asked me if he should give them to her today. I thought it best to wait for a few weeks. He did not mention the diamonds so I have no idea…'

Paul walked in. 'You've found something?'

'This…' Adam held it out for him to see. Paul took it, whistling as he saw the purity of the diamonds and their size.

'This cost the earth. I wonder where he bought it. I saw Lucy's wedding gift and I know where he bought the pearls and her ring—but he made no mention of diamonds. These would be worth a king's ransom, I think. I'm certain Mark did not buy them for Lucy or he would have mentioned it.'

'If he did buy them.'

'You didn't find a receipt for them?' Adam shook his head.

Paul shook his head. 'There was a load of receipts in a wooden coffer in the dressing room, but all for small things like gloves—oh, and a pair of pistols. I can't imagine that Mark would have been careless over something like this. If he kept receipts for his shirts, why not keep one for a necklace like this?'

'It should be here if he had one,' Hallam said.

'If?' Adam frowned. 'He must have bought it— mustn't he?'

'Mark wouldn't steal, if that's what you're implying.'

'Of course not—but what is the alternative?'

'He might have won it in a card game,' Paul suggested.

Adam nodded grimly. 'Precisely. Now supposing the previous owner came to demand the return of his property?'

'You think they might have quarrelled over it?'

'Perhaps.' Adam frowned. 'It's the only clue we have.'

'I don't see how it helps,' Paul said.

'A necklace like this will be recorded somewhere,' Hallam said. 'It must have come from a London jeweller. At least that is where I shall start to enquire as soon as the funeral is over.'

'It must be put away in Father's safe for the moment,' Paul said, a wintry look in his eyes. 'If that devil killed Mark to get this, he won't leave it there. He may return and look again.'

'Yes. I've searched all the furniture, but I haven't been through Mark's pockets yet.' Adam glanced at his gold pocket watch. 'I must take Lucy and Lady Dawlish home. I'll finish in here later.'

'Couldn't face it myself,' Paul said. 'I'll lock the necklace away—and then Father wants me to sort out the details of the service. He's feeling under the weather.'

'I ought to go home and make some arrangements,' Hallam said. 'If you wouldn't mind finishing in here alone later, Adam?'

'Of course not. Mark would understand why we have to do this. You shouldn't feel awkward, either of you—but I know how it feels.'

The cousins left the suite of rooms together. Adam then locked them and pocketed the key. He was frowning as he went down to the hall, where Lucy and Lady Dawlish had paused to say farewell to their host.

'It was so kind of you to come.' Lord Ravenscar took Lady Dawlish's gloved hand. 'And you, Miss Dawlish. Words cannot express my feelings.'

'Or mine, sir,' Lucy said, looking pale and distressed. 'Forgive me.' She dashed a tear from her cheek.

'Miss Hastings. You will come again on a happier day, please.'

'Of course, sir.' Jenny impulsively leaned up and kissed his cheek. 'I am so sorry for your loss, sir.'

'Thank you.' He pressed her hand. 'If you will excuse me now. Adam is to escort you both home.'

'How kind,' Lady Dawlish said, shaking her

head as the elderly gentleman walked away. 'It breaks my heart to see him so, Captain Miller.'

'Yes, I fear he suffers more than any of us,' Adam said. 'His health is not all it should be. This is a severe blow. All his hopes were centred on Mark and Lucy for the future.'

'Naturally he expected heirs. Well, we must leave you. You will send word of the arrangements?'

'Yes, of course. I shall come myself.'

Adam followed as the ladies went outside to the waiting carriage. He assisted them in one by one and a groom put up the steps and closed the door. Mounting his horse, Adam rode a little behind their carriage.

It had been a solemn procession that left Ravenscar for Dawlish. On their arrival Lord Dawlish came out to take charge and embrace his wife and daughter. Lady Dawlish was in tears, while Lucy was oddly pale and silent.

It was left to Jenny to thank Adam for escorting them.

'You have been so kind. Will you come in for some refreshments? I know that Lady Dawlish intended to ask, but in the emotion of the moment she forgot.'

'I should not dream of intruding at such a moment—besides, I have unfinished business,' Adam told her. 'There is something I have to do. We must bury my cousin, but my priority is to bring his killer to justice.'

'Yes, I understand that,' Jenny said. Impulsively, she reached out to take his hand. 'You will be careful, Adam. I know that you cannot rest until this evil man is caught and punished—but I think he must be very dangerous and I would not have you share Mark's fate.'

'I thank you for your concern,' Adam said and his smile came from within. 'I shall take care not to be caught off guard. We may have a clue soon and when we do I shall call on the due process of the law. Paul speaks wildly of killing the rogue, but I prefer that he shall hang for his crimes—though I may give him a good hiding first.'

'You are so angry and Paul has been torn apart by his grief. I saw it in his eyes when you were holding Mark at the first. You must not suspect him, Adam. He is so terribly hurt by this.'

'You feel things and you sense them,' Adam said. 'If I had not already decided my first thoughts were foolish, I should have accepted your opinion. Thank you for being here. Your calm presence has eased my heart more than you can imagine.'

Jenny shook her head, a flush in her cheeks. 'If I have helped, I am glad of it, sir—and I would do more if I could.'

'What we must do is men's work,' Adam said. 'But to know that I may talk to you of what is in my heart means more than I can say.'

The Dawlish family were about to go in. Adam stood back and allowed Jenny to join her friends, then mounted his horse and began the ride back to Ravenscar. For a while his thoughts dwelled on the young woman he had just left, but his thoughts soon returned to his cousin and the hunt for Mark's killer.

If Mark had won that necklace in a card game, it might have brought the former owner to Ravenscar in the hope of retrieving it—by fair means or foul. Had he tried to buy it back or had he threatened Mark? Mark would surely have allowed the rightful owner to redeem it if he could pay his debt.

Somehow Adam felt there was more here than met the eye. What was he missing? It was an expensive necklace, but surely it was not so important that it would cause a man to do murder to retrieve it? Had it been the deeds to a man's estate Adam could have understood it—but why kill for a necklace, however expensive?

There must be a further reason. Something of such importance that the murderer had been driven to desperate measures to attempt its retrieval.

In which case he would undoubtedly return to look for it.

Chapter Five

Adam returned to his task of searching Mark's bedchamber later that afternoon. Having already checked inside the drawers, he took each one out in case something had either been lodged behind or got caught up at the back, but there was nothing to discover. He then began a search of his cousin's coat pockets. As before he found various small items: a gold fob, a stickpin and several pieces of string, plus two pebbles and a trinket that took stones from a horse's hooves. It was in a velvet evening coat that he finally came across some gold coins and a handful of screwed-up papers, which, when smoothed out, appeared to be IOUs from a card game.

Mark had won what amounted to five thousand guineas and two different hands had signed the notes. One name was Stafford, which Adam knew to be Lord Jeffery Stafford, or Staffs as his fellow officers affectionately called him. His note was for five hundred guineas; the remaining notes were from Fontleroy.

Mark and Staffs were the greatest of friends. If Staffs had lost five hundred guineas to Mark, he would undoubtedly have paid him when they next met. Fontleroy was another matter. Adam had not been aware that his cousin knew the fellow well enough to play cards with him. The marquis was not a man he would care to sit down with—Adam had once witnessed him cheating, but had kept quiet, advising the victim privately to be on his guard another time, rather than causing a scandal.

Could Mark also have won the necklace from Fontleroy? There was no mention of it amongst the notes—anything to say that he would retrieve it for money at a later date.

Since Adam had now completed his search of the room and both the necklace and the notes had been removed, Adam did not lock his cousin's room when he left. He would not go there again for there was no reason.

Hallam was to take the necklace to London in an effort to discover the identity of its owner. Adam would show the notes to his cousins. They might provide a reason for Fontleroy to visit Mark, either to redeem them or come to some arrangement, but that meant little. It would be impossible to prove that he had been here or was responsible in any way for Mark's murder. They had a clue to the possible identity of his cousin's killer, but no proof as yet that would stand up in a court of law.

Paul was angry enough to take the law into his own hands, but Adam was determined to avoid using more violence than necessary. A thrashing was one thing, but murder was something else. If Paul struck out in anger, killing his victim, it could not bring his brother back.

There was nothing more they could do now until after Mark was laid to rest with his ancestors.

'I look terrible in black,' Lucy said, as she looked at herself in her dressing mirror. 'Mark would have hated me to wear something like this, I know he would.' Her eyes filled with tears as she spoke the name of the man she loved. 'Why did he have to die? I want him back, Jenny. I want him back…'

'I am sure you do' Jenny sympathised. 'I know you loved him.'

'Mark was to have given me my ring yesterday,' Lucy said, her throat tight with emotion. 'We should have dined there last evening amongst friends and our engagement would then have been formally announced to the world—with the wedding at the end of next month, for we did not wish to wait long.'

'It is so painful for you,' Jenny said, her throat tight. 'You must try to get through it as best you can, Lucy dearest. I shall help you as much as I can.'

'I do not know what I should have done had you not been here,' Lucy said and sniffed. 'I wish I need not go, Jenny. Mama says neither of us has to attend the church service unless we wish, but we must be at the reception.'

'You must decide,' Jenny told her doubtfully. 'Mama was always of the opinion that it was not fitting for ladies to attend a funeral—unless it was for a child, husband or parent. Yet it is a matter of choice. I shall abide by your decision.'

'Papa thinks we should all go since Ravenscar is one of his oldest friends.'

'For myself I feel it shows respect and I know you would not wish to be lacking in any way, Lucy dearest—but if you really cannot bear it you could tell your mama that you have a terrible headache.'

Lucy sniffed and brushed the tears from her cheeks. 'No, I shall go—but only to the reception. I do not think I could bear to attend the service and burial.'

'Then we shall go to the house and wait until your mother and father return with the other guests attending the church. I am certain Lord Ravenscar will understand you are too heartbroken to attend the service.'

Lucy gave a sob and then turned away. As Jenny moved towards her, she swung back to face her and her eyes were bright with a mixture of distress and defiance.

'Everyone assumes that I'm heartbroken,' she said, 'but the truth is I had begun to have doubts. I had intended to speak to Mark and ask if we might wait a little longer.'

'You were thinking of delaying your wedding?' Jenny was stunned. 'Oh, Lucy. I had no idea...'

'I have been in such turmoil,' Lucy told her and a little sob broke from her. 'Our marriage was always the desire of our parents—and Mark was so kind and handsome and generous. I loved him from the time I could walk and he put me up on his horse. Of course I loved him, I cared for him deeply…only I wasn't sure I wished to be his wife. Sometimes he seemed more like a kind brother than a lover.'

'Yes, I do understand.' Jenny nodded. 'It was as if you were on board a chaise with a runaway horse. You had to hang on because you were afraid to jump off.'

'You do understand.' Lucy reached for her hand. 'I am so glad you are here, Jenny. I could never tell Mama or Papa how I feel, because they would be shocked and even angry with me. I am sad and I do miss Mark—but not in the way people think. It sounds wicked of me, but in a way I am relieved that I shall not have to marry—' She broke off, her hands flying to her face. 'I am such a wicked girl to have these terrible thoughts.'

'Dearest Lucy, you are not in the least wicked,' Jenny assured her and pulled her hands away. 'You must not feel ashamed, my love. You cared for Mark as a friend and it is as his friend that you mourn him—and as his friend that you will show your respects today.'

'I have been thinking that people would think me false and horrid if they knew my true feelings…'

'Some people might not understand, but I know you, Lucy. I know that your heart is true. You did not wish Mark to die and you would have hated to hurt him had he lived—but I think you must have told him the truth. To have married with so many doubts must have made you both unhappy.'

'Well, I thought the same—and I'm not certain Mark was truly in love with me. I have thought there might be someone else he liked, but because everyone had assumed we should marry for so long he did not wish to let me down.'

'He might have been relieved had he lived long enough for you to tell him how you felt,' Jenny said. 'I did not know your fiancé well, Lucy, for I met him only once, but from what Adam tells me of him he was a very good person.'

'Mark was wonderful. Everyone adored him. I loved him, Jenny—but not…not in that way.'

'I perfectly understand.' Jenny smiled at her.

'Yes, of course. You will think me foolish, only…I feel so much better for having told you the truth.'

'I am glad that I was here,' Jenny said. 'Today must be an ordeal for everyone, but it will be over soon enough and then you may start to forget all this unpleasantness.'

'Yes…' Lucy looked so woebegone that Jenny sensed there was more, something she had not told her, but she did not press for further confidences. Lucy had unburdened herself as regards her feelings and perhaps now she would be able to face the ordeal before her with a lighter heart. 'Shall we go down now, dearest? Your mama will be waiting.'

'It was unfortunate that it should rain,' Jenny remarked to Adam later that afternoon. 'I think it must have made the proceedings uncomfortable.'

'Fortunately, it left off by the time we had Mark interred in the family crypt,' Adam said. 'I must admit the sound of raindrops against the windows was saddening as we listened to the vicar's sermon.'

'Yes, indeed.' Jenny hesitated, then, 'It may be inappropriate of me to ask—but have you discovered anything of importance yet?'

'Hallam returned from London just before we left for the church. I believe he has some important news. We have discovered a clue—something that leads us to believe Mark's death may be the result of a card game he won. It is possible that one of the losers had a grudge against him.'

'That is quite shocking.' Jenny's eyes widened in distress. 'To take a life in such a cause is wicked—but then, there is never an excusable reason for murder. I am so very sorry.'

'As you know we are all devastated. I think if Hallam has some clue for us it may help, because we must begin to track down our culprit and find a way to bring him to justice.'

'That will not be easy,' Jenny said. 'For the law to work one must have proof.' She reached out to take a glass from a footman's tray and because he jerked it away too soon the wine spilled on to her gown. 'Oh, how foolish of me…'

'It was not your fault,' Adam said to Jenny as the footman apologised.

'It does not matter. It was an accident. Do not worry, it is an old gown. If you will excuse me, I shall go to the chamber we have been given to refresh ourselves. Please do not scold the man, Adam. Truly, it was my fault.'

She smiled at the unfortunate footman and hurried from the room, running up the stairs. At the top she hesitated, trying to recall if she should go to the left or the right; then, just as she turned to the left she caught sight of a door opening at the far end of the right passage. A man emerged, turning away quickly towards the back stairs. Jenny could not but think that she knew the man, but as he swiftly disappeared from view she did not have long enough to be certain.

Shaking her head, Jenny went swiftly along the passage to the ladies' rest room. A maid was waiting there to assist with accidents and her dress was quickly sponged and dried as much as possible. She thanked the girl and went back down the stairs. Seeing Adam in conversation with his cousin Hallam, she hesitated, then decided that she ought to speak of what she'd seen.

She approached diffidently, because the men seemed to be talking earnestly. 'Excuse me, Adam—Mr Ravenscar, but I saw something just now. At the top of the stairs leading to the third floor I hesitated to get my bearings and I saw a man emerge from the bedchamber at the far end of the right passage. I seem to recall that room belongs to Mark...'

'Good grief!' Adam stared at her in dismay. 'We thought he might attempt...but today of all days...'

'We must investigate at once. Miss Hastings— did you see his face?'

'No, for he turned immediately towards the

back stairs and was round the corner and out of view before I could be certain.'

'Certain of what?' Adam's gaze narrowed. 'Did you know him?'

'I thought there was something familiar about his build, but I cannot say. I am not sure…just that I felt I ought to know…'

'You will excuse us.' Adam followed Hallam, who was already on his way from the large reception room.

Jenny watched him leave, then decided to follow. The two cousins were already at the top of the stairs when she began to ascend them. She reached the landing and saw them enter the room she'd seen someone leave a short time earlier. Instinctively, she walked quickly along the passage and stopped outside the open door. Glancing in, she saw that everything had been disturbed: drawers were left open, papers tossed out to the floor, cushions everywhere and a chair overturned. Feeling awkward and yet unable to resist, she went into the parlour and then as far as the bedroom door, which had been similarly treated.

Adam turned and saw her. 'You ought not to have followed. Had he still been here there might have been some danger.'

'I do not think he would return for he has made a thorough search.'

'Yes, indeed.' Adam grimaced. 'Had we waited to search, as we should if my uncle had not arranged for Mark to lie in the chapel, he would undoubtedly have found all that he was looking for.'

'You removed whatever it was, of course.'

'I did.' Adam's mouth thinned with anger. 'I shall tell you in confidence, Jenny—and this must not go to another soul...'

'I swear it on my honour.'

'We found a valuable item in one of Mark's drawers as well as some promissory notes. Hallam has discovered that the necklace was stolen with other jewels some weeks ago. Further inquiries have told us that the Bow Street Runners suspect the theft to be one of a series against members of the *ton*. Whoever lost the necklace in a card game—and we are convinced that Mark obtained it in lieu of gold coin for a gambling debt—must have been involved with the thieves, if not the actual thief himself.'

'Do you know who your cousin gambled with the night he won it?'

'We have two names, but there may have been others. Hallam was not in possession of all the facts when he set out for London—but he will return to town tomorrow and speak with at least one of Mark's debtors. He may be able to cast some light on what happened that night.'

'If you have a witness to what happened, you may know the name of your thief and that would make him the likely killer,' Jenny said. 'You must feel as if you are on the verge of a breakthrough.'

'Unfortunately, we have no proof that the man who lost this necklace came here to kill Mark,' Adam said and frowned. 'It would help if you could recall any detail about the intruder—did you see nothing that might trigger your memory?'

Jenny wrinkled her brow. 'Forgive me, I should truly like to help you. He was wearing a dark coat and breeches—riding clothes—which was what made me wonder what he was doing here dressed that way.'

'It is a pity you did not tell us at once,' Hallam said and frowned. 'I doubt that he would have lingered once he'd finished his work.'

'I am sorry. It was only as I thought about it afterwards that I realised I might have seen something important. Forgive me. I should have come instantly to tell you.'

'How could you know?' Adam said. 'Hallam,

you must not blame Jenny. She is not at fault here. I should have had a guard set on Mark's room. I did not imagine that anyone would dare to attempt anything of the sort on a day like this.'

'It is exactly the right moment. The house is full of people and the servants are busy. We were all distracted and concerned for our guests. He has a twisted kind of courage, Adam.' Hallam glanced at Jenny. 'Of course I do not blame you for any of this, Miss Hastings. We should have set a guard on Mark's room. It was the family's problem.' He hesitated then. 'May I ask you to keep this to yourself?'

'Yes, of course. I should not dream of mentioning it to anyone,' Jenny said. 'Forgive me for intruding. I shall go back down now and leave you together.'

She turned and left them, feeling uncomfortable. Had she been quick enough to report what she'd seen to Adam he might have apprehended the stranger.

It was unfortunate that she had not seen the man's face, but only his back as he turned away. Yet something had seemed familiar to her—but not quite as it should be. Why could she not place it in her mind? If she knew the man he was probably a gentleman, and perhaps a friend of her uncle's.

No, that was unlikely. Her uncle did not often mix in the circles Mark Ravenscar must have frequented. There were often slight similarities in people, things that made you think you knew someone when you did not.

She would have liked to give the cousins a clue that would lead to the discovery of Mark's murderer, but she could not and it would be foolish to try to perhaps steer them in the wrong direction.

Adam and Hallam were more than capable of dealing with the mystery themselves and did not need help from her. She must find Lucy. Her friend was in need of comfort and a shoulder to cry on.

'So close and yet so far,' Hallam said as the door closed behind Jenny. 'Had Miss Hastings come to us at once we might have caught him.'

'She could not know how important it was,' Adam said. 'I feel as you do—but I shall speak to the servants and the grooms. They may have seen a man in riding clothes. Everyone else is wearing formal clothes. I think someone must have noticed him.'

'It is all we can do,' Hallam agreed. 'I wish to God I'd put one of the footman on guard duty.'

'Had you done so he would have found another way—waited until it was night or come in by the window.'

'As it is he just walked in and out. How amused he must be at finding it so easy.'

'Yet he did not get what he wanted,' Adam said and frowned. 'We have Mark's notes and the necklace. You should speak to Staffs. He will recall the game and may know if anyone lost that necklace to Mark that night. We should need a witness. The mere fact that someone lost the necklace in a card game does not make him a thief. He could have been duped into buying it.'

'In which case he would be unlikely to murder in order to retrieve it,' Hallam said. 'If he were not known in society, it would not matter to him—therefore he must be a gentleman. Someone with a reputation to lose.'

'It all begins to add up—' Adam said and broke off as Paul walked in dressed in a dark riding coat and pale breeches. 'Paul, we found this mess—'

'And you did not think to tell me.' Paul glared at him. 'If you imagine I would do something of this kind…'

'No, of course not. Hallam was with me when Jenny told us of the intruder. We came straight here…'

'So Miss Hastings knows more than I…' Paul turned away. 'I've had enough of all this. It is stifling me. I'm going for a ride.'

'Don't be an idiot,' Adam said. 'Hallam has discovered something important. That necklace was stolen—'

'Are you suggesting my brother was a thief?'

'No, of course not,' Hallam said. 'For goodness' sake, man! No one is accusing Mark of theft or you of murder. Mark must have won it in a card game, as we thought—but the fact that it is stolen makes it more likely that someone might kill Mark to protect himself from discovery.'

'Yes, I see what you mean.' Paul gave them a brooding look. 'I wish to God that I knew who it was. At this moment I should need no excuse to break his damned neck with my bare hands.'

'Paul…please, do not be foolish,' Adam said. 'I know how you feel, but—'

'How can you know?' Paul demanded. 'You don't have people looking at you, wondering how you feel about becoming your father's heir. Everything was Mark's and I feel like a thief because I shall now inherit what ought to be his.'

'Ridiculous,' Hallam said. 'Mark was the elder. Now you are—of course everything will come to you in due course.'

'Even Lucy?' Paul's eyes were dark with grief. 'I've seen the way she looks at me—resentful, as if she wishes it was me who died.'

'I am sure she has no such thoughts,' Hallam said. 'You are being a fool, Paul. Lucy is grieving, as we all are.'

Paul shook his head, muttered something and walked away. Hallam looked at Adam and sighed.

'He's like a bear with a sore head.'

'We can hardly blame him. People will wonder and speculate for a while.'

'I dare say what is upsetting him is Lucy. You know how he feels about her.'

'He would never have done anything about it. She was always Mark's future wife.'

'Yes, but Mark isn't here now,' Adam said. 'Now there is nothing to stop him asking her to marry him—and yet he can't. To speak now would be like dancing on his brother's grave. It must be a terrible feeling to see what you desire most in the world within touching distance, but unable to reach out. He must feel she is still forbidden to him.'

'Yes, I see what you mean.' Hallam looked thoughtful. 'Poor devil—though…' He shook his head. 'Lucy is Paul's problem. We have more important things to worry about, Adam. If the murderer should turn out to be Fontleroy, we have to discover a way of making him reveal his identity.'

'Exactly what I was thinking,' Adam said. 'That would be difficult, I imagine. With Mark dead there are no witnesses to what happened that day—though if we could prove Fontleroy lost that necklace to Mark in a card game we could threaten him with disclosure. If he thought he might be arrested for theft, he might try to get the evidence from us.'

'It is a faint hope,' Hallam said. 'But first we have to find someone who saw him lose that necklace to Mark—if indeed it was he that lost it.'

'Do you happen to know where Staffs is staying at the moment? Is he in London or his country home?'

'It is a wonder he did not come today.' Hallam frowned. 'He was one of Mark's oldest and best friends. Come to think of it, I haven't seen a card from him—is that not strange?'

'The announcement was in *The Times* and other papers—and a notice was sent to Mark's club. I cannot think that he would not have seen it.' Adam was thoughtful. 'I believe you should set out for London this evening. If he was a witness...'

'Then his own life may be in danger,' Hallam said.

'And we should also take more care. We have been careless, Hallam. I made the mistake of thinking that the murderer would be running scared—but he may be made of bolder stuff than we imagined. He is certainly ruthless and having murdered once would not hesitate to do so again.'

'I shall speak to my uncle and leave almost at once. If I do not find Stafford in London, I shall go down to Hampshire, to his country seat—unless I discover he has gone to visit friends.'

'This grows more dangerous by the minute,' Adam said and clasped his shoulder. 'Take care, Hal—I should not like to lose another of my cousins.'

'I would say the same to you,' Hallam replied grimly. 'Be careful when you ride out alone—and keep a loaded pistol with you at all times.'

'Yes, I intend to, though the search goes on locally,' Adam replied. 'I shall wait for your return and in the meantime I shall do my best to restrain Paul from giving way to a fit of despair.'

Chapter Six

'**W**here did you go to earlier?' Lucy asked as they were leaving Ravenscar Court a little later. 'I looked for you but you had disappeared.'

'A footman spilled wine on my gown and I had to have it sponged—and then I remembered that I had left my reticule upstairs and went to fetch it.'

'Oh…' Lucy frowned. 'It was odd the way they all left—Adam and Hallam and then Paul. Lord Ravenscar looks so unwell that I felt obliged to sit with him for quite half an hour. I should have liked to tell Paul that his father was not himself, but he had disappeared.'

'Perhaps he found the proceedings unbearable,' Jenny suggested. 'I thought he looked very tense earlier. It must be hard to bear—to lose a brother you love so much.'

'Yes, perhaps,' Lucy said and sighed. 'People

think he will have it all now, but I am sure he does not care for the estate enough—' She broke off and blushed. 'Paul has the estate his maternal grandfather left him. Why should he covet what Mark had? I do not think it of him—do you?'

'Not at all. I believe he is genuine in his distress.'

'Yes. So why…?' Lucy wrinkled her nose prettily. 'I hoped he might speak to me, tell me how he feels, but he is avoiding me. Every time I approach he moves away and he will not look at me.'

'I dare say he is still too upset to think clearly.'

'It is almost as if he blames me…'

'No, how could he? No one could blame you, Lucy.'

'No—and yet Paul does blame me for something.' Lucy blinked hard. 'Oh, I do not want to talk about any of it. It is all too horrible. I wish we could go away somewhere. I can hardly bear to be near Ravenscar and know…' She smothered a sob.

'You will feel better soon, dearest.'

'Shall I?' Lucy looked at her in disbelief. 'I feel that my whole life is ruined.'

'You must try, Lucy. In a few days people will stop talking about the tragedy and you will be at peace.'

Lucy shook her head, but they had arrived at Lucy's home. As they got down, Lady Dawlish emerged from her husband's carriage and came to meet them.

'Thank goodness that is all over,' she said. 'You may change out of that gown now, Lucy my dear. I shall not ask you to wear black again. Your father and I have discussed what is right and proper and he agrees that pale grey or lilac is sufficient.'

'Thank you, Mama,' Lucy said and dabbed at her cheek with a lace kerchief. 'I wish we might go away. I feel so distressed by all this…'

'Well, we shall think about it,' her mama said. 'Your papa is not certain of what would be right for we should not wish to appear uncaring—but I do not wish to see my darling girl in such despair. We could not go to London and balls will be out of the question for some months, but we might visit Bath, perhaps.'

'Oh, Mama, if we could I should feel so much better,' Lucy declared.

'Well, we shall see in a week or two,' her mother said and patted her cheek. 'Now run along in and change, my dears. There is nothing to stop you and Jenny walking or riding as usual—and some music in the house might be pleasant. I am sorely grieved for the family, but I see no point in dwelling on something that cannot be changed. However, you must do as you wish, Lucy—for I would not push you into anything you did not like.'

Lucy thanked her and smiled at Jenny. 'We must change and then we can go for a long walk together. I feel as if I need some air after being indoors all day.'

'You will not leave the gardens this evening,' Lady Dawlish said. 'Time enough for long walks tomorrow, dearest—and then you will take a maid with you, if you please. We must not forget there may be a dangerous man at large.'

Lucy did not argue. Instead she took Jenny by the arm and they went up the stairs together.

In her room Jenny submitted to the ministrations of her maid and then chose a gown of dark blue. It had lilac tones in the stripes and she did not consider herself to be in mourning; much as she felt for Mark's family she could not grieve, as Lucy did. Instead, she felt sad for those who had loved him. His brother was in such pain, as were his cousins. She would not forget Adam's face as he held his dying cousin, but she believed he had conquered his grief, letting anger take over.

All his thoughts now would be concentrated on discovering the culprit and in that he was fortunate. Lucy had only regrets and could do nothing to help.

Jenny was upset with herself for not being quicker when she'd seen the intruder. She ought to have run straight back to Adam and told him what she'd seen. Perhaps then the killer might already have been caught.

Hallam had been very annoyed with her, but Adam had been more understanding. She knew that he was very angry over the whole affair and was disappointed with herself for letting him down.

Jenny shook her head. Adam Miller was occupying too much of her thoughts of late. With each meeting her feelings had grown warmer and she thought she liked him very well indeed. Enough to entertain thoughts of what might possibly come to be in the future. Yet she knew it was foolish to hope for more than friendship.

Even if Adam were kindly disposed to her— and his words on several occasions had seemed to indicate it—he might soon change his mind if he knew that rather than the poor dependent he thought her, she was actually a despised heiress.

She was not yet certain how much her inheritance amounted to, for although her lawyer had told her she had no need to worry he might think a mere competence sufficient for her needs—especially as she was at liberty to live either with her kind friends or her uncle. If she wished to set up her own establishment and employ a companion, she might yet find herself unable to pay her way.

She wished that she had not allowed Adam to think her in difficulties at the start, though in London he'd seemed so very arrogant and she'd initially found it amusing that he'd taken pity on her because he thought her helpless and in some distress.

She had soon learned to admire him. After witnessing the emotions he'd undergone when his cousin fell dying into his arms, she'd come to realise what kind of a man he truly was and, in the following days, she had learned to appreciate his qualities.

That he had some liking for her was evident, but that did not necessarily mean he was interested in her as anything other than a friend. Jenny bit her bottom lip. If she allowed herself to like Mr Miller too much she would be a foolish girl. And now she must hurry for she did not wish to keep Lucy waiting.

* * *

'I am so thankful that business is over,' Lucy said, taking Jenny's arm as they walked in the cool of the evening air. 'It was such an ordeal and I do not think I could have borne it without you.'

'I am sorry I was not there when you looked for me.'

'Oh…it was only that Lord Ravenscar was so kind to me. I could hardly keep from weeping. He told me that Mark had bought me a pearl necklace and a beautiful emerald-and-diamond ring. He says that they are mine and he will send them to me another day. I did not know how to answer him for I would rather not receive them.'

'But he gives them because Mark wanted you to have them,' Jenny said. 'What else is he to do with them? And they were meant for you.'

'I should not have had them had we postponed the wedding,' Lucy said and flushed. 'It makes me feel that I have them under false pretences, Jenny.'

'Yes, I see how you must feel,' Jenny said. 'But you must consider Lord Ravenscar's feelings. If you refuse them, he may be hurt.'

'I suppose so. I could never wear them…' Lucy sighed. 'Why did it have to happen, Jenny? Who could hate Mark so much that he would kill him?'

'I do not know,' Jenny replied and felt awkward because she was obliged to keep what she did know a secret. 'I believe Adam and Hallam may have some clues, but we shall know more when they manage to apprehend the culprit.'

'I pray they will do so,' Lucy said and then lifted her head. 'I shall say nothing more of this. Let us speak of Bath. If only Papa will let us go, it will be such a relief.'

'Yes, I agree with you. I have been in mourning for my father, as you know, and I should like to buy some new clothes.'

Lucy seized on the temporary escape from gloom. 'Have you thought of what colours you would like?'

'I think I should like a ballgown of peach or flame, also evening gowns of emerald green and royal blue, which is always a favourite—and a yellow muslin for mornings. You had a pretty one in town, which I admired. I thought the style became you very well. I do like the puffed sleeves and also the leg of mutton that is popular for day wear.'

'I like puffed sleeves best of all,' Lucy agreed. 'I know the dress you mean. It does suit me. I was wearing that the morning Paul asked me to save him a dance at the ball...' She flushed. 'Everyone always thinks Mark was better at everything than his brother, but it isn't true. Paul waltzes divinely—and he loves poetry. He can quote lines from my favourite poems...'

'It is always so pleasant when a friend can quote from a poem you love, isn't it?' Jenny smiled and squeezed her arm. 'We always shared a love of poetry, did we not?'

Lucy began to talk happily of poems they both enjoyed and they quoted lines back and forth so that by the time they returned to the house Lucy had laughed several times and her tense unhappy look had gone.

Dinner had been easier than it had been for some days and when they parted at the end of the evening Jenny felt that her friend was beginning to recover her spirits. She undressed, but felt unready for sleep and perched on the window seat to sit looking out at the moon sailing in a cloudless sky.

She wished again that she'd been able to be of more use to Adam in the matter of the intruder. Why had he seemed familiar to her from a distance? Had she seen his face she might have known him. She wondered if he'd noticed her sooner than she'd noticed him—and whether that was why he'd turned away so quickly.

It occurred to Jenny that if the intruder believed she'd seen him and known him, she might possibly be in some danger herself.

Adam cursed as he finished his tour of the gardens that evening. He'd put a couple of extra keepers on duty to patrol the grounds, because the intruder might pay another visit during the hours of darkness. If he were truly concerned that the necklace could lead to his being denounced as a thief and a murderer, he would possibly try to discover its whereabouts again. Yet the thought that troubled Adam most was one that had not occurred to him immediately.

Jenny might be in some danger. She had seen very little, but there was a chance she might recall what seemed familiar about the man—and he might believe she'd seen more than she had. If he did, he might consider her a danger to him—and was ruthless enough to sweep away all obstacles in his path.

'Damn it!'

Why hadn't he thought of that before? He would

have to ride over to Dawlish in the morning and speak to Jenny, because she ought to be on her guard. This man was dangerous and Adam was under no illusions that he would hesitate to murder a woman who could expose him.

It was as he entered the house that he saw Paul about to go upstairs and called to him. Paul hesitated, then came back to him.

'I'm sorry if I lost my temper earlier, Adam.'

'You've had enough to try you—but take care, Paul. This man may try to kill you next.'

'What makes you think that? I have no more idea of his identity than you have.'

'He doesn't know that and may imagine that Mark told you something of importance,' Adam said. 'It is a measure of the devil's desperation that he came here today when the house was full of guests to try to find that wretched necklace. I almost wish he had.'

'No! Why?'

'Because then perhaps other lives would not be at risk. Jenny saw him briefly. If he suspects she saw more than she did...'

'Yes, I see. If he thought she could identify him, she might be his next victim—as I might if he believed Mark told me about the necklace. Truth to tell, I knew Mark had something on his mind, but did not imagine it was of this nature.' Paul frowned. 'You will have to warn her, Adam. This is a hellish affair and gets worse. Miss Hastings must not be allowed to become his victim.'

'No, indeed. I should not like that at all.'

'I thought you quite liked her.'

'She is a sensible young woman. Very different from the young madams that my grandfather has been parading for my benefit. He would not approve, of course, because she has no fortune. He has determined that I shall marry an heiress and I may have to, Paul. His affairs are even worse than I'd imagined. He may be in danger of losing the estate while he lives. I couldn't stand by and see that happen.'

'You would not marry money for your own sake, but feel it your duty for his?' Paul arched his eyebrows.

'He loves that place,' Adam said. 'God forbid that it should come to it—but if it did I might have to find myself an heiress rather than see him go under.'

'Anyone in mind?' Paul frowned. 'Don't say Lucy Dawlish.'

'Wouldn't dream of it. She would never look at me—and I would not tread on your toes, Paul.'

'Some hope I have of marrying her.'

'In time, perhaps.'

'It is impossible. Lucy belongs to Mark.'

'Must no man have her then? Would you condemn her to remain a spinster for her whole life?'

'She will marry in time—but not me...never me.'

With that, Paul stormed up the stairs, leaving Adam to stare after him. Paul was in terrible agony, but he must battle it alone for there were no words to comfort him.

Adam walked up the stairs more slowly. In the morning he would ride over and speak to Jenny. She ought to be warned that it was possible she might find herself in some danger.

'We shall go riding today, Mama,' Lucy told her mother on visiting her after taking breakfast in bed. 'Jenny wishes to speak to Adam and I thought we would ride that way.'

'Providing that you take a groom with you— and tell him to go armed,' Lady Dawlish said. 'I do not wish to frighten you, nor do I truly think you in danger, but we must all take care until that rogue is found and tried for his life.'

'Please do not worry, Mama,' Lucy said. 'Timkins always makes a point of taking a pistol with him just in case. We shall be quite safe with him, I promise you.'

'Yes, I am sure you will. He has always been devoted to the family, Lucy. Enjoy your ride. I shall speak to Papa about the trip to Bath again today. He is a little reluctant, but I dare say I shall bring him about.'

'It would be better for all of us. I know I am in mourning and it grieves me truly that Mark should have been robbed of life so cruelly but... poor Jenny deserves a little amusement, do you not think so, Mama? She has had enough unhappiness these past months.'

'Yes, my love, I do. It is in part for her sake that I mean to convince your father. She has had months of mourning for her father and it is time she was allowed to enjoy her life.'

'Then I am sure Papa cannot refuse us.'

Lucy kissed her mother's cheek and went down to the hall, where Jenny was already waiting for her.

'That habit becomes you,' Lucy said. 'The blue brings out the colour of your eyes perfectly.'

'Papa bought it for me just before he died,' Jenny said. 'I put it away because my aunt did not think the colour fitting for a young woman in mourning, but now I may wear what I choose.'

'Fashions move on so quickly, but something like that is so elegant it is timeless,' Lucy said slightly envious. 'This is my old habit. I chose it because it is dark blue and the closest I could come to mourning wear. My favourite riding coat is red and frogged with gold braid and buttons. I did not think it suitable at the moment.'

'Very true. It is extremely dashing, Lucy, and quite the latest thing, but would not be reflective of your mood, I think. You must have a new habit made for you—perhaps grey or some dark shade.'

'We may both have several outfits made for us in Bath, Jenny. The seamstresses may not be quite up to the London standard—but I cannot wear the clothes that were intended as my bride clothes yet.'

'No, of course not.'

The groom had brought their horses forwards and helped first Lucy and then Jenny into the saddle. They walked their horses from the yard and were soon trotting happily in the direction of the Ravenscar estate, the groom following just behind them. Since neither of them was much inclined to talk, they concentrated on riding and simply enjoying the fresh air.

'Have you seen Mr Ravenscar, Simmons?' Adam asked of the head groom as he entered the stable-yard. 'I thought he meant to ride out with me this morning.'

'Mr Paul went out earlier, sir,' the groom replied. 'He—he took Captain Ravenscar's stallion.'

'Good grief—did he? Lochinvar is a devil to ride. Mark could manage him, but he kicked up if anyone else tried to mount him.'

'That is why he hadn't been exercised since Mr Mark died, sir. We'd all had a go, but the black-hearted devil wouldn't let us near him. Mr Paul said he had to be given his exercise and insisted on taking him.'

'Well, if Lochinvar didn't tip him off in five seconds he may manage him. I pray that one or the other will not be fatally injured before the day is out.'

'We must hope for the best, sir.'

Adam grimaced, mounted his horse and rode out of the yard. Paul was clearly still out of sorts despite their talk. Adam had hoped that he'd managed to iron things out, but it seemed his cousin was still too distressed to think properly. Lochinvar was a wonderful stallion and Mark had hoped to breed from him, but it took an iron will to control the beast.

At supper the previous night Paul had agreed to ride over to the Dawlish estate with Adam. Jenny needed to be warned to be on her guard—and Adam wanted to see her. He wanted to be sure she understood her situation and would take no chances.

He set out at a brisk trot. The sun was shining brightly and it was warm even though it was still early. By midday it would probably be hot. It was always best to ride early in summer because the horses might find a brisk workout too much if the day became sultry.

Hearing a shot and then a cry, Adam stiffened. The sound had come from somewhere just ahead of him—and the cry had been human. Urging his horse to gallop, Adam raced over the open ground towards a stand of trees. If he were not mistaken, the sound had come from within the trees.

'What was that?' Jenny cried as the shot rang out just ahead of them. 'I think someone has been shot.' She was already pushing her horse to a fast canter when the groom cried out a warning from behind, telling her to wait and leave it to him.

Ignoring him, Jenny pushed her horse on and within seconds she saw the figure lying on the ground a few feet ahead of her. She reined in her mount, threw herself down and rushed towards him. With no thought for her gown or her own safety, she knelt beside the fallen man and turned him on his back. He moaned, but did not immediately open his eyes.

'Are you badly hurt, sir?' Jenny ran her hands over his face and body, looking for signs of blood, but thankfully could find none. Of his horse there was no sign and she thought it must have thrown him and gone crashing away through the trees. 'Paul—Mr Ravenscar, please speak to me.'

Another horseman had arrived. Jenny did not look up, but was somehow not surprised when Adam's voice spoke to her, 'Is he still alive?'

'Yes. He moaned just now. We heard the shot, but I cannot find any blood. I think his horse must have been spooked and thrown him.'

'That is exactly what happened. He was riding Lochinvar—that horse is difficult enough at any time. If the shot were close enough to frighten him, Paul would not have stood a chance of holding on.'

'Damn and blast…' Paul muttered, his eyes flickering and then opening. He stared up at them. 'What the hell happened to me?'

'You fell from your horse,' Jenny said.

'I imagine someone took a pot shot at you and scared Lochinvar silly.'

'Damn! If he's damaged himself, Mark will never forgive me,' Paul said. A moment later his face creased with grief as he realised what he'd said. He was getting to his feet as Lucy rode up and sat staring at them all from the saddle. Paul's tone was irritable as he said, 'What is everyone staring at? I took a tumble. It happens to the best of riders from time to time.'

'Don't you realise what this means?' Adam said and offered his hand, hauling Paul to his feet. 'Someone probably just tried to kill you.'

'You needn't rub it in,' Paul muttered. 'You will frighten the ladies. It was probably only a poacher.'

'If you wish to believe that, do so,' Adam said. 'We should get you home and send for the doctor.'

'Doctor be damned.' Paul glared at him. 'Do you imagine I'm going to walk?'

'No—you will take Timkins's horse,' Adam said and signed to the groom to get down. 'The stallion made off in that direction. Would you look for it, please? If Lochinvar will allow you, you may lead him to Ravenscar stables. If not, tie him to a bush and one of us will fetch him later—do not try to ride him if you value your life.'

'I've heard of that devil's temper,' Timkins said. 'Never fear, Captain Miller. If I find him, I'll lead him or make him secure. If you are to take the ladies to Ravenscar, they will be safe until I come for them.'

'Perfectly safe, sir,' Adam said and smiled. 'You have my word on it.' He turned to Jenny. 'Let me help you up. Thank you for trying to assist my cousin. Had I not arrived, I'm sure he would have been well cared for.'

'We should certainly have done our best, should we not, Lucy?'

'Yes, of course.' Lucy was staring at Paul, almost as if she'd seen him in a new light. 'Are you hurt, Paul? Can you ride?'

'Of course I can,' he muttered, then, in a softer tone, 'Thank you, Lucy. I am bruised, but I think nothing is broken. Had it been any other horse I should not have been thrown despite the shot—but Lochinvar is a wild brute at the best of times.'

'Why did you ride him?'

'The poor beast needed the exercise and the grooms are all terrified of him. He is good breeding material, but not wonderful as a riding horse—at least for anyone other than Mark.'

'You should sell him.'

'Perhaps—and yet he is a wonderful stallion. Mark said the horse had served him well in France and deserved his time at stud. I think I shall follow my brother's plans for him as much as possible.'

Lucy nodded, but did not answer. Her face was pale and Paul averted his eyes, refusing Timkins's offer of support and mounting on his own. He rode with his eyes focused straight ahead, his mouth grim, clearly angry and in some discomfort, though refusing to admit it.

The little party had ridden at a steady trot and were soon back at Ravenscar. Dismounting at the front of the house, they were immediately surrounded by anxious servants with the information that Lochinvar had that moment returned riderless to his stable.

'We were about to send out a search party, sir,' one of the grooms said. 'That devil wants putting down—no one is safe near it.'

'You will do nothing of the sort,' Paul said. 'The fault was not Lochinvar's. We were doing very well until…a fox spooked him.'

'Give the poor beast a hot mash,' Adam said. 'And put a blanket over his back. I'll come and rub him down later.'

'Yes, Captain Miller.'

Adam offered to help Jenny dismount. She slid from the saddle into his arms and stood looking up at him for a moment before he let her go, a little smile on his lips. Adam turned with the intention of helping Lucy, but Paul had already performed the office for her. The two were staring at one another intently and Adam took Jenny by the arm, steering her towards the house.

'I was on my way to warn you that you might possibly be in danger,' Adam told her. 'If whoever shot Mark believes you saw him leave Mark's bedchamber, he may think you know more than you do. You must be on your guard, Jenny.'

'The thought occurred to me last night,' she admitted. 'We had decided to ride this way and

I meant to ask you if you thought as I did…it is most uncomfortable.'

'This whole business is a damned outrage,' Adam said and looked angry. 'Do you not think it might be a good thing if you were to go away somewhere, Jenny?'

'Lady Dawlish is thinking of taking us to Bath for a few weeks if her husband agrees. She thinks it would lift Lucy's spirits. After all, her engagement wasn't announced officially—though all her friends knew, of course.'

'I see nothing wrong with a visit to Bath,' Adam said. 'No one could take offence at it, at least in this family. I might come down for a while myself—once things are more settled here. My uncle has taken to his room. His doctor says he is worn down and should rest. I think he cannot bear to see any of us for the moment. Hallam has gone to London to discover what he can—and Paul is angry with us all.'

'Yes, I can imagine this must be harder for Paul than anyone. He is suddenly Ravenscar's heir and the full weight of responsibility must be on his shoulders. He did not wish to inherit his brother's birthright and never expected to—but he has no choice. It is a difficult thing to accustom oneself to, I should imagine.'

'Yes, I believe it is,' Adam said and looked thoughtful. 'I have always known that I am my grandfather's heir. Unfortunately, he has encumbered the estate with so much debt that I am not sure it can be recovered. For myself I should not care. Neither the title nor the estate means much to me. If I could, I would sell and forget it. I should be happy with my own small estate and the woman I loved—but that may not be open to me.'

Jenny felt her cheeks grow warm. What was he saying to her? Was he telling her that he was not free to marry where he chose, but must marry an heiress?

Was that what it had all been about in London? From the remarks she'd overheard, she'd thought him cynical and arrogant, but closer acquaintance had shown her that was untrue. Now she understood why he had been so hard to please— so angry that he found fault with every heiress in the room. He was being forced to make an advantageous marriage for the sake of his grandfather's estate.

'I suppose there is always one's responsibility

to the people of the estate.' She swallowed hard, because it was difficult to find the right words.

'Responsibility to the dependants is one thing. A good buyer could be found—one who would treat them decently and not drive them into the ground. However, my grandfather loves the house and his lands. It may be that I shall be forced to look for an heiress to set him straight. I could not allow him to lose all he holds dear while he lives. Afterwards, I would gladly sell—but for his sake…'

Why was he telling her all this? Her heart jerked, but before she could speak Lucy caught up to them and slipped her arm through Jenny's. She squeezed her arm and began to chatter about the most inconsequential things, which told Jenny she was in some distress. Forgetting her own problems, she gave her attention to her friend and Adam walked on ahead.

For the next hour Adam and Paul entertained them; they were given refreshments, and the carriage sent for to convey them home. Timkins was to ride his horse and lead the others home, but Adam considered it unsafe for them to ride back and sent two armed grooms to accompany the carriage.

Jenny had no opportunity to be private with Adam again and did her best to keep her smile in place as she took her farewell of him, but she felt very uncertain of his feelings and her own.

'Tell Lady Dawlish I shall call on you another day,' Adam said as he saw them out to the waiting carriage. 'Jenny, have a lovely time in Bath. I am persuaded Lady Dawlish will think it the safer option for you both at this time. Once she knows that rogue is still at large she may wish to remove you to Bath sooner rather than later.'

'Yes, I dare say,' Jenny replied. Her face felt stiff from smiling when all she wanted to do was cry. How foolish of her! 'Please do take care of yourself, sir—and Paul too. I fear whoever this man is, he will stop at nothing to get what he wants.'

'I have hopes that Hallam will solve the mystery in London,' he said. 'Remember what I told you, Jenny. Take care—and do not be alone with strangers.'

'You need not warn me of that,' she said and then blushed for she had accepted his offer of help when he was a stranger to her. 'That was different…I knew who you were.'

'Did you? I fear I did not know your name when I took you up.'

'I—I saw you in London at a ball and asked your name,' Jenny said. 'It was the night that Lucy asked me to stay at her home.'

'I see…' Adam frowned and bowed over her hand. 'I hope to see you again soon.'

Jenny thanked him and allowed him to hand her into the carriage. As it drew away from Ravenscar she was thoughtful, her throat tight with the tears she refused to shed.

Just how rich did Adam need his heiress to be? she wondered. She believed her own fortune was adequate rather than huge, but she was not the poor relation he thought her. If she told him the truth, would he consider making her an offer?

Oh, how shameless of her! They had met but a few times—and yet…and yet every time he came near, her heart raced and each time they met she was more certain that she liked him very well. He was exactly the kind of man she'd hoped to meet and marry one day—but would he feel the same about her? Not if he knew she had deceived him.

Her thoughts were troubled for she did not wish to be asked for in marriage just because her father's money might save his grandfather from ruin. Jenny needed to be loved for herself. She had thought that perhaps Adam might care for her a little. Oh dear, this was nonsense. They hardly knew one another—and yet she felt as if she had known him all her life. The terrible tragedy of his cousin's death had broken down all the polite barriers and made her feel bonded to the family, as if they were hers.

Was that what he'd been trying to tell her—that he liked her and might have thought of making her an offer if his circumstances were other than they were? He did not care for a fortune personally, but needed one to pay his grandfather's debts.

If she told him she had Papa's money…it still might not be enough. Mr Nodgrass had hinted that she would be well situated, but she had no idea of what she would have or how much the earl owed. It might be many times what she had—and Adam would still be unable to marry her.

Jenny's pride made her put the idea of telling Adam from her mind. Good gracious, it might sound as if she were trying to buy him, and how shocking that would be. If he'd declared his love and then told her he could not wed her because he needed a fortune, she might have confessed that she had something. However, he had not said that he cared in so many words. To presume too much would be embarrassing. She could only keep her secret until Adam was ready to speak more plainly.

Jenny scolded herself for being too forward. Whatever was she thinking of—to assume that Adam's feelings were much as hers, which, if truth were told, were all too warm to be sensible.

People did not fall in love so quickly—or did they?

Chapter Seven

Adam cursed Lucy Dawlish for interrupting when he was on the point of telling Jenny his situation. He was not sure how he'd meant to proceed. That he had deeper feelings for Jenny than any other lady he'd ever known was not in doubt. Her calmness and kindness had made him see what an exceptional young woman she was. He'd been aware of her sensuality from the first but she was so much more—so much that he admired.

In any other circumstances he would have wished to get to know her better, to court her a little, to discover if he liked her as well on closer acquaintance and if she liked him sufficiently to think of becoming his wife. He could not doubt the feeling between them. Adam was well aware that physical attraction meant very little. Passion could be white hot and urgent for a time and then fade away and what had been intensely interesting could become boring. His last mistress had been a greedy little thing and although she'd roused his desire at the beginning he had soon found that he did not truly like her. He thought that liking was very important if one were contemplating marriage. Romantic love would be the cherry on top of the cake if one were lucky enough to find it. Paul was certainly deep in love or lust with Lucy Dawlish, which was why he was so tortured.

Adam had never yet felt true love for a woman. He was a sensual man and enjoyed the chase when in pursuit of a pretty woman—but surely there must be so much more to marriage. Otherwise, one would end by being bored, taking a succession of mistresses and perhaps making one's wife miserable. Adam would hate himself if he were the cause of deep unhappiness in some unfortunate lady.

It was a curst nuisance that he might have to make a marriage of convenience. Adam had done the calculations and knew that he needed the sum of twenty thousand pounds to save his grandfather's estate. The bank was beginning to make grumbling noises and it could only be a matter of time before they called their money in. Twenty thousand pounds would pay off their loan and leave a little to spare for Adam to begin to restore the estate to at least a semblance of what it had once been.

Where was he to find such a sum? His own estate was not worth a half of that even if he sold it. He needed an heiress who would be prepared to buy herself a husband with a lump sum up front, and the promise of more to come.

Adam mentally reviewed the heiresses his friends had found for him. Only one of them actually had twenty thousand pounds at her disposal—and that was the lady with the squint. He could not recall her name for she had not registered with him, though he remembered she was the wealthiest of them all. He believed she was the daughter of a Cit, though her mother came from a good country family. Her father had no other children and was a widower.

Would he be prepared to give his daughter and her inheritance to Adam for the promise of an earldom in the future?

Why should he? Adam did not consider it a bargain worth the taking. Were he in the father's shoes he would kick any man to kingdom come who dared to offer such a debt-ridden estate to him as the marriage price. It wasn't to be thought of!

He was torn by the need to find a way of saving the estate and his preference for a marriage made out of liking and respect. Given his choice, he believed he might know the bride he would choose—but he had no right to court her, no right to allow her to expect an offer.

Adam acknowledged that he liked Jenny very much. Romantic love was something idiots like Byron, Shakespeare and others of their ilk wrote about, was it not? Adam did not dislike good poetry at the right moment—but flowery sonnets about *love*? He could only feel revolted, as young men often did. Yet now his thoughts had changed subtly. Was it possible that someone could truly die for love? Adam had felt an odd ache in his chest of late, but surely…it could not be love? The kind of love that lasted forever and was as sweet as honey and the scent of roses…

Jenny had her own perfume, unlike any he had smelled before. He found it intoxicating and wanted to bury his face in her hair—her soft warm flesh—and breathe her in, inhale her essence so that she would never leave him.

Adam laughed at himself. What a fool he was

to let his thoughts run away with him. He desired Jenny, he liked her and he respected her. She made him long to sweep her into his arms and take her to his room. She was so lovely, so gentle and honest that he could imagine living with her for the rest of his life. He could see her in his house… see her surrounded by children, girls that looked like her and a boy like him.

He shook his head. Adam had no right to dream. He could not marry anyone until he had worked out what to do about his grandfather's estate.

Was there some other way of saving it—or at least a part of it? Supposing he sold off the land and the mine, which had ceased to produce copper years ago. He might be able to save the house and park. It would mean taking out loans, which would cripple him for years, but after the old man's death he could sell off what was left of the estate.

There was nothing he could do here for the moment. His uncle kept to his room, Paul had no use for his company and Hallam was in London. Perhaps he should go down to Cornwall and take a look at the old mine. If there should by chance be an undiscovered seam of copper they might yet find a way of saving the house and park without his having to beg an heiress for her money.

'Your papa says that he now thinks we *should* go to Bath,' Lady Dawlish announced after dinner that evening when the ladies were alone in the drawing room. 'He thinks it unsafe for you here, Lucy—and, after what happened to Paul, who knows what might occur next? Papa will write tomorrow and secure a house for us. We shall leave in ten days and Papa will accompany us just to see us settled and then return here.'

'Oh, thank you, Mama,' Lucy said, her face lighting up. 'Papa is so good to allow it.'

'Well, he had his reservations for we should not wish others to think you uncaring, Lucy. In Bath we shall meet friends and choose our engagements wisely. Papa made a strict rule: there will be no balls or dances.'

'I do not think I should care to attend a ball for the moment,' Lucy told her truthfully. 'I am mourning Mark in my own way. I do miss his friendship terribly and the way he had of teasing one. But I should enjoy the shops, the views and the theatre—which I think acceptable?'

'Yes, I agree. Had the engagement taken place

I could not have contemplated the visit, but in the circumstances I think it best for you, for otherwise you might sink into a decline and that I cannot have. And that wicked man may be lingering in the district. You were known to be close to Mark and he might have it in mind to harm you. It will be safer in Bath, dearest.'

'It would not be fair to keep Jenny here in seclusion. She very much wishes to buy some new clothes.'

'Oh, you must not mind me,' Jenny said. 'I could always ask a seamstress to call here—though I admit that I do enjoy gazing into the windows of expensive shops.'

Lady Dawlish nodded approvingly. 'Of course you do, my love, and you must have had your fill of mourning these past months. Well, run along now, my dears. I must speak to Cook. I shall need to plan the menus in advance for your papa must not be neglected while we are from home, Lucy. If you need a little pin money, Jenny dear, you may look to me for it.'

'I was reliant on my aunt for my clothes, but my lawyer has arranged for an allowance to be paid into a bank for me so I may buy a new wardrobe.'

'I am glad that you will have some money of

your own, Jenny dear. We none of us knew exactly how you had been left.'

'I am not certain now, ma'am,' Jenny said, glad of the chance to raise the subject. 'But Mr Nodgrass says I shall be comfortable. He is to send on a copy of his accounts when they have been transcribed.'

'That will be a blessing for you, my love,' her kind friend said. 'For myself I care not if you have a fortune or not a feather to fly with. We are so happy and grateful to have you with us at this sad time. I hope you will not think of leaving us too soon?'

'Oh, no, ma'am. I should not dream of leaving you until things are more settled and Lucy is happy again.'

'What a sweet girl you are, and just what Lucy needs at this time to keep her cheerful. Now I must get on for there is much to arrange...'

The girls left her busy with her household plans and went out into the gardens. They walked as far as the park and then found the dry trunk of a fallen tree where they could sit and look about them, enjoying the shade of the trees and the sound of birdsong.

* * *

It was there that the gentlemen found them some thirty minutes or more later.

'Your mama thought you might have come this way,' Paul said. 'Adam and I have been making enquiries in the villages surrounding Ravenscar and Dawlish, in case anyone had noticed a stranger lurking about—someone who seemed to have no real business in the area.'

'And have you found anyone?' Jenny asked, because Lucy was deliberately staring away into the distance, as if she could not bear to look at Paul.

'We heard that a stranger passed this way yesterday. His coach was remarked for it had a coat of arms, though, as the passer-by could not recall what it was, it does not help much. However, it seems to point to the rogue being a gentleman— by birth if not by nature.'

'Yes, I see.' Jenny nodded. 'That would make sense, I think—for if there was a quarrel it would most likely be with someone Mark was accustomed to play cards with, do you not think?'

Jenny glanced at Adam, who was silent and frowning.

'I think it must have been someone Mark did not know well,' Paul said thoughtfully. 'For some reason he was obliged to sit down with him, though what happened we shall never know.'

'Unless Hallam comes up with some clues,' Adam put in.

'Can you not speak of anything else?' Lucy asked, her nerves clearly fraying. 'We are going to Bath very soon. At least there I shall have some pleasant conversation.'

She walked off as if in some distress. Jenny shot a look of apology at the two gentlemen.

'Lucy cannot bear to talk of it,' she explained. 'I should not have asked. Excuse me, I must follow her.'

'Jenny…' Adam said as she began to walk after her friend. 'I wanted to tell you that I am going down to my grandfather's estate in Cornwall. I shall be gone some days—so when I see you again it will be in Bath.'

'Yes, I see.' Jenny fought to keep her smile in place. 'We shall of course look forward to seeing you there. I dare say Lucy will be in a better humour by then.'

'She is entitled to be angry,' Paul said. 'Mark should be alive and planning his wedding. When I catch that devil he will wish he'd never been born.' He turned his horse and rode off as if pursued by all the demons in hell.

'Paul, too, is out of sorts,' Adam said. 'I assure you he is not normally this touchy.'

He got down from his horse and stood looking at her. Jenny felt her spine tingle for the look in his eyes was so intense that it seemed to burn her. She felt her insides melting with longing and looked away.

'I think no one could remain unaffected by what has happened,' Jenny said. 'It will be much better for Lucy when we are in Bath. Here she is reminded at every turn. People come every day to pay their respects and she is obliged to thank them and listen to their professions of sorrow. It is not what one needs at such times. I found the sympathy of others hard to bear after Papa died.'

'Your father's death was caused by a driving accident?'

'It appeared so,' Jenny frowned. 'I have never been certain. I know he lost a large sum of money shortly before his death.'

'You do not think he took his own life?'

'No, that is not at all what I think.' Jenny drew a deep breath. 'I think something happened—something similar to what happened to Paul yesterday, but Papa was not so lucky. His neck was broken in the fall and he died instantly…so they tell me. I am led to believe he did not suffer.'

Jenny's eyes had filled with tears. She blinked them away, brushing her cheeks with her hand.

'Forgive me, I should not have asked.'

Adam came towards her, offering his hand. He touched her cheek, which must be pale, and her hands trembled. She allowed it for a moment and then flinched away.

His touch aroused feelings quite unsuitable to the situation. He meant only to comfort, she knew, but she trembled inwardly and wished that he would take her into his arms. It seemed that a fire had begun to rage inside her. She wanted to be held close to his chest, to feel the brush of his lips against her hair—if she were truthful, to be kissed. No, no, it was too foolish of her!

'I thought I was quite over it,' Jenny said, determined to remain calm and not disgrace herself by revealing her longings, 'but my aunt and uncle were so practical. They accepted it was an accident and…' She shook her head. If she told him what her uncle had done—selling all her father's possessions unnecessarily—she would have to tell him that she was not the penniless companion he thought her. Her instinct was always to tell the truth, but she could not find the words to confess it—and it would not do to raise hopes of a fortune when she had no idea how much she actually had.

'Tears for a loved one never hurt,' Adam said and smiled down at her. His eyes seemed to caress her, then he bent his head and kissed her. It was a sweet gentle kiss that called the heart from her body and made her want to melt into him, to be his in every way.

'Adam…' she murmured. 'I think…'

He seemed to recall himself and frowned. 'Forgive me, I should not have done that. It was wrong of me. I had no right. I can never…'

'Never…' She looked up at him, trying to understand why he had withdrawn so suddenly when his body seemed to call to hers.

'My situation is intolerable,' Adam said and turned away, a nerve flicking at his temple. 'I am hoping I may discover some way of rescuing my grandfather from his problems. The mine played out its copper seams years ago, but perhaps some other use may be found for the land. I must see what I can do, because the alternative is unthinkable.'

'I hope you find something,' Jenny said. 'It must be difficult for you.'

'Difficult is not the word I should use.' Adam seemed to glare down at her, clearly in some distress. 'Excuse me, I should go after Paul before he breaks his foolish neck—and you should go to Lucy. I dare say she is in tears.'

'Yes, perhaps.' Jenny tried not to show her hurt as he remounted his horse, hardly looking at her. He had kissed her as if he meant it, but now he'd withdrawn behind a barrier of ice. She inclined her head politely. 'I am glad to have seen you again before we leave, sir. I wish you good fortune.'

'I shall need it,' he said ruefully, then turned his horse and set out after Paul at a canter.

Jenny blinked hard as he rode away. For a moment he had seemed to promise so much, but then he'd withdrawn from her. She would be foolish to let herself hope that he would offer her more than friendship. She must not expect it or let herself think of it!

Yet she had thought of it. Was she wrong to think that he liked her as much as she liked him? Or was that simply wishful thinking—a longing for the kind of happiness she'd never known?

Jenny saw Lucy some little distance ahead and ran to catch her up. As Adam had forecast she was crying, dabbing at her cheeks with a scrap of lace kerchief.

'Paul did not mean to upset you,' Jenny said. 'They think only of catching that man—and of punishing him.'

'I wish they may do so,' Lucy said angrily. 'Why will Paul not look at me? It is as if he blames me for what happened to his brother.'

'No, how could he?' Jenny was caught by her strange expression. 'I thought you blamed him for it?'

Lucy's voice caught on a sob. 'Paul would never…but now he will not speak to me or look at me. If he catches me looking at him, he scowls as if he hated me.'

'I am certain he does not,' Jenny said and put an arm about her waist. 'I think he is in so much pain that he scarcely knows what to think.'

'Even when he was thrown from his horse he would not look at me,' Lucy said. 'We all heard the shot. We know that someone tried to hurt, perhaps to kill him—but yesterday he accused me of thinking he'd arranged the accident to deflect suspicion from him. As if I would think such a thing.'

'Did you tell him so?'

Lucy's cheeks flushed red. 'He made me cross. I said that the idea was only in his mind and that only he knew what had put it there.'

'Oh, Lucy—that does sound as if you blame him,' Jenny said, her gaze narrowed. 'Why did you say such a thing to him?'

'I do not know,' Lucy confessed tearfully. 'It is just that everything is so horrid and my mind is in turmoil. I feel guilty because I was not in love with Mark, as everyone believed.'

'Yes, I know, but you must not let it affect your relationships with others,' Jenny said. 'You like Paul. Why do you not show him that you still value his friendship?'

'I…cannot,' Lucy said. 'If he would be as he was at the ball, charming and sweet…but he has changed. He is cold and bitter and angry—angry with me. I do not know what I've done to make him so.'

'I think his anger is as much frustration as anything,' Jenny said. 'He loved his brother and at the moment he can do nothing to avenge him. That is why it is so important to them all to find the rogue. Besides, if he attempted to kill Paul, he is a dangerous man. He needs to be on his guard.'

'Yes, I know.' Lucy shuddered. 'If anything happened to Paul I could not stand it—I really could not, Jenny.'

'I am sure it will not,' Jenny comforted, though she knew that it was possible unless Paul took more care of his safety. 'I dare say the rogue has left the area. He must know that he is being searched for.'

'Yes, word will have spread and people will be watching for a stranger who has no business in the area,' Lucy agreed. 'Now, please may we forget it and talk of something else?'

'I am determined to read Miss Austen's latest novel as soon as I can take it from the library,' Jenny said. 'Though there is no reason why I should not subscribe to my own copy. Your mama subscribes to parcels of the latest novels, does she not?' Lucy nodded and Jenny smiled. 'Then perhaps she will furnish me with the address of her supplier. Books are a luxury my aunt thought unnecessary. She said why buy them when it was possible to borrow—and my uncle thought both novels and poetry a waste of time. Now I can please myself and I think I shall purchase a set of

Lord Byron's works as well as Miss Austen's—
and Fanny Burney's, too.'

'I always borrow Mama's and I'm sure you
could too,' Lucy said. 'But if you wish to set up a
library of your own it would be the greatest fun.
We could draw up lists and discover what bind-
ings they come in. When you have a house of
your own your books might look very smart set
out on the shelves if you have them covered in red
or green leather.'

'I know it is possible to buy such sets,' Jenny
said, warming to the subject, because it pleased
Lucy. 'I must enquire the price. I've been used to
economy these past months, but there is no reason
why I should not treat myself to a few pleasures.'

'There is little more satisfying than a new book,'
Lucy said. 'When one looks at the cover there
is so much to discover, so much to explore. One
never knows where the author will take one or
what kind of adventures the poor heroine must endure.' She laughed. 'I think I should not like to be
the heroine in *Udolpho*, though I loved reading it.'

'Yes, so did I,' Jenny said. 'I had to smuggle it
into my bedroom so that my aunt should not see
it—but I do have my own copy of that book. It is

bound in cloth, not leather, but the story is just as wonderful.'

'Oh, yes,' Lucy agreed. 'Nothing is worse than row after row of boring books in leather. They look well, but one cannot read them—but how delightful it must be to have one's favourite books bound so. It is an indulgence, of course...'

Jenny could do nothing but agree. Lucy's spirits had lifted and, in helping to cheer her friend, she had found some ease from her own distress.

She was looking forward to the trip to Bath, and, if Adam had gone to Cornwall, she had nothing to stay here for—but she felt the loss of his company keenly. She had seen him almost every day since that fatal day when he'd taken her up from the side of the road and she was going to miss him. Her heart raced every time she saw him approaching her and she was very much afraid that she might have fallen in love. It was ridiculous of her, of course, but she feared it might have happened that first night at Ravenscar.

If only Adam felt the same. Had his grandfather not been in sore need, she was sure her fortune would have been enough to help him improve his own estate for the benefit of their children, giving them a comfortable life together. Unfortunately, she was not sure it amounted to enough to pay the earl's debts.

Jenny would not have grudged the money had it enabled Adam to do what was needed. She had no desire to wear ostentatious jewels and one simple carriage would be sufficient. A short stay in London in a house hired for the Season would content her and if Adam's fortune were modest it would be enough—but he was determined to settle the earl's debts and she was not sure it could be done.

No, she would not dwell on such things. Adam had told her he intended to visit his grandfather's estate in the hope of improving the situation and perhaps he would. Sometimes when a mine ran out of copper it was possible to find a vein of some other precious metal, like tin or silver.

How wonderful that would be!

Jenny smiled at her own thoughts. Such things only occurred in novels. It was far more likely that the land was worthless and could not even be sold.

'I was never more glad of someone's company,' Lady Dawlish said to Jenny some days later. 'Indeed, I do not know what we should have done had you not been kind enough to come here and stay. I have never seen my poor Lucy so down and

I do not know how to lift her. I am afraid that she will sink into a decline.'

'I do not think it, ma'am,' Jenny told her with a smile. 'It is true that she soars from the depths to the heights and back again, but she is stronger than you may imagine. I am certain she will recover once we are in Bath. Here, everything reminds her of Mark.'

'They were always together, even when they were little. Indeed, she and Paul were of an age and they tagged after Mark. He was always the leader, the golden god they all wanted to notice them. Until Lucy went away to finishing school I thought nothing would come of it. Then both Mark and Paul joined the army. It was when Mark was home on leave and Lucy had just returned from her school that they first became attracted to each other in that way.'

'Yet they were not engaged immediately?'

'I was determined that Lucy must have at least one Season. Dawlish and Ravenscar had always promoted the marriage, but I was not certain until Lucy told me that he had asked her to wait for him until that last campaign was over. Mark did not wish her to be a widow before she was hardly a wife and I agreed. I think her papa and Ravenscar would have liked a wedding sooner, but I wanted Lucy to be certain.'

'Yes, I see. It was very sensible of you, ma'am. What should you have done had Lucy changed her mind and decided they would not suit?'

'I should have supported her and taken her away—to Paris or the Italian lakes. Her papa would have been disappointed and Ravenscar, too—but I would not have allowed her to be pushed into a marriage she could not like. Now of course we must think of another match for her. I believe an older man might suit her, for Lucy likes to be spoiled, and I think perhaps Mark did not always dance to her tune.'

'I met him only once in London,' Jenny said. 'Was he like his brother?'

'Not at all. Mark was larger than life—one might even say arrogant at times. He was given homage and expected it, though one could not grudge him for he was a truly talented man. At riding, shooting, wrestling—any sport—he excelled. He was also clever, though his taste in reading did not extend to poetry or novels. He had a serious mind and would no doubt have taken his seat in the House one day. He laughed at Lucy for reading trash and thought she should improve her mind.'

'But Lucy loves poetry and novels.' Jenny looked at her thoughtfully. 'I am not certain he was the right husband for her, ma'am.'

'Perhaps not. I had wondered if she was beginning to realise it—and then of course he was killed. One is not certain how to behave. The Ravenscars are our particular friends, of course, and Papa thinks we should share their grief—but why should my poor girl suffer?'

'I think it very hard for her,' Jenny said. She knew more than Lucy's mother, but could not betray a confidence. 'Yet I know that she is feeling better each day.'

'Well, we are off the day after tomorrow,' Lady Dawlish said. 'I think I must ask Papa to pay a courtesy visit to Ravenscar to tell them we are leaving. However, there is no need for you or Lucy to accompany him. I think it could only distress Lucy again.'

'Yes, I believe so.'

Jenny had no desire to visit the estate, because Adam was not there. She'd heard nothing from him since he'd left the area for Cornwall and wondered how he fared. If Paul had called on them, he might have brought news, but he had not been near since that last day in the Park when he'd ridden off in a fit of temper.

Paul was suffering as much as anyone. Jenny suspected that his pain was not all due to his grief for his brother, but she had no right to speculate or to tell Lucy what she thought might be on his mind. Lucy and Paul must sort out their affairs themselves.

Was Adam finding the rich seam of tin he needed? Or would he discover that the mine was played out and there was no alternative to his problem but the marriage he wished to avoid?

'You do not think we could blast deeper into the earth and find a new seam of copper?' Adam asked the former mine manager. 'I know it would cost money, but I think I could fund it—if there's a chance.'

'I think this part of the mine is played out,' John Thawson said and frowned. 'I did hear once that there might be tin in the old mine—the one the earl closed down years ago for lack of money.'

'You've never seen it?'

'No. It was one of the older miners. He had retired then, but swore on his oath that there was a rich seam of tin if your grandfather would open the old workings up again.'

'Was the earl approached?'

'He said he had no money for chasing a forlorn hope. I dare say he thought it just a tale made up to provide work for the men in these parts. Times have been hard since the mine closed down. There are very few still working and the work is jealously guarded. Men from one mine are not welcomed at another and fights break out if they try to undercut the wages.'

'Yes, I see.' Adam was thoughtful. 'Where can I find this man—the one who saw the seam of tin?'

'He died a few months ago. He was in his sixties and that is a good age for a man who has worked in the mines.'

'A pity. Is there no one else who might know of the location of this seam?'

'Horton had a daughter and a grandson. The boy is sixteen and illegitimate—a little wild, they say. I think Horton was fond of him—and now you mention it, I've seen them close to the old workings on more than one occasion. It is possible that the old man showed him what was there—or they may just be using the old mine as a place to store contraband. I think Jake is in with a gang of smugglers that frequent this part of the coast.'

'I see…' Adam smiled. 'Well, perhaps I should speak to this young man. He may be able to help me.'

'I wish he might, sir.' Thawson frowned. 'Would you truly consider opening the mine again if a new seam of either copper or tin was found?'

'I should certainly go into it,' Adam said. 'For one thing work brings prosperity to the villagers—and that means they take more care of their homes and they cultivate the land better. Everything has been let go. I cannot put the estate back into any sort of order without help. Had I a fortune at my disposal I would do what I could—but the estate needs to pay for itself.'

'Yes, of course. Folk blame the earl for what happened, but they don't understand that no one can keeping pouring money into an empty hole in the ground.'

'My grandfather is old and tired. He has not managed things as well as he ought, but he loves this land—and it would give him pleasure to see the people prosperous again. I shall find Jake Horton and ask him if he knows where this seam is.'

'It might be best if you speak to him first,'

Thawson said. 'If you went down the old shaft alone, you could be in danger. Parts of it may be flooded—and if they're using it to store smuggled goods you might end up being murdered.'

'Then I shall visit the Hortons at home and speak with them,' Adam said. 'At least there is something I can do. If there's anything worth opening Wheal Margaret for, I would be willing to have a go. It may come to nothing, but there is always a chance.'

'You never know with a mine, sir,' Thawson said. 'I'll go down the newer workings myself and take a look. Now that I know someone is willing to open them up again, it's worth exploring a bit further...'

'I'll come with you,' Adam said. 'Could we go today? I can call on Jake Horton this evening.'

'Best leave it until tomorrow,' Thawson said. 'He will probably be out with the Gentlemen if it's a moonless night.'

Adam nodded. 'Aye, you're right. But I could speak to his mother. She might sound him out on the idea—and if they need to move a few barrels I'd rather give them time to do it than cause bad feeling.'

Thawson laughed. 'You'll make a good master

here, Captain Miller. You understand men better than your grandfather ever did—but that's to be expected after what you've been through out there.'

'War teaches you to respect your fellow men, the troopers as well as the officers,' Adam said, a grim light in his eyes. 'We might as well take a look at Wheal Sarah now, while it's still daylight.'

'Won't be much light down there. We'll need hard hats and lamps to see what's what. I just hope it isn't completely flooded.'

Chapter Eight

'So, here we are then, Lucy,' Lady Dawlish said, looking fondly at her daughter. 'Tell me, can you be comfortable here, do you think?'

'Oh, yes, Mama. Father has taken a beautiful house for us. The Crescent is one of the most fashionable areas of Bath. Jenny and I are looking forward to our walks for there is so much to see here.'

'It is a particularly beautiful area,' Lady Dawlish agreed. 'Some of the beauty spots are close enough to make it possible to drive out in an afternoon and be back in time to change for dinner. We may hire an open chaise if we wish— but I dare say we shall be invited to drive out with friends. I am certain we shall find several of our acquaintance settled here for the summer. Picnics would be quite acceptable for you to attend.'

'I hope we shall make new friends,' Lucy said. 'I think that many people who frequent Bath seldom visit London.'

'Yes, indeed. I dare say a great many visitors come here for their health—but I am certain they will have young relatives with them. You may meet some young ladies and, indeed, gentlemen that you have not met before.'

'I only wish to have friends so that I may talk and laugh,' Lucy assured her. 'I would not think of… It is too soon, Mama.'

'Yes, of course, my love—but acquaintances made here may become more in time. I would not encourage you to think of marriage for at least a year, Lucy. This visit to Bath is merely the start of my plans for you. I think in the autumn we might travel to the Italian lakes, if your papa can be prised from his home—and perhaps even if he cannot. We might find some other travelling companions.'

'I think I should like that,' Lucy said. 'I feel better already. At home everything seemed so grey and dull.'

'Yes, I saw how you were feeling.' Lady Dawlish hesitated, then, 'Would I be right to think that you were a little unsure about the wedding, dearest?'

'Would you think less of me if I said I had considered asking Mark to delay it? I could not be certain of my feelings for him. I loved him dearly as a friend—and he looked so handsome in his uniform when he proposed that I was swept away by emotion—but I was not certain I was in love with him. I thought it might be better to wait so that we could both be sure of our feelings, for I am not certain he was in love with me, Mama. Though I know he cared for me, I think he felt our marriage was expected and did not wish to let me down.'

'Thank you for your confidence. I had thought it might be that—you have been feeling guilty, have you not?'

'Yes, Mama. It was so terrible of me. I grieved for Mark, truly I did—but my heart is not broken, as it must surely have been had I been in love.'

'I quite understand. We shall not speak of this again, dearest. Nevertheless, neither Papa or I could countenance an engagement before a year has passed. It would look very bad and we should not wish to give offence to the Ravenscar family for they are our oldest friends.'

'I do understand, Mama,' Lucy said and held back a sigh. 'But you would not think me wicked if I fell in love with someone else?'

'If you should meet someone you like very much, I should be happy, my love. We should continue to socialise so that you could meet in company, but there would be no formal agreement for twelve months.'

Lucy nodded. 'Thank you, Mama. I feel better for our talk. May I walk out with Jenny now, please?'

'Providing you take one of the maids with you.' Lady Dawlish smiled. 'Do you intend to go shopping?'

'We have spoken of it. Jenny wishes to have some pretty gowns made and I need one or two evening gowns in grey or lilac.'

'Yes, you must have at least one of each and perhaps a dark-blue silk,' her mother agreed. 'I think you need three afternoon gowns, two at least for mornings—but you will not need a ballgown. By the time we attend such an affair you will be wearing colours.'

'I should not wish to dance just yet.' Lucy kissed her mother's cheek. 'It would be disrespectful of me. I did think the world of Mark, truly I did—

only not in that way. Jenny is waiting for me. I must not keep her any longer for I only came to tell you of our plans.'

'I shall visit the Pump room to take the waters. It is nasty stuff, but I dare say it may do me good. Once I am seen there we shall receive invitations to the kind of affair that will be perfectly suitable to our situation—but this evening we shall attend the theatre. I believe they are showing a performance of *Othello*.'

'That will be a treat. I love a play—and it is such a passionate story, a man driven to such extremes for love…' Lucy said and then her face turned pale. 'Do you think that such a story might be likely to occur in real life, Mama?'

'It is merely a piece of drama,' her mama said. She had been sorting through her own gowns and missed the stricken look in her daughter's eyes. 'But I think one of Shakespeare's finest works.'

Lucy murmured something appropriate and left her mother's room. She saw Jenny standing in the hall and ran down to greet her.

'Have you been waiting long?'

'Only a few minutes,' Jenny said. 'An invitation to a card party was delivered just now. I have seen it lying on the hall table on the salver. I do not think you will have time to brood here, Lucy.'

'I am glad of it,' Lucy said and tucked her arm through Jenny's. 'Mama is taking us to the theatre this evening—it is a performance of *Othello*.'

'One of my favourites,' Jenny said, then her gaze narrowed. 'It will not upset you?'

'Because the theme is jealousy?' Lucy shook her head. 'No, I do not think so. I could hardly think Paul jealous of his brother. He has hardly looked at me since that day he fell from his horse. He did not even come to say goodbye to us.'

'We do not know the circumstances,' Jenny said, sensing her friend's hurt. 'You know that Lord Ravenscar has been ill. It may be that Paul was reluctant to leave his father at such a time.'

'Yes, I suppose it might be that,' Lucy said and her frown cleared as she nodded. 'We shall not talk about him. I am determined to buy a new bonnet this morning and as many silks as take my eye…'

'I thought you would go straight to Bath,' Paul said and frowned at Adam. 'Were you not engaged to Lucy and her mother in Bath?'

'It is my intention to go down soon,' Adam said,

'but I had a mysterious and alarming letter from Hallam. He said that he had news of a serious nature and wished to impart it to me in private. Since he wanted you to hear it too, he suggested that I come here. He will join us tomorrow.'

'I hope to God he has something positive to tell us. It is driving me mad, Adam. To see Father so worn down...I think this business has broken him. He was quite ill and I feared for his life for some days, but he seems to have made a recovery. His physician tells me that his heart is not all it should be, but he has a strong constitution and a will of iron. I am assured that his death is not imminent. He wants me to join you in Bath for a few days, thinks the change will do me good.'

'Let us see what Hallam has to say tomorrow. Our plans may change, according to his news. If he can tell us something positive about Mark's killer...'

'I want that murdering rogue dead or on trial for his life!'

'You know we all want that,' Adam said and placed a hand on his shoulder. 'It has taken longer than I'd hoped to find him out—but you know what they say, revenge is best taken cold.'

Paul nodded. 'What of you—have you news of your own?'

'I'm not certain. I was told of a possible vein of tin that one of the old miners swore he'd seen. I persuaded his grandson to take me down and show me where it was found, but unfortunately the way was blocked. The mine had flooded and the force of water had brought down some of the roof. Thawson said they can dig it out once the pumps have dealt with the flooding. Unfortunately, it isn't a quick fix, but I've authorised the work to go ahead.'

'That will cost a pretty penny.'

'Yes, it will. I was ready to finance it myself, but Grandfather produced a Rembrandt that should be worth perhaps a thousand pounds. It had been damaged, but should still sell for enough to cover the work we have in mind. As he said, it was a drop in the ocean as far as his debts were concerned, but if we should find that seam of tin the bank would be willing to allow us to run on and we could repay the loans over a longer period of time.'

'You know my father might be willing to help if you asked, Adam. I should certainly not object to a long-term loan should the bank refuse to accommodate you.'

'You are my friend so I shall not take offence,' Adam said, 'but you must know my answer to that, Paul. I do not mind taking a further loan from the bank or simply extending the repayment term—but I will not borrow from family or friends.'

'I meant no offence. I know Father would offer to loan you the money if the earl was about to go under.'

Adam shook his head. It was for this very reason that he had not been able to tell his cousins how large his grandfather's debts had become. He'd always known that Ravenscar would make him a loan if he asked, but he would almost prefer to marry an heiress.

'I thank you for the kind thought, but my answer will always be no. I shall not take a loan that I might not be able to repay from either you or your father.'

With that the subject was dropped. They talked some more and then parted, Adam to pay his respects to his uncle and Paul to go riding.

'An attempt on Staffs's life?' Paul cried, staring at his cousin in horror. 'Hal, this grows worse by the hour. How is he? Is he close to death?'

'He was wounded, but not fatally,' Hallam said. 'I visited him at his home, where I found him in bed being fussed over by his mother and sisters. He was a little groggy at first, but after some strong coffee and refusing to take more of the laudanum his mother pressed on him, he was able to tell me what happened.'

'Good grief,' Paul said. 'I would not be in his shoes for the world—I hope he has the wit to refuse that damned awful stuff. Laudanum may dull the pain, but it robs your mind of sense.'

'He was in a deal of pain at first, I believe. It seems he was set upon when out riding, dragged from his horse and beaten to an inch of his life. He has several broken ribs, bruises all over and a lump the size of a cricket ball on his head. It was the head wound that laid him low and robbed him of his senses for days.'

'Has he any idea of who attacked him or why?'

'He had none until I told him that Mark had been murdered—and asked him if he recalled a certain diamond necklace...'

'I dare say he was pretty cut up about Mark,' Adam said, looking thoughtful.

'Yes, extremely. Overcome would probably fit the bill—but he recovered and told me something very interesting. It would seem that the night Mark had a run of luck, there were two others involved in the game. Fontleroy was one of them, as we suspected—and his friend Henry Lichfield was the other. Staffs saw Fontleroy hand over his IOUs and he thinks Lichfield owed a similar amount for both had been gambling recklessly—and he says Lichfield had been drinking heavily. He remembers that he had a wild light in his eyes.'

'So we have two possible candidates for our murderer.' Paul nodded grimly.

'What of the necklace?' Adam asked. 'Did Staffs see it?'

'No, not that evening,' Hallam said. 'He believes someone asked if Mark would take a necklace in settlement. Staffs cannot recall which of the two suggested it, but thinks it was probably Lichfield. He thinks Mark agreed, but the game had ended and he was called away by someone. The next day Mark showed him a diamond necklace and asked what he thought it worth.'

'Would he remember the necklace?' Paul asked.

'Yes, he is sure of it for he thought it very fine. He believes it may have been Lichfield who redeemed his debts that way—and since we did not find any notes from him it may be that he did.'

'So Lichfield and not Fontleroy?' Adam frowned. 'This has muddied the waters, Hallam. We now have two suspects rather than one…'

'Yes, but Staffs said he saw Fontleroy leaving Mark's lodgings the day he saw the necklace and that he was in a foul mood. Says he was muttering something like "…the damned fool, he'll hang us all…" Can't be certain, but he thinks that was it.' Hallam frowned. 'You must understand that these things came out as we spoke and were but half-remembered. Staffs did not think of everything immediately and he cannot vouch for having remembered it all correctly. He is afraid that his illness may have made him either forget something or remember it wrongly.'

'So it may have been something he dreamed up in his fever?'

'I suggested the same thing, but he refuted it hotly. I think he was probably right, though not as clear as I should like. Apparently Mark told him that morning that Fontleroy had wanted something from him—something that he had refused to sell. I imagine he would have been furious if the necklace could implicate either Lichfield or himself in these jewel thefts.'

'You think that Fontleroy tried to recover the

necklace in London—offered to buy it back and Mark wouldn't sell…' Paul frowned. 'Then he knew where the necklace came from—that it was stolen?'

'It sounds to me as if they may both have been involved with these stolen goods. Perhaps Fontleroy had given him the necklace in settlement of a debt and told him to have it broken up before selling—but Lichfield offered it to Mark to redeem his vowels.'

'So he was the fool and Fontleroy tried to redeem it to save their necks, but Mark would not sell. I wonder why Mark did not just take the money and be shot of it?'

'Perhaps Fontleroy offered something other than cash—Mark didn't tell Staffs, but he thinks Mark suspected something was going on. He thinks he may have intended to investigate further.'

Adam's brow darkened. 'If either Fontleroy or Lichfield believed they were in danger of being exposed as thieves or simply in possession of stolen goods…'

'Mark is dead,' Paul said harshly. 'It's obvious what they did—I've been shot at, Staffs was beaten nearly to death. They are as guilty as hell. Where are they? I'll have the truth out of them.'

'You will not have it out of Lichfield,' Hallam said grimly. 'He was found three days ago at his London house—with a pistol in his mouth and his brains spilled out on the floor.'

'Suicide or murder?' Adam said, a low whistle escaping him. 'Either way it simplifies things, don't you think?'

'I think we can safely assume that Lichfield was involved in these thefts or in handling stolen goods,' Hallam said. 'We can surmise that Fontleroy made the attempt on Paul's life, had Staffs beaten and killed Mark—but we have no proof.'

'He has either killed or attempted to have killed anyone who might have some knowledge of his part in the affair,' Paul muttered, lips white with anger. 'I shall delight in teaching him what it feels like to be on the receiving end of a beating.'

'If you are allowed near enough to attempt it,' Adam said. 'For the moment we have no proof. I do not wish to see you hang for murder and if you kill Fontleroy without proof that is what may happen. No, we have to put him under pressure, make him sweat. If he thinks we know it all, he will wonder what we're waiting for. He will become nervous and make a mistake and then we'll have him.'

'What are you suggesting?' Hallam asked.

'We must discover where Fontleroy is and follow him. I shall endeavour to engage him in a card game and somehow we shall let him think that the necklace is for sale.'

'Why would he believe that?' Paul asked, eyes smouldering.

'Because I need money to save Grandfather's estate—and, having found the necklace, which neither of you two know about, I am willing to sell it for the sum of ten thousand pounds.'

'It is a beautiful necklace, but not worth that sum.'

'I am not selling the necklace—I am selling his freedom, his security. While we have the diamonds we could expose him. Remember, he does not know if Mark told any of us—or if a letter naming him exists. He found nothing and therefore assumes that one of us found it. He must be on thorns, waiting for our next move. If I accepted his bribe and let him have it back, he would be in the clear.'

'If you let him believe that, your life is at risk.'

'I know—but that is where you two come in. We watched each other's back while we fought Boney. Now we have another enemy, perhaps more dangerous and definitely less honourable. It might be best if I seemed a little at loggerheads with you both. I must allow him to think that I am willing to sacrifice my honour in order to settle Grandfather's debts. He will lead me on, but then he will try to murder me—that is when you—and the others we shall enrol—will pounce. Take him in the act.'

'Supposing he employs a gang of rogues to do his dirty work for him?'

'He has already tried that with Staffs and it didn't work. For all we know it was a hired assassin that fired at you, Paul. No, I believe that he will do the deed himself if he can. He will want the necklace in his hand before he kills me—in case I have left a letter telling one of you where it is hid.'

'It might work,' Hallam said and frowned. 'You will be taking a hell of a risk, Adam. If we happen to lose him, he could kill you and we should be none the wiser.'

'That is a risk I am willing to take.' Adam smiled. 'It so happens that I trust you—and a few of the men who served under me.'

'We just have to discover where he is. He may be lying low, hiding like the rat he is,' Paul said.

'No, he has gone down to Bath,' Hallam told them with a slight smile. 'I was told that he was interested in a girl, but I have no further information.'

'To Bath?' Adam frowned. He would have preferred their little masquerade to be played out elsewhere, but he must follow where the marquis led. 'Are we agreed on our strategy, then? You and Hallam will go down separately, Paul. If anyone asks where I am, be a little off-hand, but say nothing. I am out of favour with the pair of you, but do not give a reason. If I am any judge of character, Fontleroy will be intrigued. And if you are asked if there are any clues as to the reason behind Mark's death, say you have no idea. Say a search was made of Mark's room—and, if you are asked, say it was I who made the search, but do not volunteer the information.'

'Yes, we must let it appear that we know nothing—while you may know everything.'

'Exactly.' Adam smiled. 'Are we agreed?'

'I don't see why you should take all the risk...' Paul objected. 'Mark was my brother.'

'Which is why you would never dream of concealing Fontleroy's guilt. I, however, am in a desperate situation—so desperate that I might go against my conscience to save my grandfather's estate.'

'Adam has to do it,' Hallam said. 'You can't—and I don't think I have the temperament for it. I should want to choke the life out of him the moment I saw him.'

'Do not imagine you are alone in wanting that,' Adam said. 'But I am more interested in seeing him hang for his crimes and there is only one way to prove him guilty—and that is to provoke him into trying to kill again.'

The three looked at each other grimly. Fontleroy was a dangerous enemy and if they were right he'd killed once and attempted two other murders. Adam's life was at risk and they would have to watch his back or he might end with a knife in it.

Jenny sighed as she accompanied Lady Dawlish and Lucy to the Pump room that morning. They had been in Bath more than a week now and every day she'd looked for Adam, but thus far she'd seen no sign of him. His business in Cornwall must have delayed him or some other reason had kept him from joining them, as he'd promised.

It was foolish of her to look for him each day, but she could not help scanning the rooms wherever they went. It seemed an age since she'd spoken to him, though it could not be much above three weeks—but that was such an age.

Jenny had told herself a dozen times that it was useless to think of Adam. Even if she told him that she had her inheritance at her disposal and risked his censure for deceiving him, her fortune might not be enough to solve his problems.

And did she wish to be wed for her money? Jenny had spent more than one sleepless night trying to resolve the problem. She would be happy to offer what she had to help Adam out of his difficulties—but only if he loved her.

Perhaps the idea would revolt Adam even had she sufficient funds to repay his grandfather's debts. She remembered that night in London, when she'd heard him jesting with his friends as he laid down his requirements in an heiress. At the time she'd imagined him arrogant, the veriest coxcomb for finding fault in blameless girls, but she understood him better now. He had been protesting in jest, because he did not wish to marry an heiress for her money. The idea offended his pride and he would be humiliated at having to beg for a lady's favours simply because he needed her fortune.

Jenny knew she could not offer hers without some encouragement. He thought her a penniless girl in a difficult situation and had gone out of his way to help and protect her. If she told him the truth, might he not feel that she had been laughing at him behind his back?

Only if he declared his love could she declare hers—and then she might tell him that she had some money. Perhaps a drop in the ocean of the earl's debts, for she could not know the extent of them—or indeed of her own fortune—but surely it would help to stave off the bank's demands until Adam could make improvements to the estate, which might make it profitable.

She thought it a little odd that it was taking Mr Nodgrass so long to send her the accounts he'd promised, but supposed that he must have wanted them checked before giving her the total of her expectations.

The problem went round and round in her mind endlessly, but there was never an answer to her questions.

For the moment she must think of the Dawlish family and not of her own situation. They had several acquaintances in Bath now and were sure to see them wherever they went, particularly in the

Pump room, which was a favourite meeting place. Ladies and gentlemen nodded as they entered and walked to the seats where an attendant was offering glasses of the foul-tasting water. Neither Lucy nor Jenny had tasted it, though urged to try a sip by Lady Dawlish, who managed to swallow a few mouthfuls each morning in the hope it might do her some good. Why she should bother when she was in perfect health was a mystery to Jenny, but Lady Dawlish said one could not come to Bath and not take advantage of the waters.

That good lady was soon settled with other matrons and gossiping happily. When Lucy suggested that she and Jenny would walk to the lending library and bring back a parcel of books, she merely nodded her permission and smiled.

'I thought we might take a cup of chocolate at the little cake shop near the library,' Lucy said, tucking her arm through Jenny's as they left the Pump room and emerged into bright sunshine. 'And I have decided that I shall buy that green-silk bonnet we saw in the French milliner's the other day. It becomes me well and even though I ought not to wear it for the moment I shall as soon as Mama says I may.'

'It hardly seems fair that I may wear colours while you are forced to wear only grey or lilac.'

'Oh, pooh,' Lucy said and hugged her arm. 'It is only a few weeks since you left off your blacks. I am pleased to see you in colours again—besides, you often wear dark or rich colours, whereas I prefer pastels.'

'Pale colours do not become me as they do you,' Jenny said. 'If I wear yellow, it must be a deep—' She broke off and caught her breath as she saw a man approaching. 'Whatever you do, do not leave me, Lucy.'

Her friend glanced at her, surprised at how pale she was. 'What is wrong, dearest? You are not unwell?'

'No, not at all. It is the Marquis of Fontleroy. He has come down to Bath. Of all the unlucky chances! One of the reasons I left London was so that I should not have to see him. He was determined in his pursuit—and my aunt thought I should accept him.'

'Oh, Jenny, poor you,' Lucy said. 'Did she try to force you to wed him? That must have been so uncomfortable. I do not like that gentleman at all. The way his eyes seem to…strip away one's clothes is most unpleasant.'

'You feel as I do,' Jenny said. 'In London he would not leave me alone and my aunt encouraged him.'

'Mama will not do so,' Lucy assured her. 'She thinks him unsuitable as a husband for me and would feel the same regarding you, Jenny. It is different in Lord Mallory's case. He must be fifteen years my senior, but Mama has been encouraging me to see him as a possible suitor when I am ready to begin a relationship again. Mallory has a fortune and is so very kind and funny that one cannot help but like him.'

Jenny could not answer for Fontleroy was upon them and, as he lifted his hat, she was forced to acknowledge him.

'Miss Hastings,' he said, his thick lips seeming to curl in a sneer over white teeth. 'How very fortunate to find you here. I had not looked for such pleasure.'

'Sir, you must excuse us,' Lucy said and drew a scowl from the gentleman. 'I fear we have an appointment and may not linger.'

'Yes, forgive us. We are already late.' Jenny blessed her friend for thinking of the excuse. 'Good day, sir.'

Jenny dare not look back as they hurried away,

but she sensed that he watched them to the end of the street and she knew he would be scowling.

'He will not like that,' she said to Lucy. 'You must be careful of him, because he is not a nice man. I know he wants me, but I do not know why he should.'

Lucy's laughter rang out. 'Oh, Jenny, you goose. He looked at you as if he could gobble you up. Mama would scold me for saying it, but…he wants you in his bed and, since he knows that the only way to achieve that is to marry you, he is determined to have you if he can.'

'I would rather die,' Jenny said.

She shuddered at the thought and wished that Adam were here. She had missed him more than was sensible and longed to see him again. He was such a strong man that she felt comfortable in his presence. If he were to show an interest in her, she would be safe from Fontleroy and others like him.

Chapter Nine

It was that evening at the theatre, where they were to attend a concert, that Jenny saw Adam enter a box opposite them with a party of friends. Her heart caught and she felt a little hurt for he had obviously been in Bath long enough to make contact with some friends, but had not come to the house to pay his respects.

Had she read too much into his kindness? He had said that he would call on them in Bath, warned her to take care and not to be alone with strangers—but perhaps he now thought his duty towards her done? So his attentions to her had been merely duty because of the circumstances in which they found themselves.

After all her heart searching! Jenny's throat felt tight with misery and for some few minutes she was unable to listen to or enjoy the music. However, looking up at the first interlude, she caught his eye and saw him smile and nod in her direction. In another moment he left his companions and made his way to Lady Dawlish's box. They had arranged for refreshments to be brought rather than join the crush in the public refreshment rooms and the first knock at their door was the arrival of lemonade, water ices and wine. A few moments later, Adam looked round the door and asked if he might join them for a moment.

'I was going to offer to fetch you some refreshment,' he said, 'but I see that you have been served.'

'Dawlish never likes the crush at affairs like these,' Lady Dawlish said and smiled. 'One pays for these little attentions, but it makes the evening so much more enjoyable. I am glad to see you here, sir. Your cousins were at the Pump room this morning, but I did not see you?'

'I travelled down alone, ma'am,' Adam said and frowned. 'I fear Paul is a little out of sorts with me for various reasons and Hallam bears him company.'

'I dare say Paul has had much to try him,' Lady Dawlish said. 'He will recover. You have always been the best of friends.'

'Yes, and hope to be again. I think it is but a misunderstanding,' Adam said and glanced at Jenny. 'May I sit beside you for a moment? You must forgive me for being away so much longer than was planned, but there was more to do than I had imagined.'

'Did your trip go well?'

'I have hope that something may come of it,' Adam told her. 'Nothing is certain in such ventures, but we may find something of interest and if we do things should improve—otherwise...' He shrugged his shoulders. 'I fear things are difficult for the earl.'

'I am so sorry. If there was anything I could do...'

'How kind of you,' he said and for a moment his gloved hand rested over hers. 'I fear it is beyond your help—and mine unless our fortunes change.'

'I am sorry to hear that,' Jenny said, her mouth running dry. If only she dared speak, but she feared to see the warmth in his eyes turn to disgust, as it surely must if he believed she had deceived him deliberately. Besides, she would seem a braggart if she spoke of her fortune and it should prove negligible after all. 'Would—forgive me, but would the bank not grant you a little more time?'

'Perhaps if we should find this elusive seam of tin,' he said. 'It is perhaps merely an old man's wishful thought. If there was reason to open the mine once more, it would bring much-needed work to the area and be good for them as well as my family.'

'Yes, of course. The benefits would be for many families besides your own.'

'Indeed. Nothing would please me more—but even to pump out the water and clear a rock fall is expensive. If we do not find anything within a few weeks...' He shook his head. 'It is not a fit subject for the theatre. We are here to enjoy ourselves. I may perhaps find a way to come about.' Jenny arched her eyebrows and he shook his head. 'It is merely a chance, nothing certain.'

'I must wish you good fortune in your attempts to restore your grandfather's estate, sir.'

'Would that I could...' Adam sighed. 'The financial world is an odd one, I fear. If one has money, the bank is eager to lend one more, but if not... These things are sent to try our mettle, I suppose.'

She laughed. 'One must make light of one's

troubles for otherwise they might drag one under. If ever I could help you, Adam, I should be happy to do so.'

'How like you to offer. If I think of something you might do, I shall ask.'

Jenny's heart beat faster. When he sat beside her and looked at her so intently she could almost be certain that he liked her very well. She smiled at him and then something made her glance at the box opposite. They were being closely observed and, as the man lowered his opera glasses, she saw that it was Fontleroy. A shiver ran down her spine for there was something about him at this distance that made her turn cold.

'I should return to my friends,' Adam said and stood. 'I shall call tomorrow afternoon if you are at home?'

'Yes, we are, after three,' Jenny replied. 'We are invited to luncheon with friends, but we should be at home by three and thirty at the latest.'

'Then I shall definitely call—and perhaps we could go driving one morning?'

'I should like that very much, though Lucy must be one of the party. I do not like to leave her alone.'

'She looks much better. Have her spirits recovered?'

'She is in better spirits than she was at home. We are always out and about, meeting people and enjoying ourselves. We do not attend the assemblies or dances, but there are enough soirées and card parties to amuse us. A play or a concert at a public theatre is always acceptable.'

'Yes, I dare say you enjoy a good play.'

'Well, I do and so does Lucy, though she is much quieter than before. Lucy loves to dance above all things, but she did not plague her mama to be allowed the treat, even though she was pressed to attend the assembly last night. She is still grieving for Mark, though she tries not to show it in company.'

'I suppose you could attend, but dancing is the business at such affairs and that would not be acceptable just yet, I think.'

'No, not at all. If Ravenscar learned that Lucy had attended a ball I think he would be offended—and rightly so.'

'My cousin was foully murdered.' Adam looked grim.

'That word sends shivers down my spine.' Jenny looked at him anxiously. 'I suppose there is no news?'

'None, I fear,' Adam said, but looked so odd that

she suspected he was keeping something from her. 'Excuse me, I shall call tomorrow.'

Jenny gave him her hand. He bowed over it, but did not kiss it as he had been in the habit of doing in the country. She was conscious of disappointment once more. It did seem as if she had been making too much of his attentions to her.

Foolish, foolish girl. He was such a handsome, charming man that he could have his pick of the young ladies wishing for a husband, despite his grandfather's difficulties. Thank goodness she had not allowed anyone to see her own partiality for him, even though her pulses leapt to life when he touched her. She must certainly curb her feelings in future—and perhaps look elsewhere. If she wished to marry, and she surely must for she could not live with Lady Dawlish for ever, and did not wish to return to her uncle's house, this would be one of her best opportunities to meet someone suitable. She had taken little interest in the various gentlemen presented to her by Lady Dawlish, but now she must begin to look about her in case a gentleman she could encourage paid her some attention. Love was not imperative, she supposed, as long as one could be comfortable. Yet her heart was not in the idea and she felt oddly listless.

After Adam had gone back to his friends, Jenny was aware of an ache in her chest. She had been foolish to agonise over whether she should offer her fortune to him. He would be embarrassed for it had been made clear to her this evening that he had no intention of offering for her.

Adam was thoughtful as he left Jenny and her friends. He had been aware that they were under surveillance from Fontleroy. Why had the fellow been so interested? Adam had not even begun to lay his trap yet, but it seemed that the marquis was already intent on watching Adam's every move. Or was it only Adam that he watched?

Fontleroy would be aware that Jenny had seen him leaving Mark's bedchamber on the day of the funeral—if indeed it had been he. Adam believed it must have been. He believed the marquis must have been desperate to attempt it even though the house had been filled with people who would have known him. He could not be sure if Jenny had recognised him, even though he'd turned away hurriedly. The possibility that she could accuse him must be in his mind.

Adam had seen her glance at the marquis once and been aware of her discomfort as he lifted his quizzing glass to stare at her. She clearly did not like the gentleman—but had she realised that it was he who had ransacked Mark's bedroom? If she'd remembered anything, she would surely have told him so he must assume she had not. Why, then, did he make her feel so uncomfortable?

Adam knew that the marquis had an unsavoury reputation. More than one young maidservant had been seduced forcibly—and he'd heard it whispered that Fontleroy had once persuaded a young heiress to run off with him, but her family had discovered the plot and prevented her from making a terrible mistake.

If Fontleroy were interested in seducing Jenny, he might seek to take advantage of her vulnerability. Lady Dawlish and Lucy were in lieu of guardians to her, but Adam was not certain that either of them were watchful enough of her safety. She could be snatched away and forcibly seduced—but what then? Fontleroy must know that her friends would avenge her. He would surely not seduce and then abandon her? She was a lady and he would do much better to snatch a country girl if he had mere seduction in mind.

Could he be thinking of marrying her? Adam

was not certain of Fontleroy's circumstances. He was a reckless gambler and might now and then find himself in the suds, but he had not heard that he was ruined. If that were the case, he would not think of offering marriage to a girl with no fortune. So what was his interest in Jenny? Did he think she might endanger him—or was his passion for her sufficient to overcome his qualms?

Adam pondered the idea, but came up with no conclusions. He would simply have to watch from a distance for the moment. His plan was to lure Fontleroy into a sense of security, which would not happen if he challenged him on Jenny's behalf—though a ball through the heart would have the same result as his more elaborate plans might bring about if they succeeded. Paul would not hesitate to take that route if he could be certain the marquis had killed his brother. Yet if he were not careful such a reckless act could have unpleasant repercussions. Without proof of the man's guilt, Paul could be accused of murder. If Fontleroy would meet him in a duel, it might solve his problem.

Somehow he could not see it happening. Adam was known to be a crack shot and excellent with the sword. A man who sneaked in to kill another at close range in his own home was hardly likely to respond to a challenge for honour's sake. No, Adam had to force the marquis to demand the return of his necklace; it was the only way to bring him out of the shadows and force him to risk everything to save himself from exposure.

Adam wished he might have gone to the assembly with his cousins that evening. He could have done with talking things over with Hallam, but he needed to keep this mask of indifference in place until Fontleroy had taken the bait. If Fontleroy saw them together, he would not believe that Adam was about to betray them for the sake of money. It was in truth the last thing Adam would ever do and he must act his part well if he were to deceive the marquis.

He had chosen his path, but he had not reckoned with Fontleroy being interested in Jenny. Many young ladies in Jenny's unfortunate situation would be flattered by the interest of a marquis. Fontleroy was not ill looking and could offer her a home of her own and much that she might desire—but Jenny had been uncomfortable under his scrutiny. She had not liked it!

Adam knew in his heart that Jenny would not consider an offer from Fontleroy. He flattered himself that her feelings for him were more than mere friendship. Had he been free to do so he believed that he might already have spoken to her, because he liked her more than any other young lady of his acquaintance. He had given little thought to marriage in the past, but must do so at some time—and Jenny was suitable in every way but one.

He must concentrate his mind on his plans to trap the marquis and not allow himself to be distracted by a delightful young woman, who was in danger of turning his world upside down without even knowing it.

Whatever Fontleroy was planning in his devious mind it did not bode well for Jenny. Adam sensed without being told that she was nervous of him and would not accept an offer if the marquis had marriage in mind. Therefore, Adam must watch out for her, which might make things awkward in the circumstances. His concern for Jenny and his need to solve his cousin's murder might be in direct conflict, forcing him to choose one path or the other. If he antagonised Fontleroy, there would be no chance of luring him into the trap.

Adam swore beneath his breath. He must seek

Fontleroy out at one of the gaming clubs as soon as possible. Contact must be established so that he could hint at a certain necklace within his possession.

The stolen necklace was, in fact, in a bank in London, awaiting collection by its rightful owner, but Hallam had managed to purchase a copy—or something that looked similar from a distance. It would fool most people in a poor light. Of course, if Fontleroy ever laid hands on it he would know that he had been taken for a fool.

Adam knew that there was no way the marquis would part with ten thousand pounds to recover the necklace. Therefore, he would either arrange for an assassination or attempt it himself once he could be sure of getting his hands on the incriminating necklace.

Adam had risked his life too many times to find the prospect daunting, but he would not throw it away heedlessly. He trusted his cousins and a handful of old comrades to watch his back. Fontleroy must be taken in the act, which meant that his friends had orders to wait until the last moment. Only then would they be able to avenge Mark's murder and make sure that the marquis paid the price of his villainy.

* * *

'Would you care to drive out with me one morning?' Lord Mallory asked Lucy when they met at the Pump room two days later. 'I was thinking we might make up a little party. Miss Hastings might drive with one of my friends—and perhaps your mama and one of her friends might accompany us in her chaise. I could have a picnic basket put up for us.'

'That sounds delightful,' Lucy said and smiled at him. 'Who were you thinking of asking to accompany us?'

'I had considered Sir James Justus—or Fontleroy?'

'Sir James would be acceptable,' Lucy said, 'but not the marquis. Jenny does not like him.'

Lord Mallory frowned. 'Has he offended her in some way? Fontleroy's estate is close to my own. I would vouch for him, Miss Dawlish.'

'I know that Jenny would not wish him to be a part of our group, sir. If you insist on his accompanying us, I must decline your kind invitation.'

'To be frank, he asked me if I could arrange it,' Mallory said and frowned. 'Naturally, I should not dream of disobliging you or your friend—but

I am sorry that Miss Hastings has taken him in such dislike.'

'Pray speak to Mama about the outing,' Lucy said. 'I am sure she will agree—but please ask Sir James rather than the marquis.'

'Certainly, of course,' Lord Mallory said and frowned. 'I am sorry to have distressed you by mentioning it. As the suggestion came from Fontleroy, I must find some excuse to put him off—but do not fear, I shall find a means of doing so. I would not distress you or Miss Hastings for the world.'

'You are very kind, sir.' Lucy smiled at him. 'Jenny has one or two admirers and I know Sir James is one of the most devoted. I believe she likes him.'

'Then it is settled,' he said. 'If you wish, I shall speak to your mama at once and arrange the outing for the day after tomorrow.'

Lucy thanked him. They strolled across the room to where Lady Dawlish was speaking with one of her friends. Jenny was actually talking to Sir James, and, as they chose to join Lady Dawlish at the same moment, the suggestion was put and received by all with evident pleasure.

'I should be delighted to make up one of your

party,' Sir James said. 'I am thinking of having a little card party myself at the end of this week and I should be happy if you will all join me. I shall send cards, of course. It will be an intimate affair with just a few of our closest friends.' He hesitated, then, 'It is a pity that you do not attend the assemblies, Lady Dawlish. Lord Padstowe is giving a dinner followed by a small dance this weekend. He was asking me if I knew any more young ladies to swell the numbers—but I thought you would refuse an invitation?'

'One of our closest friends met an unfortunate end recently, as you know,' Lady Dawlish replied. 'I brought Lucy away to Bath, because she felt so very low—but I do not feel that she ought to dance just yet.'

'Could you not attend, even if Miss Lucy sat the dances out and just watched?'

Lady Dawlish hesitated, then sighed. The situation was awkward for she had not explained the full consequences of Lucy's situation.

'I suppose we might attend the dinner—and of course Jenny could dance if she wished.' Lady Dawlish looked at her daughter doubtfully. 'What do you feel, dearest? We had said we should not attend any dances...the public assemblies are out of the question, but a private dance might be acceptable. However, you would have to sit and watch as others dance, Lucy.'

'It is a little unfair to Jenny if we do not go,' Lucy said. 'I should not mind sitting with you and watching—if that would be acceptable, Mama? I do not wish to dance yet, but there is no reason why Jenny should not.'

'I do not like to deny either of you,' Lady Dawlish said and looked at her daughter. 'Are you sure you would not feel left out of things, dearest?'

'It would be pleasant to listen to the music and I should be quite content to sit with you and watch, Mama,' Lucy said and smiled. 'We have both bought a new ballgown, though we did not expect to be wearing them just yet. Mine is pearl grey, so it would not be too bright…'

'No one could think ill of you, Miss Lucy. You were not engaged to Mark Ravenscar, though I believe it might have been intended?' Lord Mallory said.

'I was considering it,' Lucy replied with perfect truth, though she did not add that his family and her closest friends had expected them to marry that summer.

'Then it must be quite unexceptionable.' Lord

Mallory smiled down at her. 'I shall be delighted to sit with you. We might even have a hand of cards, for Padstowe is sure to set up his tables—and the dance is but a few couples and quite informal.'

'Then you may tell Padstowe to send us an invitation,' Lady Dawlish said. 'I have thought it a little unfair on Jenny that she has come to Bath and not attended one assembly.'

'You do not need to feel concern for me, ma'am. I am quite happy to go on as we are,' Jenny hastily assured her. 'Just being here with my kind friends is enough for me.'

'But you were out of mourning in London and attending balls,' Lady Dawlish said, 'and since you hardly knew the Ravenscar family it would be quite acceptable for you to dance.'

'You must agree, Miss Hastings,' Lord Mallory said. 'You have several admirers who long to dance with you.'

'Oh, no…' Jenny blushed and shook her head. 'I do not think…' She looked at Lucy. 'Would it not distress you, dearest? I should not like to dance if you could not.'

'Not at all,' Lucy assured her. 'I should be sorry

if you did not have the chance to dance at least once while we are in Bath, Jenny.'

Jenny shook her head, but she could see that her friends were quite determined on her behalf, and she suspected that Lady Dawlish was hoping that Sir James might make an offer for her. Her kind friend would naturally think it a suitable match for her, and perhaps it was, for the gentleman was sincere, comfortable if not vastly wealthy, and attractive. He was also a widower with one child, a little girl three years old. Jenny knew that he was looking for a wife who would be a mother to the child and was not averse to the idea. His first wife had died in childbed and she believed he had loved her very much. When he spoke of his loss, Jenny had offered him ready sympathy and she imagined that it was the reason he had paid her more attention, believing that a girl of little fortune would find such a match advantageous.

Jenny regretted that her uncle had sold all her father's property without consulting her. His act had led everyone to think that she had no prospects, which was not the case. However, she was not certain whether her fortune was large enough to satisfy a gentleman with a more prestigious title, and to drop hints that she might have a substantial fortune might seem to be bragging.

Since coming to Bath, Jenny had sat quietly to one side, watching the proceedings at the various affairs they attended, content to observe and listen or to play an occasional game of cards. It was true that she had attracted one or two elderly admirers, the youngest and most acceptable to her being Sir James. So far she had managed to avoid being alone with the Marquis of Fontleroy. She had hoped that Adam would call to ask her to go driving, but they had been out when he left his card and she had not seen him since that night at the theatre, though he'd promised to call the next day. He must have changed his mind for some reason, though she could not think what she had said or done to cause him to avoid her. This seemed to confirm what she had suspected at the theatre. Although he liked her as a friend, and had been concerned for her because of what had happened at Ravenscar, he did not care for her as she cared for him.

It would be sensible of her to encourage one of her suitors if she wished to marry. Once they were in the country she might not meet many single gentlemen. Most of Lady Dawlish's friends were married or already engaged to someone they had known for years. Had they been to all the balls, dances and dinners that had been planned, it might have been different, but amongst their immediate circle at home, only Paul Ravenscar and Adam Miller were single.

Most evenings in Bath they had attended either a dinner or a soirée at the houses of Lady Dawlish's friends and Adam had not been present at any of the affairs they'd attended. It was almost as if he were avoiding her and that was hurtful.

Fortunately, in Jenny's opinion, the marquis had not been invited to many of them either. She'd seen him once or twice at the Pump room or in the town, but avoided speaking to him if she could.

'Yes, Jenny must certainly dance,' Lady Dawlish said, making her blush as she gave her an arch look. 'I must think of Jenny as well as my darling Lucy. I am as a guardian to her and must promote her welfare as much as I can.'

Sir James looked pleased with himself. Jenny felt a little apprehensive. Clearly, he'd pressed the invitation for Jenny's sake, so that he could dance with her himself. She realised that his pursuit of her was serious and knew that she must be careful, for it would not do to encourage him too much and then refuse the offer she was certain he meant to make. She had been thinking of him as a friend, but he wanted more from her.

'That is excellent news, ma'am,' he said and beamed at Lady Dawlish. His gaze moved on to Jenny. 'You will please save me the first set of dances, Miss Jenny—and the dance before supper if you will.'

Jenny could only smile and thank him. If her situation had been as others perceived it, she would undoubtedly have been fortunate to receive an offer from Sir James. Had she no money of her own and no kind friends, she might have been forced to consider him—but happily for her she was able to choose for herself.

Her situation was far from desperate and even if Captain Miller had no interest in her she did not need to marry. She would consider her options for the moment.

The trip to a local beauty spot was organised for two days ahead and the party broke up. Sir James had an appointment elsewhere and took his leave, looking very pleased with himself. Lord Mallory stayed with them until Lady Dawlish sent for her carriage and then left them regretfully.

'Well, my dears,' Lady Dawlish said and smiled at them both as they were driven back to their house. 'I think this little trip may turn out most fortunately for both of you. I would never dream of interfering, Jenny—but if Sir James were to offer it would be such a chance for you.'

'You are very kind, ma'am,' Jenny said. 'I find the gentleman kind enough, but I have no thought of marriage just yet.'

'Too soon?' Her kind hostess raised her brows. 'Well, you must do just as you wish, my love. You are very welcome to stay with me for as long as you wish—and to accompany Lucy and me to Italy later in the year should you care for it. However, Sir James is a good catch—as is Lord Mallory for you, Lucy.'

'I do like him, Mama,' Lucy admitted. 'But pray do not expect me to think of marriage for at least nine months or a year, for I could not.'

'No, no, of course not. I should not dream of pressing you,' her mother said. 'I just wanted you to be aware that a match like that does not come along often. Similarly, you should consider seriously before you turn down an offer from Sir James, Jenny. He is a gentleman I would trust and you might not receive another offer as good.'

Jenny took a deep breath and smiled. 'Thank you for your kind sentiments, ma'am, but I would prefer not to marry unless it is for love or a warm affection. I do like Sir James—far more than certain other gentlemen who have paid court to me— but I do not wish to marry him. At least, I have no wish to think of it as yet.'

'Well, it is not for me to press you, but I am a little anxious for you, Jenny.'

'I am quite happy as I am for the moment, ma'am—as I told you, my lawyer says I am not penniless.'

'Of course, my dear.' Lady Dawlish nodded. 'However, I still think you might consider Sir James. He would, I think, be a kind husband and that is most important after all.'

Jenny did not argue further. She was uncertain of her feelings on the matter. A part of her wished to be married with a home of her own and a husband who loved her—but she would not wish to settle for second-best. Much as she might long for her own home and a family, Jenny knew that only one man had made her heart race. Only one man had made her want to be held in his arms and kissed until she melted into him.

If Adam Miller had cared for her—as he'd

seemed to at the start—she would gladly have married him. She would be a fool to settle for less, even though she did not wish to be a spinster all her life.

She thrust the troublesome thoughts to the back of her mind. She need not decide in a hurry, for in the autumn she could travel, either with Lucy and Lady Dawlish or an older companion. By then she would know for certain what Adam Miller thought of her...

Chapter Ten

Adam frowned as he approached the house Lady Dawlish had taken and saw the small cortège of three carriages set out. It was a lovely day and he'd hoped to find Jenny at home this morning and take her for an impromptu drive in his phaeton. However, this was the third time he'd meant to call, only to find the ladies not at home, though he'd left his card but once—having seen them leave the house on two occasions and turning away. It would seem that they were popular and enjoying the visit to Bath.

A flicker of something like jealousy went through Adam. He was not the only man to have noticed how good natured and pretty Jenny was—and there were plenty of men with sufficient fortune not to worry over her lack of it. If he could not speak others would and if the right one asked,

Jenny might accept him. The thought of her as another man's wife smote him, making him aware of a pain in his chest.

Damned fool! He could not afford to fall in love with her. He had struggled with his feelings and his frustration at not being able to ask her—but he might not have the chance to ask, for someone else might do so first.

He ought to have called sooner, but his thoughts had been focused on one thing and that was to trap Fontleroy into making a mistake. It had taken some time and effort to run the marquis to ground, but he'd succeeded the previous evening, finally cornering him at a gentlemen's gaming club. Adam had joined a table at which Fontleroy was seated and had managed to lose every hand, rising some five hundred guineas down at the end of the evening and cursing his luck.

'Another time, Miller,' Fontleroy suggested as he gathered Adam's gold. 'I will give you your revenge tomorrow if you wish.'

'Happy to oblige you, if you will take my notes,' Adam replied carelessly. 'I fear my pockets are entirely to let.'

'I know the feeling,' Fontleroy said and smiled oddly, 'I am always willing to take another gentleman's notes. I am certain you will come about another day.'

Adam cursed just loud enough to be heard. 'If it were my own debts alone...' He shook his head, as if regretting he'd spoken. 'I must not say, but things have come to a desperate pass. I need a large sum of money for another's sake and I am not sure how to obtain it.'

'The answer is not at the gaming table,' one of the other players remarked. 'You will find yourself staring into the abyss, Miller.'

'I was not thinking of relying on Lady Luck,' Adam said and glanced at Fontleroy. 'It so happens that I may have another way to redeem my fortunes...'

He'd risen from the table then, only to be followed from the room by the marquis. It was raining outside and Adam called for a cab to take him back to his lodgings.

'Do you have something to sell?' Fontleroy asked.

Adam looked at him, surprised by his direct question. 'I'm not sure I understand you, sir?'

'Oh, I think you do,' Fontleroy said and smiled thinly. 'You have never sought me out before. I know you've been looking for me; I've been told of your enquiries. Your little charade this evening was unnecessary. You should just have stated your price. You have something that belongs to me— how much do you want?'

'Ten thousand pounds.'

Fontleroy's brows lowered. 'It is not worth as much.'

'But what I know about it is worth at least that sum. I'm not a greedy man. Ten thousand will set me right and keep the bank from foreclosing. It's that or nothing.'

'Damn you, that's blackmail.' Fontleroy glared at him, a deadly glitter in his eyes that warned Adam he was treading on dangerous ground.

'Is it?' he asked innocently. 'What have I said that leads you to such a conclusion?'

'You do not need to. We understand each other perfectly.'

'Yes, perhaps.' Adam's pulse was racing. 'Do we have a deal?'

'The necklace and any letters pertaining to the damned thing?'

'Of course. One would be no use without the other, I think. One is perhaps more damning than the other…' Adam's lie was calculated to thrust home and he saw the marquis's jaw tighten. His meaning could not have been clearer and Fontleroy's guilt was written all over him. He was Mark's murderer.

It took all Adam's strength of will not to fly at the man and take him by the throat. He longed to thrash the devil to within an inch of his life, but controlled the urge, because it was his word against the marquis's. Nothing had been said that could convict the man of murder—it was merely innuendo. A casual observer would have heard nothing that might lead him to understand what was being said here.

'So he did leave something. I suppose he trusted you more than his brother. Paul had everything to gain from his brother's death, whereas you had nothing.'

'Nothing but what I might gain from the sale of a very charming necklace and a letter explaining the whole,' Adam replied, a cold smile on his lips. 'Were I not in such dire circumstances I should have taken both straight to the authorities, but needs must when the devil drives.'

'None of us are very different when the chips are down,' Fontleroy said. 'Damn Lichfield for being a fool. He should never have used the necklace to pay his debts. If I'd guessed what he meant

to do, I should have stopped him—but I didn't realise until it was too late.'

Fontleroy had been careless, but there was no
one close enough to hear. The very fact that the
marquis was willing to speak so frankly told
Adam that his fate was sealed. Fontleroy could
not allow him to live—though he would pretend
to go along with the blackmail.

'I suppose he was afraid of being hanged.
Thought he would save the hangman the trouble by blowing his brains out?' Adam arched his
brow, his manner making it clear he did not believe one word he was saying. Fontleroy had killed
the man who had betrayed him, though Adam
could never prove it.

'Since you know so much you may as well know
the whole,' Fontleroy said and scowled. 'I guided
his hand—he was too much of a coward to go
through with it, though it was his idea. He was
afraid of the consequences if he were caught. I'll
pay your ten thousand pounds, Miller—but betray me and I'll kill you.'

'Naturally.' Adam arched his brows. 'Yet why
should I? I should ruin myself with you, should
I not? You may rest assured that if you play fair

with me I shall return the compliment. Where and when shall we exchange?'

He made the offer, knowing that Fontleroy had every intention of killing him. His carelessness in confessing his guilt had made that plain. Adam would always be a danger to him for he could demand further payments. Fontleroy now had no choice but to murder him.

'I am going to a small dance on Thursday evening. Shall we say at midnight? I should be free by then.'

'Yes, of course. Furnish me with your direction and I shall meet you there.'

'I'm engaged to Padstowe for the evening...'

'As am I,' Adam said and smiled. 'We shall attend to our business after we leave, I think.'

'Yes. Good lord, I don't want any of the guests to see the exchange. You leave at eleven-thirty and I'll follow. We'll meet by the statue in the square just beyond Padstowe's house. I'll give you the money and you can give me my property.'

'Delighted,' Adam said and extended his hand, only to have it ignored. 'Suit yourself. There are others who would pay as much for the privilege of catching a gang of jewel thieves...especially one with so much inside knowledge.'

Fontleroy glared at him, but made no answer. The marquis would see him dead as soon as he had his property safe.

He could only hope that his friends would cover his back and catch Fontleroy in the act.

'Hallam, my dear boy—and Paul,' Lady Dawlish said and extended her hands. 'It is good to see you both. How is your dear father, Paul?'

'He was recovered enough to insist that Hallam and I came down to Bath for a few weeks,' Paul replied. 'We have called twice before, but you were out, ma'am. I trust that both you and Lucy are well.'

'Yes, we go on very nicely. Lucy has gone walking with Jenny. They enjoy the good weather as much as possible. We have been driven out to several beauty spots—and two days ago we had a lovely picnic up in the hills overlooking the city. Tomorrow, we have accepted an invitation to Padstowe's dance.' She hesitated, then, 'I hope you will not be offended, Paul? Lucy does not mean to dance, but I felt that Jenny should have her chance. We do not attend the public assemblies.'

'I have noticed your absence, ma'am,' Paul said. 'We attended one the other evening, but, like

Lucy, we do not dance.' He smothered a sigh. 'I had hoped I might see her—is she bearing up?'

'Her spirits have recovered a little, sir,' the doting mother said. 'Jenny is very good for her and they enjoy the simple pursuits that are acceptable in the circumstances. It is not what we had all hoped for this summer…but nothing can be done to bring your dear brother back.'

'No, I fear not.' Paul's jaw tightened. 'I hope to see the devil who took his life brought to justice sooner rather than later.'

'Have you discovered who it was?'

'We have few clues,' Hallam replied hastily, giving Paul a warning glance. 'Well, we shall leave you now, ma'am. We do not go to Padstowe's dance for we have a prior engagement. Pray give our regards to the young ladies, ma'am.'

'Yes, of course. They will be sorry to have missed you. Had I not been feeling low with a little headache I should have gone with them—so I am glad to have seen you. Please send my regards to your father, Paul.'

Paul promised he would and the gentlemen took their leave. Outside, he looked at Hallam.

'I should not have told her for she is a rattle and

Fontleroy would have heard of it sooner rather than later.'

'Adam has placed himself in great danger,' Hallam said and frowned. 'Even though we have someone watching his back all the time, I know that something could go wrong.'

'We know Fontleroy is guilty because he practically confessed it.' Paul's eyes were glacial. 'Adam should allow me to call him out and have done with it.'

'He would not meet you in a duel,' Hallam warned. 'If it were that easy Adam would already have done it—besides, he confessed the necklace was his, but said nothing of Mark's murder. We still have no proof—and he would deny it all in a court of law. Adam's way is the best, Paul.'

'I know...' Paul cursed and clenched his hands. 'I just want to see him dead.'

'We all want that,' Hallam agreed. 'Hanging is best, as Adam says, but if need be I shall shoot to kill. It is all set for the night of Padstowe's dance. We shall wait with the others, taking turns in watching Adam's back so that Fontleroy does not become suspicious.'

'Supposing he decides to kill him before then?'

'He would not dare. Adam might have left the

necklace with someone he trusts; he might have left a letter to be given to one of us if he is killed. Fontleroy has heard that we have fallen out with our cousin, but he cannot be certain that Adam has not protected himself in some way. No, he will take the necklace from him and pay him the money—then shoot him in the back and take it back.'

'We must hope his plan is that simple,' Paul said. 'But he will know that Adam has the necklace with him.'

'He cannot be certain,' Hallam said. 'I think he will wait to shoot when he has it in his hand.'

'I wish I could be at the dance tomorrow. We ought to be there to see what is going on.'

'Padstowe did not invite us. Besides, Adam said it was not a good idea. He was afraid we might give ourselves away by a look or a glance.' Hallam laid a hand on his shoulder. 'Patience, my friend. It is all set. All we have to do is wait…'

'You look lovely in your new gown,' Lucy said, admiring the dark-blue silk Jenny had chosen for her ballgown. 'It is very unusual and it suits you.'

'Yes, I think it does,' Jenny said and glanced at herself in the mirror. She had taken a risk by choosing such a deep shade of blue, because most girls of her age wore pastels or white. The gown was of heavy silk and trimmed with silver lace at the shoulders, on the puffed sleeves and at the waist. She had chosen to wear a necklace of moonstones set in silver, which had been her mother's favourite, and a matching bracelet. She had tiny eardrops of moonstones and diamonds and her slippers were leather with silver buckles. 'Your gown is also charming, Lucy.'

Lucy glanced at herself in the mirror; her gown was a silver-grey lace and charming. She wore it with a chain of silver links with tiny pink sapphires hanging from it about her neck. 'I prefer white or pink, or perhaps yellow, but those colours would not be suitable. This gown will do very well for the moment.'

Jenny reached for her hand. 'How do you feel now, dearest? Sometimes you seem almost your old self, but at others I see that you are still unhappy.'

'I do not feel as guilty as I did,' Lucy confessed. 'Mama says she understands that I had doubts about my wedding—and she would have supported me had I chosen to draw back. It is not my fault that Mark was—' She broke off, unable to say the terrible word. 'I do miss him, Jenny—but there are others I miss as much.'

'It would have been a mistake to marry him then, for unless one is loved...' said Jenny. 'Do you care for Lord Mallory at all? I noticed on our picnic that he was very attentive to you.'

'I like him, of course—and Mama thinks him suitable—but if he asks I shall say I am not ready. I do not wish to form an attachment yet. Next time I shall be certain of my heart before I accept a proposal of marriage.'

Jenny nodded. She suspected she knew what was troubling her friend, but so far Lucy had not confessed it.

'It was a pity that Hallam and Paul called when we were out,' she said, watching Lucy's face intently.

'Yes...' Lucy sighed. 'I had hoped they might be at Padstowe's dance, but it seems they have another engagement.'

Jenny agreed. She was almost sure she was right in thinking Lucy cared for Paul, but would say nothing until her friend decided to confide in her.

'Lucy, Jenny...are you ready?'

Lady Dawlish's voice calling from downstairs made them turn as one towards the door. It was time to leave for the evening and Jenny could not help feeling pleased because she had been told that Adam would be there that evening. He'd called more than once since that night at the theatre and they had unfortunately missed him. Now at last she would see him and, despite knowing that he probably felt merely friendship towards her, she longed to see him, talk to him.

Adam saw Jenny across the crowded room and swore beneath his breath. No one had mentioned that they would be here this evening. He knew that Lady Dawlish had refused to attend the public assemblies and he'd imagined she would feel the same about this dance. Here she was and he could not help looking at Jenny and wishing that he were free to go at once to her side and ask her to dance with him. She looked cool, charming and beautiful, a young woman that any man might wish to make his wife. Adam would have been a fool had he not noticed the eyes turned in her direction. She did not laugh often, but when she did her face lit up from within and the sound was enchanting. He wanted to take her in his arms and dance with her all night.

However, it would not do to become involved

with her this evening—his business with Fontleroy was too dangerous. He did not want to chance something happening to her. If the marquis knew that she meant something to him, he might try to use her against him. Much as he wanted to speak to her, it would be best to wait—to make the meeting casual rather than show his eagerness.

Lady Dawlish had taken her place with the other dowagers and those ladies who had no intention of dancing. Seated at a little table, where other ladies were playing cards or eating some of the tempting morsels being served by waiters, she glanced about the room and nodded to him. Lucy had taken her place beside her mama and was looking about her with interest—and a gentleman had immediately taken the seat next to her.

So Mallory was interested in Lucy? He was a decent enough fellow, but Paul would not care to see the familiarity in his manner towards the girl. Lady Dawlish had seen Adam and was beckoning to him. He smothered a sigh and began to make his way towards her. As he did so, he saw Fontleroy approach the table and ask something of Jenny.

He was clearly asking her to dance, but in the next moment another gentleman had presented himself. Jenny appeared to apologise to the marquis and accepted Sir James Justus's hand. A set was forming for a country dance and she had clearly promised it before the evening began.

Seeing the annoyance in Fontleroy's eyes, Adam knew that the marquis was furious, but trying to conceal it. He waited until the man walked off before presenting himself to Lady Dawlish.

'Adam, my dear,' she said and smiled up at him. 'At last we meet. I understand you called again the other day, but we were all out once more.'

'I have been unfortunate several times for you were either out or I saw you leave.'

'That is a pity,' the lady said. 'Your cousins found us at home the other day. They were unable to come this evening, because they had other engagements. I wanted to ask—you will not be offended if Jenny dances a few times this evening?'

'Why should she not, ma'am?' His eyes followed her as she made her way gracefully through the dance. 'She is not in mourning. She did not know my cousin.'

'Lucy does not intend to dance—but I wished Jenny to have the chance. She was in mourning all last winter and this spring for her father. I think Sir James likes her very well, but she may meet other gentlemen. I fear she does not like Fontle-roy, though he is persistent in his suit of her. He called at the house several times, but I was forced to deny her for she would not see him.'

'Do you know why, ma'am?'

'I think it just a young woman's fancy,' Lady Dawlish said. 'If you should decide to dance, I would take it kindly if you were to ask Jenny for the waltz. I know she loves it of all things.'

'I did not intend it,' Adam said. 'I came for cards and conversation—as you do, ma'am.'

'Yes, I thought it might be so.' Lady Dawlish sighed. 'Jenny cannot dance more than twice with Sir James or it will be remarked and I do not think she is ready for that yet.'

'Indeed?' Adam's mouth suddenly tasted of ashes. It was a highly unsuitable match in his opinion. Sir James was a dull dog and would not make her happy. His resolve to abstain from dancing crumbled. 'Perhaps one dance—to oblige you, ma'am,' he said. 'I will ask Miss Jenny to reserve it when she returns.'

He watched Jenny as she danced with her admirer. She smiled at him and laughed once, as if at a joke, but he could see nothing in her manner to suggest that she thought of him as a future husband. Of course she had little choice in her circumstances. If she wanted a home of her own, she must marry sooner rather than later—and Sir James was very suitable, if too old and too set in his ways. Far more suitable than the marquis, who Adam noted was staring at her in a brooding fashion.

Clearly the marquis felt he had rights over her and resented the attention Sir James was paying Jenny. When the dance ended and they began to make their way back to Lady Dawlish, Fontleroy intercepted and caught hold of her arm. She tried to pull away, a look of such disgust in her eyes that Adam was stung into action. Without thinking of what he risked, he walked quickly to her side.

'I believe this is our dance, Miss Jenny?'

She turned to him with such a look of relief that Adam's heart caught. He knew then that, even if he risked his carefully laid plans to trap the marquis, he had done what must be done.

'Yes, thank you, sir,' she said and avoided looking at the marquis. 'I believe this is our dance...' then, looking at Fontleroy, 'I shall dance only twice this evening for Lucy may not dance and I shall not desert her. Perhaps another time, sir.'

Fontleroy looked at her and then at Adam. His

hands clenched at his sides and it was clear that he was battling his temper. His jaw hardened and he turned and walked away, heading for the card room.

'I fear you have made an enemy of him,' Adam said, gazing down at her. 'You should be careful for he is not to be trusted.'

'He…he asked me to marry him in London,' Jenny said. 'I refused him, but he will not take no for an answer and persists in pursuing me. I dislike him very much. I cannot understand why he thinks he will change my mind—or why he wishes to marry me.'

'You are very pretty,' Adam said and guided her on to the floor. The music they were playing was a waltz and he held her at the correct distance, a gloved hand in the middle of her back. 'How fortunate that it should be a waltz. Lady Dawlish told me that you love to waltz.'

'Yes, I do. It is my favourite dance of all, if my partner is accomplished, and you certainly are, sir.'

Adam laughed, for it was just the sort of answer he had expected her to give. He was beginning to know her and to like her more and more—she was exactly the kind of woman he had always hoped to marry. Amusing, pretty, good tempered and intelligent. He wanted time to spend with her, time to discover if they liked the same music, books and pastimes.

'Waltzing was a requirement for all Wellington's officers. He thought it a part of our duty to entertain the ladies and we were all instructed to attend the duchess's ball the evening before Napoleon was sighted and we had to leave quickly…'

'Yes, I heard about it,' Jenny said, her face glowing as she looked up at him. She was so lovely and as light as thistledown in his arms. Adam felt the desire burn deep in his loins, which was inconvenient when dancing, but it seemed that whenever she was close to him he felt the need to hold her tighter and kiss her until she melted into him. He wanted to draw her nearer, to feel the softness of her body pressed against his, but, had he done so, she must have been aware of his urgent desire and so he maintained the required distance by exerting his iron will. 'It is pleasant to see you here this evening, sir. I had hoped to see you sooner.'

'I have called,' Adam said. He had never felt this way with a young woman of quality before and his throat caught with emotion as he gazed down into her lovely face. God, how he wanted her! His breeches felt uncomfortably tight—but he should not be thinking of his own needs or desires. He had important business this night and must keep a cool head. 'Forgive me, Jenny. I have much on my mind at the moment—and my business is dangerous. I would not involve you at such a time.'

He felt the shiver run through her, her eyes dark as she gazed up at him, concern in her face. 'Have you discovered who the...culprit is?'

'Yes, I have, though as yet I do not have sufficient proof,' he said. 'After our dance I shall go into the card room and then in a little while I shall leave. I have business this evening, which, with luck, may solve our little problem.'

'Will you be in danger?' she asked, her eyes opening wide. Her hand trembled a little in his and he held it tighter, wanting to comfort her.

'Yes, perhaps I may...' Adam hesitated, then, 'If anything should happen to me—or you should hear ill of me—promise me you will keep your distance from Fontleroy.'

'The marquis...' Jenny's gaze narrowed. 'I think I see...yes, now it comes to me. What I saw that day... It struck a chord with me, but I could not think what was familiar, but now I see it. There is the way he hunches one shoulder. It was there at

the back of my mind all the time. I believe it was
he I saw coming from Mark's room. The wicked
man...'

'Forgive me, I should not have said. If he
guessed that you had remembered, you might be
in danger.' Adam pressed her hand. 'Yet I had to
warn you for I could not bear that anything should
harm you.'

'Thank you,' she whispered, her cheeks pink.
She kept her eyes down and would not look at
him. 'I shall remember your warning, sir—but I
pray you to take care. I would be distressed if...'
She was too emotional to continue. He pressed
her hand and she glanced up, her eyes revealing
so much that had been better concealed. He felt
the pain slash through him, for he could not say
the words he needed to say—the words she was
entitled to hear.

The music was coming to an end and she
shook her head, as if recalling that they were in
a crowded room. Adam smiled and stood still for
a moment, his hand still pressed against her back,
one finger stroking as if to comfort her. Then he
released her, but kept hold of her right hand, leading her back to Lady Dawlish.

'I shall hope to call on you soon,' he said. It was

with reluctance that he bowed to her and left her with her friends.

Given the freedom to do so, he would have liked to continue to dance with her throughout the evening and then perhaps to lead her outside into the garden as the dance ended and kiss her. Her mouth looked so soft and ready to be kissed, but he could not risk it. Should Fontleroy be the winner of their contest this night, Jenny could suffer if he'd paid her too much attention. He had already risked much by coming between the two earlier.

Besides, his own problems were unresolved. His grandfather's estate was still deep in debt. As yet Adam had no prospects and nothing to offer the girl he found more and more delightful each time they met. Why should she take him when there were others with more fortune to recommend them?

Forcing himself to walk away from her, Adam made his way to the card room. He saw that Fontleroy was watching the proceedings, but had not sat down at the tables. As soon as Adam was seen, he was hailed and invited to join one of the tables. He smiled and accepted the invitation, noticing the scowl on Fontleroy's face as he sat down.

So the marquis was impatient to get on with the evening's business and recover his property. It could not be better. Adam was of a mind to keep him waiting for a while. The more frustrated the marquis became, the more likely he was to make a mistake.

Jenny was asked to dance by several gentlemen after she sat down with her companions. One of them was a very handsome gentleman with large side-whiskers. He was dressed in the uniform of the Hussars and looked at her as if he truly wished to dance with her. However, having told the marquis she would dance only two dances, she could not change her mind.

'I do not dance again this evening,' she told him and smiled. 'Forgive me, but my friends are still in mourning and Lucy may not dance. I shall not do so again tonight—but perhaps another time?'

He bowed and clicked his heels and then went off to dance with someone else. Jenny felt only relief. She had enjoyed her dance with Adam so much that she did not wish to dance with anyone else. It had been the most perfect moment, transporting her to a place she had never been. As he held her she had known such exquisite happiness—and something she realised must be desire. She had danced with many handsome gentlemen in the past, but never had she felt such exquisite pleasure. Adam's unique scent had made her pulses race and her stomach spasm. She had wished their dance might go on for ever and felt bereft as he walked away.

Had he not had another engagement she would have hoped for another dance later, but he'd made it clear he would not ask again that evening. She knew that he had more important business and feared that he might be in danger. He could not think of her at such a time.

Yet he had looked down at her in such a way! Insensibly, Jenny felt her heart soar. Once again he had seemed to show some preference for her— she was the only lady he'd asked to dance and surely that meant something?'

'Captain Miller did not intend to dance this evening,' Lady Dawlish told her, smiling comfortably. 'I asked if he would dance with you just once— and I see he did so. Why will you not dance again, my love? Lucy does not mind.'

Had he asked only because Lady Dawlish asked? Jenny considered, but decided that Adam would dance only if he wished—and the way he'd held her suggested that he, too, had felt pleasure as they danced.

Jenny had noticed her friend's foot tapping to the music and knew that, despite her determination not to, Lucy was longing to dance. To continue dancing throughout the evening would have made it unbearable for Lucy to sit and watch.

'It is hardly fair when Lucy may not dance,' Jenny said and smiled at her friend. 'Besides, there is no one else I wish to dance with—and I told the marquis I would not.'

'Ah, then you may not,' Lady Dawlish said. 'Pray tell me if you can, my love—why do you dislike him so?'

'It is something in the way he looks at me— and when I danced with him in London, he held me too close. I was aware of his…I felt very uncomfortable and decided I should not dance with him again.'

'Indeed, then you must not dance with him, especially a waltz, for it is unpleasant to be held close to a man one does not like. Well, you can enjoy yourself watching for the rest of the evening— and we'll have a hand of cribbage if you wish, for a board can be brought and we have friends to play with,' Lady Dawlish said and passed a bonbon dish. 'These are very good, Jenny. They taste of almond.'

Jenny thanked her and took one. She looked towards the card room, but there was no sign of Adam, though she continued to look for almost an hour and a half at intervals.

It was at ten thirty that she saw him leave and go out of the house. A moment or so later she saw the marquis follow. Her heart began to thump and she could not help being afraid for Adam.

He'd warned her that he was involved in something dangerous—and if Fontleroy was responsible for his cousin's death, as she now suspected, Adam might be in danger.

She glanced about her, but there was no one she could ask for help or tell of her suspicions concerning the marquis. If only Hallam or Paul was here, she would not hesitate to communicate her fears. What could she do? Knowing she was helpless, Jenny fretted over her inability to do anything for some minutes. Then it occurred to her to wonder why they were not present for the cousins had almost always done everything together and she knew that they were all in Bath. A comforting thought occurred to her and her expression lightened.

Adam Miller was not a fool. She suspected that he would not risk his life without taking some precautions.

Were Hallam and Paul watching and waiting for whatever was to happen that night?

Jenny wished with all her heart that she was able to follow and watch what happened, but she knew she must not attempt it. Lady Dawlish would demand to know where she was going—and if Adam had something planned, she would only be in his way.

'Please be safe,' she whispered beneath her breath. 'Oh, please be safe, my dearest…and come back to me soon.'

A rueful smile touched her mouth, because she knew that Adam did not belong to her. Even if he came through this night safe there were so many barriers between them. Yet if Jenny were sure that he truly cared for her she would tell him that she was an heiress.

It might be that her fortune would at least be sufficient to enable him to at least begin to restore his grandfather's estate. She wished that she might have Mr Nodgrass's report for then at least she would know the truth of her situation.

Chapter Eleven

Adam walked purposefully towards the meeting place. He kept his pace measured, knowing that Fontleroy was not far behind him. He had taken the precaution of hiding the necklace earlier, before he entered the ballroom, and was far enough ahead of the marquis to recover it without being seen by his pursuer. In his pocket was a pistol, which he had left with the necklace and a sealed letter—a letter he hoped would fool Fontleroy into handing over the money. For his plan to work, the marquis must believe that both the necklace and letter were real for long enough to attempt to recover his ten thousand.

Since Fontleroy could not be certain that Adam was carrying either the letter or the necklace, he would not attempt to attack from the rear—and if he did so, he would find only a few words from

Adam in the letter and a fake necklace. He could, of course, kill Adam and hope that no one else knew of either the necklace or the letter Mark was supposed to have written. Adam could only trust that his friends were in the appointed place and the men he had served with in France watching his back even now as he walked through dimly lit streets.

'Miller—wait, this is far enough…'

Adam heard Fontleroy's voice from close behind him and hesitated. The marquis was no one's fool. He had probably suspected a trap and decided to do his deal before they arrived at the meeting place.

'Hold, I say—or I'll shoot and take my chances.'

Adam turned, waiting for the marquis to come up to him. They were two streets away from where Hallam and Paul waited, but some of the men who had served under him in France should be nearer, though they'd been warned to keep their distance until the meeting place was reached. The light fell on the marquis's face as he paused beneath the street lamp. His skin looked white and his brow was beaded with sweat. He moved out of the light into the shadows and Adam could only just see the pistol in his hand.

'Give me the necklace and the letter,' Fontleroy ordered. He sneered at Adam, a mocking tone to his voice. 'Did you truly imagine I should give you money for them?'

'How can you be sure I have them on me?'

'I had spies watching as you left. They saw you take something from the municipal flowerbeds— a package and a pistol. You were a fool to think I would let you live, Miller.'

'You murdered my cousin and Lichfield,' Adam accused in a ringing tone. 'You are a double murderer and either a jewel thief or a fence for stolen jewels—do you deny it?'

'Why should I? We are alone and you are about to die. I had Staffs beaten just for knowing the little he did—and Lichfield was a blundering idiot. He put all I had worked for at risk by his stupidity. I disposed of him. Do you imagine you can threaten me and live?'

'Why did you kill Mark?' Adam persisted. 'You could have recovered the necklace. He would have allowed Lichfield to redeem it.'

'Ravenscar was a self-righteous prig,' Fontleroy sneered. 'He suspected it was stolen because of Lichfield's guilty looks—and he planned to unmask us. I had intended to buy the necklace back, but he would not allow it—so I shot him. It was his own stupidity that caused his death.'

'You are a murdering devil and I hope they hang you,' Adam said. His hand went to his pocket, but before he could reach his pistol Fontleroy fired. Another shot rang out an instant later, but the marquis's ball had found its mark. Adam fell to the ground moments before the marquis buckled at the knees, a look of startled surprise in his eyes.

'Damn you…' he muttered as his voice slurred.

As he slumped face forwards to the pavement, several shadowy figures came running. The first bent over Adam, running his hands over his still figure in desperation.

'My God, forgive me,' Paul cried. 'I was a second too late.'

'Is he dead?' Hallam asked and bent to take his cousin's pulse.

A moan issued from Adam's lips, but he did not open his eyes. Blood was oozing through his coat, running down over his hand.

'He's alive, thank God,' Hallam said. 'He took the ball in his shoulder. Another inch to the right and he would almost certainly have died.' He glanced over his shoulder at the ex-soldiers clustered around the marquis. 'Is he dead, Trigger?'

'He's alive, Major Ravenscar,' the man said. 'Captain Ravenscar's ball hit him in the back, but the ball merely scraped his flesh and passed into his arm. Had it penetrated his back, he would've been a goner.'

'Damnation,' Paul muttered. 'The pistol misfired or I should have killed him.'

'It is perhaps just as well,' Hallam said, eyes glittering in the smoky yellow light of the candle that flickered from the street lamp above their heads. 'We all heard his confession. He will be tried for this and with all the evidence we now have he must hang.'

'I hope to God you are right,' Paul said. He looked at his cousin grimly. 'It seems your gut feeling was right, Hal. Had we waited at the meeting place, as Adam instructed, he would be dead. Fontleroy might have got off a second shot before the men could fire.'

The troopers had been instructed to follow, but not to fire until the last moment. Paul's finger had been on the trigger before Fontleroy fired his pistol, but his hammer had not come down true and the difference of half a second meant that Adam was wounded.

'We must get him to his lodgings,' Hallam said

and signalled to one of the men, who whistled, bringing a carriage and horses into the street.

'What shall we do with the other one?' Trooper Jones asked. 'He's out for the count, but I reckon he'll survive. It's not a deep wound.'

'Take him to the magistrates,' Hallam said. 'Let them deal with him—and say that I shall be along tomorrow to lay all the evidence of Fontleroy's guilt before Sir Michael.'

Sir Michael Alderny was the Justice of the Peace for the district and Hallam had taken the precaution of telling him a part of the story earlier that day. Adam had warned him to tell no one for they could not know whom they might trust, but Hallam had known Alderny for years and trusted him not to reveal what he had been told—which was merely the bare bones of the affair. He already had proof of the necklace being stolen property, which would be backed up by the owner and the magistrate in London, to whom Hallam had confided the tale. This evening's work, combined with Stafford's story, was surely enough evidence to convict in a court of law. Fontleroy was done for. He would be charged with his crimes and must surely be punished for them.

Eager hands reached out to lift Adam's unconscious body and carry him gently to the waiting chaise. Hallam dispensed one of the troopers to fetch the doctor, who had been warned to be on stand by earlier and would be at Adam's lodgings almost as soon as they were. He looked down at his cousin's white face and cursed. They had the marquis where he deserved to be—but at what cost?

'Forgive me,' Paul said and his eyes were bright as if with unshed tears. 'I let you both down, Hal. I said that I would shoot, but I was an instant too late.'

'Your pistol was not true,' Hallam said. 'No blame attaches to you. I thank God that Fontleroy's aim was also off its mark. Adam lives. Mark was fatally wounded. We must pray that Adam's wound is not as severe as it might have been.'

'I shall never forgive myself if he dies. Never!'

'Courage,' Hallam said, though his expression was grim. Adam had survived the shot but these wounds often led to fever and poisoning of the blood and they both knew from past experience that any wound however slight might prove fatal. 'We shall do all we can for him. If God wills it we shall pull him though.'

'Pray God he lives,' Paul said, a look of bitterness in his eyes. 'Why did I wait—why did I not shoot as soon as I saw the pistol in Fontleroy's hand?'

'Because Adam wanted the confession. He risked his life to prove Fontleroy's guilt and he got what he wanted. Adam would not blame you, Paul—but had you shot too soon he would have been furious.'

'Yes, I know...' A rueful smile flickered in Paul's eyes. 'He has avenged Mark for Fontleroy is done—if he lives long enough to stand trial they will hang him.'

'Or send him to the colonies,' Hallam said and saw the quick frown in Paul's eyes. 'He has influence and friends, Paul. He will protest his innocence and even though we have proof he may convince the judge to give him a more lenient sentence.'

'If that happens, I shall kill him. And next time I'll make sure my aim is true.'

Hallam climbed into the chaise, but did not answer. He had gone along with Adam's desire to see the marquis punished by the law, but he knew that the law did not always deal in justice. A poor man might find himself hung for stealing bread—

but a rich one with influential friends might escape his just punishment.

All they could do was to pray that Adam lived to give evidence at the marquis's trial—and that the judge was a man who could not be corrupted by promises of fortune or privilege.

Jenny glanced at herself in the mirror as the maid finished coiling her heavy hair into a neat knot at the back of her head. She was feeling happy, because the magic of her dance with Adam had given her beautiful dreams. The look in his eyes and the way his finger had stroked her back as if to comfort her made her blood sing. For a moment a prick of fear took the smile from her eyes. Had anything happened the previous night? She'd seen Fontleroy follow Adam from the ballroom—had they come to blows later? She was on thorns to know, but there was no way she could discover anything for herself. She must just wait for information.

It was just as she was about to leave her bedchamber that she heard the rap at the front door. She reached the top of the stairs as their early visitor was admitted. She gasped as she saw Hallam Ravenscar and started down the stairs at once.

'Have you news?' she asked. 'Is Captain Miller harmed?'

'You know something?' Hallam stared at her. 'Did he tell you?'

'I knew he was doing something dangerous.' She took his arm and drew him into the parlour. 'Please tell me, is he hurt?'

'Fontleroy shot him last night,' Hallam said and Jenny gasped. 'Forgive me, he is not dead, but has a wound in his shoulder. Paul shot the marquis and he is being attended by a doctor, but is in custody. They tell me he is conscious and protesting his innocence, but the evidence is in place and he will be charged with murder and attempted murder—as well as jewel theft.'

Jenny's hand trembled as she placed her fingers to her mouth. 'Is Captain Miller badly hurt?'

'I think he will survive, but he is feverish…' Hallam hesitated, then, 'He called your name several times in his fever. I do not know…I came to beg you to visit him, Miss Jenny. It is not truly proper, of course, because I know you are not much acquainted—but I think it would comfort him if you would just talk to him.'

'Yes, of course.' Jenny spoke without hesitation. She looked round as Lady Dawlish entered the parlour and the whole story was related again.

'Jenny…' Poor Lady Dawlish was astounded and hardly knew how to answer. Her lace kerchief fluttered and sent waves of lavender water towards them. 'I am not sure…it is a little irregular, my love—but Captain Miller is such a good friend and…'

'I must go to him as a friend and a good neighbour,' Jenny said, keeping her voice strictly controlled. 'He has no female relation here to care for him—and I must do what I can to see that he is properly cared for.'

'You would not think of nursing him?' Lady Dawlish was shocked.

'No, indeed, ma'am,' Jenny replied, but crossed her fingers in the folds of her skirt. 'But I must satisfy myself that he is being properly cared for.'

'Yes…well, to be sure…' Lady Dawlish floundered in the face of Jenny's determination. 'I shall send Mary with you. It will be perfectly proper if she is with you all the time.' She nodded, pleased with her solution. 'Mary is a sensible girl and she will make sure that your reputation does not suffer.'

'Thank you so much, ma'am.' Jenny was grateful for Lady Dawlish was making a considerable sacrifice in offering the services of her maid. 'Once the arrangements for his welfare are in place we shall return.'

'Yes, please do so for we shall be anxious,' her kind friend said. 'But do not leave him if he is in danger of his life… Oh dear, this is most irregular. I would nurse him myself, but my duty is to Lucy.'

'Yes, of course it is, ma'am.' Jenny smiled at her, then impulsively kissed her cheek. 'You know that I am very sensible and shall do nothing improper.'

'Of course, my love.' Lady Dawlish's frown disappeared. 'There is no more level-headed girl to be found. Fetch what you need and go with Hallam. I shall not be anxious about you for I know that I may trust you to do what is right and proper.'

Hallam added his thanks to hers and Jenny hurried upstairs to collect her things. In the meantime Mary was summoned from the kitchen and had assembled the things she thought might be needed by the time Jenny was ready.

'This is most kind of you, Miss Jenny—and you, Mary,' Hallam said as he assisted them into his chaise. 'My cousin will soon be better now that you are to oversee his nursing, I am sure.'

Jenny nodded, but made no more than a murmur of assent. She was accustomed to the sickroom, for her mother had suffered several fevers before she succumbed to the last terrible illness that had robbed her of life.

Jenny knew that fevers were very difficult to control for they might seem to abate and then suddenly return stronger than before. She could only hope that the doctor who had bound Adam's wound was to be trusted and that he himself had a strong constitution.

Jenny's heart caught as she saw Adam's pale face. He had thrown the covers back in his fever and the top of his body was naked, apart from the swathes of white bandages that bound his shoulder. The doctor was still with him when they arrived and he turned to her with a look of relief.

'Have you come to nurse Captain Miller, ma'am? I am heartily grateful, for I do not have a nurse I can send at this moment. There is a woman who might come, but I cannot recommend her.'

'We shall look after him for the moment,' Jenny said, causing Mary to glance at her sharply. 'Tell me, Doctor, how is he? Is his wound severe?'

'It is a clean wound for the ball was lodged at

the edge of the shoulder and I was able to remove it easily. I do not think there will be infection, but none the less you must change the bandages twice a day and be careful to keep the wound clean. I have left some pomade to use with the linen strips, which may help to heal the wound. Also laudanum for the pain.'

'What of a mixture for the fever?'

'I shall leave a receipt, which someone must take to the apothecary. Such mixtures must be freshly made or they may do more harm than good.'

'Yes, I know. My mother taught me how to make something that is useful for fever—if someone could buy the ingredients we need I could make it up myself.'

'Ah, a sensible young woman,' the doctor said. He offered his hand. 'I shall leave our patient in your capable hands, ma'am—but do not hesitate to call on me if he should take a turn for the worse.'

'I shall see you out, Dr Harnwell,' Hallam offered. He sent Jenny a grateful smile. 'In a moment I shall return for that receipt and purchase whatever you need.'

'Thank you.' Jenny moved towards the bed as they left and placed a hand on Adam's forehead.

His skin was warm and damp and he moaned as she touched him, but his eyes did not open. She turned her head to look at Mary. 'I think we ought to bathe him a little. He is burning up with the fever.'

'Do you think that wise, miss?'

'I did it often for my mother. It seemed to ease her for a time.'

'That was not what I meant, Miss Jenny. I will bathe him if you wish—but you ought to leave the room.'

'Captain Miller is not fit to ravish me—nor will he notice what we do to him,' Jenny said with a smile. 'I think I am quite safe.'

'It was your reputation I was thinking of, miss.'

'You are with me—and no one else will know, unless we tell them.'

'I should not dream of it, miss.'

'Thank you. I was sure I could trust you.'

At that moment Adam cried out and flung his arm out in an arc, clearly in some distress. Jenny turned back to him, stroking his forehead.

'Rest easy, sir,' she said in a firm but gentle tone. 'We are going to cool you a little and then you will soon feel better. Bring me some cool water from the washstand, Mary.'

Mary was already pouring water into a bowl, which she brought and stood on the bedside chest. She turned back the bedcovers, taking care to cover Adam's modesty. There was a cloth and a yellow sponge that had been taken from some warm sea and brought to England with others of its kind. Mary took the cloth and Jenny the sponge. Jenny began with his face and then his neck. She could not sponge his shoulder on her side, because it was covered in bandages, but Mary bathed his right shoulder and down his arm. Jenny sponged down his left arm and hand, then leaned across his chest, marvelling at the firmness of his stomach muscles and noticing the dark arrow of hair that disappeared beneath the sheet Mary had folded for modesty just below his navel.

'Do you think we can turn him?' Jenny asked. 'Or will it disturb his wound?'

'I think perhaps we ought not to try,' Mary advised. 'If we cover the top half of him now, I could turn back the sheet from the bottom so that we can bathe his legs—that should cool him sufficiently, I would think.'

'Yes, perhaps you are right,' Jenny said. She drew the covers up over his chest, placing his hands inside the covers and keeping her back turned as Mary arranged the covers to protect Adam's privacy once more. Then they bathed and dried his feet and legs before replacing the sheet and one light blanket. Jenny put a hand to his brow and discovered that it was cooler and dry. 'I think that has helped him…'

The door opened and Paul entered. He approached the bed, a haunted expression in his eyes as he gazed down at his cousin.

'How is he now?'

'A little cooler,' Jenny said. 'Once we have the fever mixture he should soon start to feel easier. Hallam is going to take the receipt to the apothecary and bring back the ingredients for me to make up.'

'Give it to me and I will fetch it,' Paul said. 'I feel so helpless. You were very good to come, Miss Hastings, since we hardly know you.'

'I have felt a part of your family since that day,' Jenny said and saw the pain in his eyes. 'I am sincerely glad that Fontleroy has been taken into custody. At least now you may start to put the past behind you, sir.'

'Would that I could…' Paul's face worked with his emotion. 'I thought it would suffice when that devil was caught, but I find it does not. I wish I could go back somehow—stop what happened.'

'We cannot turn the clock back, sir,' Jenny said and reached out to touch his hand. To her horror, he started to weep bitterly. Hardly knowing why she did it, she reached out and drew his head down to her shoulder, patting his back. 'I am so very sorry, Mr Ravenscar...so very sorry. I fear there is nothing I can say to comfort you.'

Paul drew back, stared at her and then, startling Jenny, he suddenly kissed her. She allowed it for a moment, then placed her hands against his shoulders, pushing him away.

'No, sir. You must not...'

Paul jerked away and looked at her shamefacedly. 'Forgive me. You were kind and I...' He turned and went hurriedly from the room.

'The gentleman...' Mary said, making Jenny turn to look at her.

'He was in distress, please forget what you saw. It meant nothing.'

'I know that, miss.' Mary pointed towards the bed. Turning, Jenny saw Adam looking at her, his eyes wide open and angry. 'The gentleman saw...'

'Adam...you are awake?' Jenny went to him at once. 'Has the fever broken?'

'What are you doing here—and why were you kissing Paul?' he asked hoarsely. 'Water…I need water…'

'Here you are, sir.' Mary had guessed his need and was there at his side. She assisted him to swallow a little from the glass. He thanked her, lay back against the pillows and immediately closed his eyes.

'Adam?' Jenny placed a hand on his brow. He felt cooler. 'Adam, are you conscious? You must know that Paul kissed me—he was in distress. It meant nothing to either of us.'

'Go away…' he muttered. 'You shouldn't…I don't need you here…'

'You asked for me…Adam…. You can't think I wanted Paul to kiss me?'

There was no answer. Adam was sleeping deeply, as a little snore bore witness a few moments later. She frowned and drew back as Hallam entered the room once more.

'I just saw Paul leaving in some distress. Adam isn't worse, is he?'

'He is a little better, I think. For a moment he was conscious, but now he is sleeping. His fever has broken for the moment, but we cannot be certain it will not come back. In my experience they often wane and then return with more vigour than before. You should still fetch the ingredients for that mixture, I think.'

'Will you stay for a while until I return?'

'Of course. His bandages need changing twice a day...'

'I can do that,' Hallam said. 'I asked you to come because he called your name so desperately, but I did not expect you to nurse him, Miss Jenny. The landlord knows of a reliable woman and he has sent for her. If you tell her what is needed, I am sure she will be quite capable. It would not be fitting for you to stay here and nurse him—even if Mary stayed with you.'

'Are you certain you can manage?'

'We ought to do as Captain Ravenscar says,' Mary put in. 'For your sake, Miss Jenny.'

'Yes, I dare say you are both right,' Jenny said. She took a little silver-cased notebook from her purse and used the tiny pencil that was attached to it. Writing down the ingredients she needed for her mixture, she gave it to Hallam. 'I shall sit here with him until you return—and then you may send us home in your chaise, sir.'

'Of course. I am grateful that you came. If

Adam saw you when he woke, he will know that you were here.'

'He told me to go home,' she admitted. 'He would not think it suitable if I stayed to nurse him.'

'I shall be as quick as possible,' Hallam said, took her receipt and left the room.

'Mary, will you empty the water we used and bring fresh, please?' Jenny instructed. 'Also ask the landlord for a large jug and some wine and sugar. The mixture I make needs both or it is foul to drink.'

'But, miss…' Mary hesitated, but Jenny's look told her that she must obey and she went off, though reluctantly.

Jenny stood by Adam and looked down at him. He was certainly cooler for the moment and he looked peaceful. She hesitated, then bent down to kiss his lips.

'Please get better, Adam,' she said softly. 'I love you so very much. I do not think I could bear it if—' She caught back a sob, because it was ridiculous of her to cry when he seemed to be recovering. 'You must know that I meant only to comfort Paul. It is you I love…you I care for, my dearest one.'

Adam slept on, not hearing her. She wiped the tears from her face, feeling foolish. If only he would wake up and talk to her for a moment, but she must not wake him for he needed his rest.

Would he recall what he'd seen when he woke? She thought it would possibly seem like a part of his fever to him.

Mary returned quickly and out of breath. She had clearly hurried, fearing to leave her mistress's protégée alone in a bedroom with a gentleman— even if that gentleman was fast asleep. Jenny hid her smile and busied herself by setting out what she had.

Hallam returned within a short time, during which Adam did not stir. He had brought all the ingredients that Jenny needed, as well as a mixture the apothecary had recommended himself. Jenny made up her own and poured a small measure, which she handed to Hallam.

'This is the amount he should take three times a day. If you or the nurse give it to him, make sure you do not exceed the dose. It is not dangerous, but it might make him sick if he had too much—

and I would not use what the apothecary sent unless you trust his remedy more than mine?'

'I trust you implicitly,' Hallam said, and poured the other mixture into the slop basin in the washstand cupboard. 'And now I shall arrange for my driver to take you home, ladies.'

Jenny glanced at Adam regretfully as she followed him from the room. She did not look back as she closed the door behind her.

Adam opened his eyes as the door shut. He pushed himself up against the pillows gingerly, feeling the pain in his shoulder start up. Jenny had left the glass beside him on the chest. He picked it up with his right hand, thanking his lucky stars that it was his left shoulder that had taken Fontleroy's ball. Sipping the mixture tentatively, he discovered it tasted reasonable, though there was an underlying bitterness. He swallowed it all in one go and then pulled a face as he caught the aftertaste that the wine and sugar had masked.

'Trying to poison me, Jenny?' he murmured and smiled oddly.

His mind was a little hazy, but he was vaguely aware of two female voices in the room. He thought that they might have bathed him and it was after that that he began to feel a little easier. He'd woken for a moment and seen Paul in a woman's arms. He'd been kissing her—then she'd turned and he knew she was Jenny.

Why was she kissing Paul? He recalled telling her she should go home and asking for water... then he'd fallen into a deep sleep. He thought he might have dreamed for a while, because he'd heard a woman's voice telling him that she loved him.

Was it Jenny's voice? Had she truly been here?

Adam felt bewildered. His shoulder hurt like the very devil and he felt weak, which he knew from experience was par for the course after losing a deal of blood. He would come about in a few days—but what had happened in this room a short time ago?

Had Jenny truly told him she loved him? Had she kissed him on the lips—or was that a part of the whole mad dream? She could not have been kissing Paul so he must have dreamed it all. Had she been here in the room at all?

Yet as he lay back again and closed his eyes he thought he could smell her perfume—and someone had prepared that mixture for him. Someone had told Hallam that he should take it three times a day…which there was no way he would if he had a choice. The taste was awful and Adam would be better in a day or so…

Adam was not better immediately. Later that evening, when Hallam and the nurse returned to change his bandage, they discovered that his fever had returned. He was talking wildly and thrashing his arms and legs and Hallam had to hold him down while the nurse changed the bandage. He then poured the required dosage and forced it between Adam's lips. Adam fought and muttered, but most of it went down as Hallam intended.

'Damn you…foul…' Adam muttered but slumped back against the pillows almost at once.

In a few moments he was snoring. Hallam decided to follow Jenny's instructions and instructed the nurse to fetch cool water. Between them they bathed him and saw a distinct improvement.

'He should rest for a while now, sir,' the nurse said. 'If you would like me to stay for a few hours, you should get some sleep yourself.'

'I shall return in three hours so that you can get off to your other patients,' Hallam said. 'It was good of you to come, ma'am.'

'I always try to help Dr Harnwell's patients. He

don't trust many, sir, though I says it myself. I do my best for folk and there's some as take your money and do nothing.'

Hallam thanked her again and left her to care for Adam. He decided to write a note and deliver it to Miss Jenny. She was sure to be anxious for news.

Chapter Twelve

'Who is your letter from?' Lady Dawlish asked when Jenny opened it. They had been out to dinner and were just returned after a pleasant evening that had been a little overshadowed by Jenny's unspoken fear for Captain Miller.

'It is from Major Ravenscar,' Jenny said. 'He says that Captain Miller's fever returned, but the mixture I left for him seems to have eased him again. He is sleeping peacefully once more.'

Thank God! Oh, thank God. She could not have borne it had he gone into a decline and died. She had been keeping herself on a tight rein and now she almost collapsed with relief.

'How worrying,' Lady Dawlish said. 'I had an uncle who died of a gunshot wound sustained in a duel. It was the fever that killed him, too.'

'Please do not,' Jenny said in a faint voice. 'I

pray that Captain Miller will not succumb to his fever. Do you think I should go round to his lodgings again, ma'am?'

'He has a nurse and Hallam is quite capable,' Lady Dawlish said. 'You know that I would not forbid you for the world, dearest—but I think I must advise against it.'

'I know you are right,' Jenny said, her throat tight with suppressed emotion. How could she stay away when Adam needed her? And yet she must. She could not visit an unmarried gentleman in his bedroom without incurring censure. The first time had been risk enough, but to go again now when he had an efficient nurse would be thought highly improper in her. 'There is sufficient of the mixture to last three days. I shall ask if more is required then.'

'Then I am certain he is as comfortable as possible and there is nothing more you could contribute to his welfare.'

'Of course you are right, ma'am,' Jenny agreed, though her heart rebelled.

She kissed Lady Dawlish goodnight and then went up the stairs to the landing, where she met Lucy. She said goodnight to her friend, who seemed a little odd, quite pale and distressed, then went into her bedroom. She sat down on the bed, feeling close to tears. If only she could be there with Adam—if only she were able to nurse him herself, but she had already risked her reputation by visiting him once. Besides, Adam would not want her at his bedside. If she insisted on visiting him when he had his cousins and a nurse to care for him, she would lay herself open to gossip— she might compromise herself, and that would be unfair to Adam.

As a gentleman he might feel compelled to ask her to marry him and that would be most uncomfortable. Much as she longed to be his wife, she did not want it to happen that way.

Brushing a hand across her eyes, she tried to think of other things. A small posy of flowers had been delivered that afternoon, and a note of apology. It had not been signed, but she knew it had come from Paul.

Lucy had been curious, smelling the sweet roses and glancing at the letter, as if she wished to know what was in it.

'Who is your admirer?' she asked. 'Has he begged you to flee to Gretna with him?'

Her tone was teasing, but Jenny knew she was very curious about the posy. Unable to explain what had had happened with Paul in Adam's sickroom, Jenny shook her head and pretended not to know who they had come from.

She had screwed up the note and placed it amongst the kindling in the fire grate in her room, where it would be burned the next time a fire was lit. Jenny had forgot it while they were out for the evening, but when she returned to her room she thought it best to set it to the candle and burn it. However, when she bent to retrieve the note, she could not find it at first—then discovered it had been torn into several pieces.

Now how had that happened? Had one of the maids seen it and read it before tearing it into shreds?

She recalled Paul's words, which had been ambiguous to say the least. He'd thanked her for her kindness, blamed himself for his careless action in kissing her and begged her to forgive him. He had been overcome by his emotions and forgot himself and hoped he had not distressed her too much.

Jenny suddenly felt cold all over. Had Lucy entered her room and read the note—had she known it had come from Paul, even though it was unsigned? If she had, it would explain the way she had stared at Jenny so oddly—almost as if she disliked her.

Jenny felt most uncomfortable. She had not told Lucy about the incident because she felt it embarrassing to Paul. He had wept in her arms and the kiss had been the kiss of a man in terrible distress. All he'd wanted from her was comfort—but to someone who had not been there to witness it, it might seem so much more.

If Lucy had read that note and recognised Paul's handwriting, she might think Jenny had encouraged him to kiss her. How could she explain? If she'd told Lucy when the flowers arrived it would have been easier, but the mere fact that she'd kept it secret and then tried to dispose of the note seemed damning.

Jenny was almost certain that her friend was in love with Paul. Lucy had not said so in as many words, but Jenny had seen something in Lucy's eyes that told her she was not indifferent to him. If she'd read the note, she would naturally feel that Jenny had betrayed her.

Ought she to go to Lucy's room and try to explain? She hesitated for a moment, because it was not something she wished to do, but her concern for her friend made her leave her room and go along the hallway. She reached Lucy's room, which was slightly ajar. She hesitated, hearing Lady Dawlish's voice and the sound of Lucy's weeping.

'What is the matter, dearest?' Lady Dawlish was asking. 'You cannot be crying for nothing.'

'I am,' Lucy said thickly through her tears. 'It is nothing, Mama—and I shall not tell you. Please go away and leave me alone...'

Jenny turned away with a heavy heart. She could not intrude at such a moment. Lucy obviously thought the worst. She would have to find a way of telling her the truth soon, because she did not want a foolish incident that meant nothing to her to come between them.

Adam opened his eyes and looked at his cousin. Hallam had yet another glass of some foul mixture in his hand, but he pushed his hand away and inched his way into a sitting position against the pillows.

'Enough, no more, Hal,' he said. 'Unless you want to kill me off?'

'Miss Jenny's mixture has served you well,' Hallam said and grinned at him. 'She warned me it was foul stuff when she made the second batch for me, but she added a little honey this time to try to make it more palatable.'

'Well, she did not succeed,' Adam said. 'I feel as if I have been run over by a coach and horses—how long have I been stuck in this damned bed?'

'Four days,' Hal told him. 'We thought the fever had gone twice, but it came back again. It's no wonder you feel weak—you've been ill, Cousin.'

'I shall survive.' Adam looked grim. 'What happened after that devil shot me? Did you get him?'

'Paul shot him an instant later. His pistol misfired or he would have shot first—he feels bad about it so do not criticise him too harshly.'

'I dare say I may thank him and the rest of you for my life. Is Fontleroy dead?'

'Merely wounded in the arm. Unlike you, he suffered no fever. He was conscious by the morning and I understand he has recovered well. Naturally, he claims he was innocent and set upon by a gang of rogues. However, the evidence is too damning. He will come to trial no matter how he wriggles and twists.'

'I hope they hang him, but you know there's a chance he'll get away with it—he's not without friends.'

'Will they stand by him now that he's been revealed as a jewel thief? My agent tells me that he has been stealing from quite a few gentlemen who have sat down to cards with him in the past—at least they have all suffered thefts when at a party that Fontleroy knew they were to attend. I think he is finished in society for the tale is already circulating and we've received messages of sympathy and outrage. He made a point of being at the affairs his victims attended, which means he either employed rascals to do the actual burglary—or it was Lichfield who committed the crime.'

'Of course, Fontleroy was too clever to risk his own neck. Dead men don't talk.'

'Which is why Fontleroy disposed of him as soon as he discovered what he'd done with the necklace.'

'Fontleroy will not confess.'

'Never! He'll protest his innocence until the last—but he'll get a shock when you testify in court against him.'

'One man's word...'

'Not quite. We all heard him and we all saw him shoot you—we'll have him for that if nothing else. It was attempted murder, Adam—and he should hang for that without the rest.'

'If the law fails, I'll kill him myself.'

'Paul has already sworn to do it.' Hallam smiled coldly. 'I believe he will be tried and found guilty—but he may get away with transportation, if that *is* getting away with it. A man of his ilk would find it hard to accept.'

'No doubt he'd find a way to ease his burden.' Adam frowned. 'I pray they hang him.'

'Amen to that.'

'Hal…' Adam hesitated, then, 'Did I imagine it—or was Miss Jenny Hastings here in my bed-chamber alone with me?'

'She was here with a maid. I was here and the doctor—and Paul for a moment. He was very cut up about it all, Adam. Felt he had let you down—and that he should have been the one to face Fontleroy. I've never seen him in such distress, even after Mark died.'

'He knows why it had to be me.' Adam was thoughtful. 'So she came to visit me here and she made that mixture for me—I wasn't sure if I'd dreamed it.'

'I left her and the maid with you while I went to buy a few things she needed for her fever mixture. She might have sent the maid for something—why does it bother you that she was here?'

Adam rubbed at the bridge of his nose. 'It

wouldn't do her reputation much good if this got out, Hal. She has nothing, you know. Lady Dawlish took her in, but if there were a scandal...'

'No reason why there should be. None of us are likely to say anything. Too much respect. She is a lovely person, Adam. If you thought of marrying her, I'm sure you could hardly do better.'

'If only I had the choice,' Adam said with a wry twist of his mouth. 'You know my situation, Hal.'

'Have you heard nothing about the mine?'

'They were digging deeper the last time I had a letter—but I doubt there's much hope. Even if a seam is found it will hardly be enough to pay off the earl's debts, though it might help us to maintain the estate and pay the interest. Given a chance I might bring us about.'

'The earl should not expect you to pay his debts. You must just do what you can to stave off bankruptcy, Adam—and when the time comes sell off what is left to pay the bank.'

'I believe it may come to that...' Adam sighed. 'How can I ask a girl with no fortune to marry me? I shall likely be repaying Grandfather's debts for years—though if she were compromised I should feel compelled to ask.'

'I thought you might quite like her? You called for her repeatedly in your fever.'

'Did she hear me? Damn it! Did you ask her to visit me?' Hallam nodded and he swore again. 'I may have ruined her good name for nothing. Even if I ask her to be my wife I have nothing to give her. My own estate would be adequate for us to live quietly, but...' He shrugged and then groaned as his shoulder hurt. 'I do not know what to do for the best, Hal. I admire Jenny more than any other lady I know.'

'Are you in love with her?'

'What is love? I'm not sure—are you?'

'Oh, yes, I know just what it feels like,' Hal said and a nerve flicked at his temple. 'I was in love once and it hurt like hell when she—' He broke off. 'I try to forget her. No sense in living in the past—but real love takes a long time to die and the pain is worse than you are suffering now.'

'Then I'm sorry for you,' Adam said, struck by his cousin's tortured look. He had not realised Hallam had suffered from a devastating love affair. 'I'm not sure if that's how I feel for Jenny. I know I want her...but that's not love. I respect her and I should not wish to harm her, but the kind of love you're talking of...I don't know. Perhaps I don't wish to know, because it is impossible.' Yet even as he denied it, he felt the odd ache about his heart and knew that the day he asked another woman to wed him would be the day he gave up all chance of happiness.

How could he not love a woman who had come to him when he was lying on his sickbed and nursed him, regardless of her own reputation? She was brave, lovely and kind…and he was very much afraid he was already deep in love with her. Yet how could he ask her to wed him, knowing that it would be years before he could give her the kind of life she deserved?

'You could ask Ravenscar for a loan to help you recover the earl's estate,' Hallam suggested. 'No, no, don't poker up. He would not want to see you or your grandfather go under. It is possible to repay a loan in time, Adam. A few prudent investments and you might earn more than you think. I am considering setting up a wine import company and you might join me if you wish. With various schemes you might prosper in time.'

'I was hoping to have my stables up and running as soon as possible—but if I can raise sufficient capital for both I should be glad to be your partner.'

'You must be able to raise a few thousand, even if the bank is not willing to help.'

'Do you think I have not tried to think of a way—but to ask for a loan from my uncle...' Adam shook his head. 'I suppose...I know he would make it easy for me, but I fear my pride stands in the way.'

'It would be a solution, that's all I'm saying.' Hallam laughed. 'Do not be angry, Cousin. My own estate is hardly in much better case. I think I can manage to set it straight in time. My father's debts do not equal the earl's and the bank has not asked me to repay them—but I know how you feel.'

'I had not realised you were also in trouble, Hal.'

'Fortunately, I think the bank may give me more time,' Hallam said. 'Besides, I do not have a beautiful young woman in love with me.'

'You think Jenny cares for me?' Adam's gaze narrowed. 'Hal, have I allowed her to hope? I am all kinds of a cad if she thinks I may offer for her.'

'I have no idea what you may have said to her,' Hallam said. 'But she was very willing to nurse you—and I believe she cares for you deeply. It was there in her eyes—though it is wrong in me to say so, but you did ask. She did all she could for you, Adam. Indeed, were your problems not so very difficult I should say that you owed it to her to offer her marriage.'

Adam swore. 'Then I must consider my options again,' he said. 'I did not think I had aroused expectations, but if I have…' A rueful laugh broke from him. 'If someone would discover tin or copper in the mine everything might yet be perfect. I should much prefer to marry Jenny than any other lady of my acquaintance.'

Prefer it? It was what he wanted with every nerve in his body, but he knew it was the last thing he should be thinking of…for his grandfather's sake and for hers.

'Then perhaps you'd best get up from that bed and court her?'

Adam shook his head. 'You may laugh, Hal—but it is the very devil. You are certain she does not prefer Paul?'

'Good grief—what makes you ask?'

'I thought I saw him kissing her. She had her arms about him and did not seem to dislike being held by him.'

Hallam grinned. 'It's the fever, dear fellow. The things one sees when in a fever. You wouldn't believe what I saw when I was wounded in France.'

Adam laughed. 'I may have a good idea. I've been wounded before, you know—and some of the stuff those quacks give one make one go out of one's head.'

Jenny stared at the letter from her solicitor with a mixture of elation and despair. It seemed that she had far more money than she'd dreamed. Why on earth had her uncle sold her father's possessions when there was absolutely no need? It just did not make sense. She knew her uncle was a nipcheese and hated to waste money. He'd thought she did not need to keep a large house going and could perfectly well live under his roof, thereby saving the expense—but why all Papa's carriages and horses? And without consulting her wishes? It really was too bad of him!

And now so much money, more than she really knew what to do with. How could she ever confess to Adam that she was an heiress, after she'd allowed him to assume that she had nothing?

He would think the worst of her, imagine that she had tried to entrap him. Her throat tightened and she was close to tears, because she loved him so very much and when he knew…he would despise her…

'Oh, there you are.' Lucy's voice brought her out of her daze. 'Mama is ready to leave. She sent me to find you.'

'Yes, of course. I must just fetch my shawl. I had a letter…I am sorry to have kept you waiting…'

'Lucy…' Jenny slipped her arm through the other girl's as they were walking to the Pump room to join Lady Dawlish, after having been to the lending library. 'You've been quiet all morning—are you upset with me?'

'No—should I be?' Lucy asked, but her eyes flashed an accusation. 'Was there something you wanted to tell me, Jenny?'

Jenny sighed. She'd tried to broach the subject once or twice, but Lucy had turned away or someone had interrupted them. There was no avoiding it now.

'You read the note from Paul, did you not?'

Lucy's cheeks went bright pink. 'You admit that the flowers came from him—that you let him kiss you? How could you? Are you in love with him?'

'No, Lucy, I am not,' Jenny said. Lucy had dropped her arm and stood facing her accusingly. 'Paul broke down and cried when he saw Adam lying in his fever. He was in such distress that

I put my arms about him to comfort him—as I would you or a brother, or any friend in distress. For some reason he suddenly kissed me. I allowed it for a moment because he was in such anguish, then pushed him back. He apologised and rushed off in a hurry, much embarrassed.'

'So you did let him kiss you.'

'Only out of sympathy,' Jenny said. 'It meant nothing to either of us. Please believe me, Lucy. I did not flirt with him, nor did I want or encourage him to kiss me—it just happened.'

'He has fallen in love with you, because you offered him sympathy and held him while he cried,' Lucy said, two red spots in her cheeks. 'You deliberately tried to steal him from me...'

'I did nothing of the kind,' Jenny said. 'Please believe me, Lucy. I am not in love with him—and he does not love me. It was the kiss of a man in terrible grief, nothing more. I think he is embarrassed over it. Besides, you did not say that you considered Paul yours.'

'No, but you knew...' Lucy choked on her tears, brushing them away angrily. 'You must have guessed that it was Paul I—' she broke off and pulled out a lace kerchief, dabbing at her cheeks. 'Oh, no—I have no right to accuse you. I thought

Paul cared for me, but it is obvious he does not. If—if he offers for you, you must accept him.'

'Not for the world, especially now that I am sure you care for him,' Jenny said, feeling troubled. She had suspected what lay behind her friend's unhappiness, but it was worse than she'd thought. 'How can you be certain Paul does not care for you, Lucy? Has he said something?'

Lucy's eyes filled with tears again, but she blinked them away. 'That night we danced I thought…the way he looked at me, held me…but he has never once said that he loves me, and since Mark…died, I think he hates me.'

'I am very sure he does not,' Jenny said. 'I think he is very mixed up in his head. If you had seen his distress over Adam…'

Lucy brushed away her tears. 'I am sorry for suspecting you, but you did not tell me and I thought…I thought you wanted him for yourself.'

'I promise you I do not.' Jenny's cheeks flushed. 'I like someone else, but I am not certain he feels the same for me.'

'Do you mean Sir James?' Jenny shook her head and Lucy frowned. 'Are you speaking of Adam—surely you know that is impossible? He must marry someone with a fortune because of the earl's debts.'

'Yes, he told me,' Jenny said diffidently. 'I do have some money of my own, Lucy.'

'Do you? Your uncle sold everything, so we thought... Everyone assumed there was nothing left for you.'

'My uncle behaved very foolishly.' Jenny sighed. 'My lawyer has told me that neither the house nor the carriages need have been sold. I could set up my own establishment and employ a companion if I wished.'

'Really?' Lucy looked astonished. 'Does Mama know?'

'I did tell her that I had more money than I believed at the start—you were in the carriage when I mentioned it.'

'Was I? I did not take it in. My mind must have been elsewhere.' Lucy was thoughtful. 'Does that mean you will leave us when we go home? I was hoping you might stay longer—at least until we go abroad. You could come with us if you chose, couldn't you?'

'We may talk about that when it happens,' Jenny said. 'Are you sure you don't want me to go away?

If you think I've been flirting with Paul behind your back...'

'No, please don't.' Lucy blushed. 'It was mean of me to accuse you. I didn't understand why he sent the flowers and the note. I thought he was in love with you.'

'Oh, Lucy. I should hate to part bad friends over such a silly thing,' Jenny said as Lucy tucked her arm through hers once more. 'We are neither of us very fortunate in our love affairs, are we?'

'Not at all,' Lucy said. 'Though perhaps if Adam knew the truth...'

'I do not wish to tell him—at least until I know how he feels about me,' Jenny confided. 'I should not wish to embarrass him by mentioning my money—and he imagines I am a sort of unpaid companion.'

'Why should he think that? I've told everyone you are my friend—and so has Mama.'

'He assumed it when he helped me after my carriage broke down—and I sort of allowed him to think it. Most people assumed that Papa had lost all his money, whereas, although the loss was large, he was much richer than anyone knew.'

'Really?' Lucy squeezed her arm. 'Was he a nabob or something of the sort?'

'Yes, perhaps you could say that.' Jenny laughed. 'The lawyer said his money was made in trade with various steel companies, mills and factories, which is why he did not broadcast it to the world. Trade is a dirty word in my uncle's house. He considered the house and land all my father owned, discounting all his shares in industry—which my lawyer is going to discreetly sell for me. He tells me I shall have quite a large sum at my disposal when the money is all in his client account. I already have ten thousand pounds from the sale of the estate and house, but I know that would not be enough to pay the earl's debts.'

Lucy looked stunned. 'That is a huge sum, Jenny—and you may have some more. Do you know how much?'

'My lawyer wasn't sure exactly. He estimated it might amount to a similar sum but did not want to arouse expectations that might fail. I should be grateful if only a thousand or two was raised from the sale for every little extra must help, do you not agree?'

'So I should think,' Lucy said and squeezed her arm. 'I shall have ten thousand when I marry—so we are both heiresses. I am sure you would have many more suitors if people knew the truth.'

'Please do not mention it,' Jenny begged. 'I prefer that people think I have little or nothing. I should hate to be courted for the sake of money.'

'Yes, it is unpleasant. Mama warned me to beware of fortune hunters when I was first out—but I had little trouble with them because everyone thought me promised to Mark, even before it happened.'

'Well, they will not now,' Jenny said. 'You have some suitors already—but once you are out of mourning you will have more.'

'There is only one I want,' Lucy said and her voice suddenly rose to a squeak. 'Oh, he is coming this way. Do not leave me, Jenny. Is my face stained with tears?'

'Not at all,' Jenny reassured her. 'You are a little pale. Pinch your cheeks, dear one. He has seen us and we cannot avoid him.'

'Miss Lucy, Miss Jenny,' Paul said and swept off his hat. 'You both look beautiful. I trust you are both well?' He sent an oddly shy glance at Jenny.

'We are very well, Paul,' Lucy said, her chin up. 'We expected you would call on us before this— how is Captain Miller?'

'Adam is recovering, I am glad to say. He is aware how much he owes to you, Miss Jenny—

but I know he will call to thank you as soon as he is able. He was out of his bed this morning and I do not think Hal can keep him in his room much longer.'

'I am relieved to know Captain Miller is recovering,' Jenny said and her heart beat faster. 'However, I did little to help—my offering was merely a mixture I knew to be useful. I am glad it worked for him, as it did for my mama.'

'We were wondering if we might get up a party to drive out into the hills and take a picnic one day soon,' Paul said. 'I know Adam wishes to thank you, Miss Jenny—and we all feel much more the thing now that my brother's death has been avenged.'

'How evil that man must be,' Lucy said, her fingers playing nervously on Jenny's arm. 'We are so pleased he has been arrested, are we not, Jenny?'

'It is a relief for us all,' Jenny agreed. 'I am sure we should all look forward to the picnic, sir, when Captain Miller feels able to take such a trip.'

'It was he that suggested it for next week. Perhaps on Wednesday? We shall call for all of you, Lady Dawlish and any friend she cares to invite included.'

'Mama will be delighted,' Lucy said. 'I do not

need to ask for I know we have no prior engagements that day.'

'Then we shall settle on Wednesday at ten in the morning. Now, I have some errands to perform for my cousins—if you will excuse me, ladies?'

He made them a little bow and walked off down the street, leaving both girls breathless and staring at each other.

'Do you think…?' Lucy asked with a catch in her voice. 'Do you think he looked easier than he has since…?'

'Yes, I thought so. A little embarrassed at first, but then…I would say he has begun to cope with his grief, Lucy. Not to forget, but to accept. It is because Fontleroy has been taken, of course.'

'Everyone knows Paul had nothing to do with it now,' Lucy said. 'I think a shadow has been lifted from him.'

'You must not expect too much too soon, but it is clear that he feels a little better—they must all do so to offer us the invitation to a picnic.'

'Paul said that it was Adam's suggestion,' Lucy said and looked at her. 'Do you think?'

'I am trying not to think anything,' Jenny said, but could not quite hide her pleasure. 'I dare say he merely wishes to thank me for making up that mixture—or simply because they all wish to relax now that the mystery is solved.'

'We were none of us able to relax while that devil was at large,' Lucy said. 'It has been terrible for the family, but perhaps now things may become a little easier for everyone.'

'Yes.' Jenny squeezed her arm. 'It does not solve my problem—but perhaps if things go well on Wednesday…'

Jenny knew it was foolish to hope, but insensibly she found that she *was* hoping this invitation meant more than merely a pleasant outing. For Adam to arrange it as soon as he was able, it must be important to him. Had he realised while he lay close to death that he wished to marry her no matter whether he could pay his grandfather's debts or not?

And if he had—how soon could she tell him that she had money of her own, money that might at least help to solve his problems?

'Adam…' Paul hovered on the threshold of the bedchamber. 'May I come in? I need to talk to you about something awkward.'

Adam was sitting in an elbow chair with a cushion to support his arm. His shoulder was still uncomfortable, but the pain had been dulled by a glass of the best French brandy.

'Of course, Paul—what may I do for you?' He indicated the brandy. 'Do you care for a glass?'

'Not at this hour, gives me a headache before dinner,' Paul said, 'Unless it's medicinal, of course. Being shot hurts as I remember only too well. Are you feeling any better, old chap?'

'Much. I should have gone out this morning had Hallam not declared he would tie me to the chair if I attempted it. However, I wished to be recovered in time for the picnic otherwise I should have ignored him.'

'Rather...' Paul wiped his hands nervously on his breeches. 'Tell me to mind my own business if you like—but do you intend to ask Miss Hastings to marry you?'

'Mind your own business,' Adam said pleasantly. 'Anything else?'

'I ought to tell you that I kissed her,' Paul said, his neck turning dark red. 'Damned cheek, I know—but I was in tears and she put her arms round me, just to comfort me, you know. I lost my head and kissed her. She was very good about it, just smiled the way she does and forgave me—but I'm wondering if I should ask her to marry me.'

'Are you in love with her?'

'No, not at all. It's…well, you know what I want, but that is impossible. Lucy was Mark's—besides, she is grieving for him. I just thought perhaps I owed it to Miss Hastings. Loss of reputation, you know?'

'Paul, you're an idiot,' Adam told him good-naturedly. 'Well meaning, but a fool. Please do not embarrass yourself or her by asking her. She would refuse you.'

'Yes, well, I rather thought she might like you…'

Adam sighed, looking at him in a rueful manner. 'Since Hallam thinks the same, I believe you are right. If anyone owes her a proposal of marriage, it is I.'

Paul's face cleared and he grinned. 'Ah, right, then that's the end of it. You didn't mind my asking?'

'You did just as I would expect of an honourable young idiot,' Adam said and laughed. 'I shan't tell you to ask Lucy to marry you, though you might be surprised if you did. I dare say you ought to wait a few months, perhaps a year—but don't give up on her yet, Paul.'

'I wish I could think…' Paul shook his head. 'I have dreams of Mark accusing me of letting him die…perhaps they will stop now that Fontleroy is behind bars.'

'Mark is dead and we can none of us bring him back,' Adam said. 'Give yourself time to grieve, Paul—but do not give up all hope and don't shut Lucy out. Mark would not wish you to suffer more than necessary, either of you. Try to explain how you feel to her if you can.'

'Yes, perhaps…' Paul's body was tight with tension. 'You're a great gun, Adam. I'm glad we've had this talk. I don't think I could've got through this business without you and Hal.'

'It's what friends are for,' Adam said and smiled. 'I thought the world of Mark—but you're my cousin too. Remember, it's one for all and all for one.'

'Yes.' Paul blinked hard. 'Excuse me, I have somewhere I ought to be.'

Adam's mouth set in a thin line as Paul left before he disgraced himself by shedding unmanly tears. His own eyes felt gritty, though his grief had become muted, perhaps because of his illness. He could face Mark's loss now and begin to remember with fondness and amusement. It would take longer for Paul to be able to do the same, but in time he would remember the fun and comradeship they'd shared.

His brow furrowed as he thought of Jenny. Had he not understood the motive for Paul's tentative question concerning her he might have been tempted to punch him—if he could, of course, which was doubtful for the moment. When had he begun to become possessive over her?

'Jenny Hastings.' He spoke her name aloud, testing it, bringing her pretty face and trim figure to mind. What was it about her that had got beneath his skin, making her the only woman he would ever want to marry—the woman he could not live without? She was lovely, but not the most beautiful woman he'd seen, but there was something in her smile, in the tilt of her head…and the way she had of bringing calm to his soul in the midst of disorder.

He was going to have to propose, of course. In all honour he had no choice but to ask her to be his wife. Yet in his heart he knew that it was what he wanted deep down inside.

His grandfather would not be happy, but there was nothing Adam could do. He'd never wanted to marry an heiress for her money; the idea revolted him and made his flesh creep. He would have felt humiliated having to ask for money from his bride, and though he would have done his best to make any young lady happy, he felt any such marriage to be doomed from the start. Marriage to Jenny would be a constant delight.

Having decided on a course of action, he began to feel better about the whole thing. Jenny was the only woman he'd ever wanted to marry and he believed they would make each other happy. Somehow, Adam must find enough money to prevent the bank foreclosing—at least during his grandfather's lifetime. Perhaps five thousand on account and the promise of more each year would do it—he might have to approach his uncle. Unless that seam of tin was found in the mine, or he took a loan on his own estate…

Suddenly, Adam was smiling. It was as if a dark cloud had lifted. Even if he had to sell his own estate and take Jenny to live at that mausoleum the earl loved so much he would find a way—and he would have the woman he cared for at his side to help him do it.

Chapter Thirteen

Jenny jumped out of bed and ran to the window as soon as she woke that morning. It was the day of the promised picnic and, looking out, she saw that the sun was already shining. They would have a glorious day for their outing.

She had spent many hours debating what to wear and had finally settled on a new yellow-silk walking gown, which had been delivered only two days earlier by the seamstress. It was perhaps a little unfair to Lucy, who would be wearing either light grey or lilac, but she was sure that her friend would understand that she wanted to look her best for the occasion.

As she was stroking her gown with loving fingers, the maid brought in a tray of hot chocolate and sweet rolls. Jenny decided to eat her breakfast sitting in an elbow chair by the window and the maid placed the tray on a table beside her.

'I shall bring water in half an hour, miss,' she said.

'Yes, please.' Jenny smiled at her. She felt as if she would burst with happiness, though she was trying to be sensible and not allow herself to hope for too much. An invitation to a picnic did not mean that she would receive a proposal from Adam, though she'd felt that it was important to him. She hoped that he did not imagine he was obliged to ask her simply because she'd visited him in his bedchamber, but even that small cloud could not dim her feeling of anticipation and pleasure.

Lucy came in as Jenny was washing behind her screen. She asked if she might wait and Jenny replied that she would be out in a moment. Emerging from behind the screen in her petticoat, she saw Lucy trying her perfume at the dressing table.

'I like this scent,' Lucy said. 'What is it called?'

'Oh, something like Essence of a Garden,' Jenny replied. 'Papa brought it back from a trip to Paris and I liked it so much I only use it on special occasions.'

'I thought it must be French,' Lucy said. Jenny

stepped into her yellow gown and pulled it up, then the maid fastened the back for her. 'You look lovely, Lucy—that dress suits you.'

Her pale-lilac gown was set off with silver tulle beneath the bosom and around the squared neckline, the little puffed sleeves very becoming to Lucy's slim arms.

Jenny sat patiently as the maid brushed her hair back from her face and fastened it with clips.

'Is there anything more you need, miss?'

'No. Thank you, Lily. My hair looks very nice.'

'I was up early,' Lucy said and sat on a stool as Jenny hunted in her jewel box and found a silver pendant with a tiny pearl drop. 'I can hardly wait for the gentlemen to arrive.'

'We are so fortunate that the day is warm.' Jenny laughed. 'I do not think I have seen you so excited before, Lucy.'

'Is it foolish of me? I know that if one expects too much, things are never as wonderful as one imagined.'

Jenny rose and went to her, holding out her hands. 'You are hoping that Paul may say something, are you not?'

'I know it is foolish,' Lucy said. 'It is much too soon for a declaration. I should not know what to say if he asked…but of course he will not. He could not…it is too soon to hope for so much.'

'I think you must not expect a proposal, dearest, but if Paul is easier in your company—if you can be friends again—that would be something, would it not?'

'It would be everything,' Lucy said and her eyes glowed. 'I have missed him so much. When we danced in London that time I was certain that he was in love with me. I believe he would have told me had he not known I was to be engaged to Mark. I had almost decided that I must break off my engagement when…it happened.'

'So you were certain of your feelings?'

'Yes, I think so,' Lucy said. 'Mark had never made me feel the way I did when I danced with Paul…but I liked him so much and he was so generous and sweet to me. I found it difficult to tell him that I had changed my mind and then it was too late.'

Jenny leaned forwards to kiss her cheek. 'Should you not tell Paul how you felt? If he understood that your marriage would not have gone ahead, it might relieve his mind.'

'Yes, perhaps—only he might be angry with me for letting his brother down, and he might think

I am saying it because Mark is dead and I cannot marry him. He might think I am interested in the title and the estate—which is not true.'

'Well, only you can make him understand that,' Jenny said. 'You must do what you think is right.'

'What shall you do if Adam asks you to marry him?'

Jenny blushed and turned aside to pick up her bonnet, reticule and a light silk stole to drape over her bare arms.

'I am not sure that he will,' she said. 'It would make me happy, I think—but I must not presume too much.'

'Surely you are entitled to expect it after what you did for him?' Lucy said and swung the strings of her own bonnet. 'He asked for you to visit and by doing so he committed himself to a relationship. Any gentleman would propose after what happened.'

'I merely helped to make him comfortable,' Jenny said, a faint flush in her cheeks. 'I trust that Adam does not imagine he has compromised me for it is nothing of the sort. I would not have him ask me out of a sense of duty.'

'Oh, I did not mean that, of course I didn't,' Lucy apologised instantly, her own cheeks flushed. 'I am sure he likes you very much and would be happy to marry you.'

Jenny's shining happiness evaporated slightly. If Adam were under the impression that he had compromised her and must ask her to be his wife she would not know what to do. She loved him and wanted to be his wife—but unless he loved her she was afraid that her heart would break: not all at once, but little by little over the years.

'Well, he may not ask,' Jenny said, blinking fast so that she should not shed a tear and make herself look foolish.

'Jenny, I'm so sorry.' Lucy's hand found hers. 'I spoke without thinking. I am sure Adam cares for you—you can see it in his face when he looks at you.'

Jenny smiled. 'I know he likes and respects me,' she said. 'Perhaps that is enough for marriage— but we both presume too much for very likely he will not ask me.'

Adam had just finished tying an intricate knot in his pristine cravat when a knock at his door heralded Hallam's arrival. One glance at his face told Adam that something was very wrong. He frowned and brushed an imaginary speck from his immaculate coat, waiting for his cousin to speak.

'Well, what is on your mind?' he asked when Hallam continued to hesitate.

'I have no choice but to tell you, though I know it must overshadow the day,' Hallam said apologetically. 'Fontleroy has escaped from custody.'

'How the hell could that happen?' Adam said, glaring at him.

'They were transferring him to London, where he was to be tried for his crimes. I do not know whether he was bound, but it seems that when an accident to the carriage occurred he overpowered the man supposed to be guarding him and escaped. A shot was fired, but missed. Although a search was made, he could not be found.'

'Damnation!' Adam stared at him in dismay. 'So now the rogue is at large again. It could not have happened at a worse time. Well, I suppose we know what to expect. He will be looking for his revenge on us.'

'Shall you cancel the picnic?' Hallam asked. 'I suppose it would be sensible, though the ladies will be disappointed and it is a beautiful day for it.'

'No! Why should we let that devil dictate our

lives? We are forewarned and I shall take my pistol with me. You must do the same, Hal. Have you alerted our men?'

'Yes, even before I came to you. Fontleroy is a wounded beast and dangerous. He knows he has nothing to lose, which means he may be reckless. I dare say he will try to kill as many of us as he can—even if it means his own death.'

'He has little left to live for,' Adam said grimly. 'What did Paul say?'

'I haven't told him yet. Shall you—or shall we leave him in ignorance for the moment?'

'I would prefer not to tell him, but I feel we must. He has a right to know—and must be able to protect himself, Hal, and the ladies.'

'Fontleroy can know nothing of our plans. He will surely lie low for a few days at least, before trying to assassinate one or all of us—do you not think so? I dare say we may enjoy our picnic.'

'Yes, perhaps,' Adam agreed. 'I refuse to cancel our plans. We are on our guard and there is as much danger in a Bath street at night as out in the open. Our men will follow at a discreet distance—and if we choose the site for our picnic carefully he cannot come close enough to do any real damage without being seen by one of our men, who must be warned to shoot on sight.'

'Yes, I have already given instructions that the marquis is to be shot if he comes within firing distance of any of us.'

'And the ladies. They must also be protected, just in case his vicious mind seeks to take his revenge that way.'

'He must know that we shall be on our guard,' Hallam said. 'In his shoes I might go for the more vulnerable target—which must, of course, be the ladies.'

'We must make certain to keep together on the picnic,' Adam said. 'No wandering off alone to make it easy for him…though, as you say, I imagine he will lie low for a while, until the search dies down a little.'

'Yes. It is what a sensible man would do,' Hallam agreed and glanced at his pocket watch. 'Are you ready? I think we need to be leaving if we are to be on time.'

'We shall not tell the ladies until after the picnic,' Adam said. 'They must be warned of the possible danger, of course—but I would rather not spoil the day by throwing a shadow over the proceedings.'

* * *

'You look lovely,' Adam said as he assisted Jenny into his chaise and sat beside her. He had planned to drive her himself, but because of Hallam's news, he had brought not only his groom, but a rather ferocious-looking man, who rode at the back of the chaise. Both were armed with pistols, as was Adam himself. 'I do not think I have seen you in buttercup yellow before?'

'No, I have not often worn it of late,' Jenny said and her heart fluttered as she looked at him. He was so very handsome and such a powerful man that he made her tremble inwardly. 'I wore dark colours for Papa for many months, but this is a new gown I have just had made for me.'

'It is a colour you should wear more often— though you are beautiful whatever you wear.'

Jenny blushed at the compliment, glancing at him shyly. She was aware that his manner was both warm and caring and her heart skipped a few beats as he smiled at her. When he looked at her in that way she was convinced that he did truly care for her.

'Thank you, I dare say I shall choose yellow more often in future,' she said. She met his eyes for a moment and then glanced away, her pulses racing. If they were alone she was certain he would kiss her and she felt a stirring of need deep inside her, wanting to be held in his arms, to melt into him and lose herself in his kiss.

'Have you ever been to Paris?' he asked. 'It is beautiful in the spring when the chestnuts are out, but there are many lovely places to visit in France. I know my sister bought her trousseau in Paris.'

'You have not spoken of your sister before.'

She looked at him in surprise, noting the firm lean cut of his jaw and his soft sensuous mouth. A tiny pulse was beating at his temple and she sensed that he was tenser than his tone implied.

'Have I not? Marion is married to Lord Henry Jarvis and lives in Hampshire for most of the year, though she likes to visit London for the Season, when she is not…in a delicate way. This year she was unable to visit and I hear she has a new son, which will please Jarvis. He now has his heir and a spare.'

'Your sister has two sons? How fortunate for her,' Jenny said, feeling warmed by the turn of his conversation. It made her think of a large country house filled with children, dogs and lots of noise and laughter. How she would love to live that way with Adam by her side. By telling her these details of his family he was preparing her to meet them and that must mean… She blushed for she must not let her thoughts show in her manner. 'Her husband must be so pleased.'

'Yes, indeed he is,' Adam said. 'Marion has always wanted a large family—there were just two of us, you see. Mama died when we were but nine and ten, and Papa never remarried. He said that no one could replace our mother. I believe he found consolation in friends, but he honoured my mother's memory until he died two years ago.'

'He must have loved her very much?'

'I am sure he did,' Adam said. His smile was warm, caressing, making her heart skip a beat. Jenny felt her cheeks a little warm, but she did not lower her gaze for she wanted to let him see what was in her heart. 'I have always felt that I would wish for such a marriage—a meeting of minds as well as of the flesh, companionship and affection combined. Do you not think it the best foundation for a marriage?'

His eyes were on her again, making her spine tingle with anticipation. Her throat tightened and she knew a longing to be in his arms, to be kissed until she could barely breathe.

'Yes, I do. My parents were happy enough, I

think. Mama was a beauty when she was young and Papa thought himself fortunate to have married her.' Jenny laughed at the memory. 'After she died he told me that he always wondered why she'd chosen him, because he was not the best looking of fellows.'

'Perhaps she loved him?'

'Yes, I think she must have,' Jenny replied a little shyly. Could he see the love in her eyes, could he know that she longed for his touch? Was she shameless in wanting him to take her in his arms and kiss her? No, surely there was no shame in feeling this way...if he felt the same. 'It is the best reason for marriage—love and respect also.'

'Much the best if one is lucky enough to find love, though affection and respect are good reasons to marry,' Adam said. 'Too many marriages are made for reasons of a practical nature. I suppose money and position are important for many. It is the way families maintain their fortunes and their status—but I have seen the unhappiness this type of match can cause if there is no affection on either side. Some of my friends married for money and are unhappily situated.'

'I should never wish to marry for money or position.'

'Nor I—unless I were forced,' Adam said. He reached for her gloved hand, playing with the fingers for a moment. 'You know my circumstances, Jenny?'

'Yes…' Her voice was hardly above a whisper. What was he trying to say to her? Her heart fluttered like a caged bird and she had to fight to stop her hand shaking.

'To save my grandfather's estate I must find a way to stave off the bank so that they do not foreclose. I am trying various things and I hope to keep the estate going while he lives, though it may have to be sold after he dies. To keep it for him while he lives I may have to raise a loan on my own estate—or sell it, which would mean I would have nowhere to take my wife other than Grandfather's estate. It is not a house I would choose to live in…or to inflict on my wife.'

'Perhaps a part of it might be made cheerful. Sometimes it is possible to make a few rooms pleasant on very little money—if one has the knack.'

Adam nodded and looked thoughtful. 'I had hoped to give my wife her own home and all the pretty things she required. As things stand, I should not have very much to offer her, Jenny.'

'Perhaps she would not mind that…or she might have a little money of her own…' Her heart beat rapidly. Was this the moment to confess that she had at least ten thousand and might have almost as much again? If only he would not think her deceitful and believe that she had deliberately set out to fool him!

'Yes…' Adam's hold on her hand tightened. 'This is not the proper place to ask—but perhaps later…' He smiled at her. 'I think we understand one another, do we not?'

'I—I think so…' Jenny glanced down at her hands. She wished that she'd found the courage to speak, but it was so very hard. Far from understanding, she did not know if he meant to ask her to be his wife or to explain why he could not—but she must not let him see her anxiety. She raised her head, looking at the two carriages ahead. Paul was driving Lady Dawlish and Mrs Beeton, who was a good friend of Lucy's mother—and Hallam was driving Lucy in the leading carriage.

'I rather thought Paul might drive Lucy,' she said, her cheeks pink as she changed the subject. 'I am sure she expected it.'

'We thought it best if Paul drove Lady Dawlish and her friend,' Adam said. He looked a little stern and Jenny wondered what was in his mind. 'Perhaps on the return journey.'

Jenny caught the inflection in his voice and turned to look at him. Something was wrong; she could see that from the little pulse at his temple. Her nerve ends tingled and she sensed that he was hiding something from her—from all of them.

'Has anything unpleasant happened?' she asked. 'You have something on your mind, do you not?'

'Yes, Jenny, I do,' he replied, smiling a little grimly. 'I would rather not tell you if you do not mind. Please do not press me. This was meant to be a happy occasion and I would hate to cast a shadow over things—or to alarm anyone.'

Jenny stared at him, then the icy shiver passed down her spine. 'It is to do with that man—Fontleroy. Have they let him off?'

'Not exactly...' Adam sighed. 'You will not tell the others? We have taken precautions, but Lady Dawlish might feel we should have cancelled the outing. Fontleroy was being transferred to a London prison and escaped when there was an accident to the carriage. He was searched for, but not found.'

'Do you think he had help? Was the accident arranged?'

'That is possible,' Adam said and smiled grimly. 'I'd hoped to keep it from you rather than spoil the day, Jenny, but you are too clever for me.'

'I could see you were under some stress.' She smiled and placed her gloved hand on his briefly. 'The marquis could not spoil this day for me, whatever he does. It is a pleasure for me to be with you on such a lovely morning. Never fear, I shall enjoy myself despite what you have told me—but it might be best not to mention it to the others. Lady Dawlish is a sensitive lady and might have hysterics.'

'You are so sensible,' Adam said. 'I believe that is a part of your charm for me. I feel as if you are a true friend—as Hal and Paul are. I can talk to you and I know you will not fly into the boughs. A life with you in it would be comfortable and a pleasure.'

Jenny's heart turned over. He seemed to be saying that he intended to make her an offer when they were alone. He had not spoken of love, but perhaps that was asking for too much. She knew that he cared for her—and desired her—and if they were to be friends it would be a wonderful way to live. To ask for romantic undying love was perhaps more than she ought to expect.

'You may rely on me to keep your secret, Adam,' she said. 'You asked earlier if I had been to Paris and I believe I did not answer you. Papa took me for a brief visit once, but I should very much like to visit again—and to purchase some clothes there, though I already have most of what I need.'

'Every lady needs at least three new gowns made in Paris,' Adam said, 'and perhaps several more...'

The picnic spot was found near, but not too close, to the ruins of an old abbey. There were some ancient trees in what had once been the park of the great monastery, but was now a beauty spot beloved of local people and visitors alike. Adam had sent servants ahead of them with a wagon loaded with everything needed to make the picnic a success.

Rather than expect his guests to sit on blankets on the ground, a table had been provided, which was spread with a white cloth and folding chairs were set up. There were indeed blankets on the ground for those who wished to stretch out in the sun or the shade of a tree, but the sumptuous picnic was laid out on the table, together with wine flutes, silver cutlery, pristine napkins and good china, also wooden wine buckets filled with ice and bound with silver.

'Now this is what I call a picnic,' Lady Dawlish said approvingly as she inspected the silver dishes and discovered all manner of treats. There were lobster tartlets, pasties of chicken or beef, pastries filled with creamy sauces and prawns or ham. A green salad, also cold new potatoes and peas with a white sauce, quantities of crusty white bread, fresh butter, fingers of cheese with crisp biscuits and fresh fruit. She picked up a tiny strawberry meringue and nibbled at it. 'I cannot resist. One gets so hungry in the open air...'

Adam had brought a servant to wait on them and he poured wine into glasses, while another served Lady Dawlish with food from the various dishes. Her friend joined her at the table, but Lucy and Jenny chose to sit on a blanket under the sheltering branches of a tree.

'A picnic must be eaten this way,' Lucy said and smiled as she accepted the plate of delicious food that Paul had selected for her. 'Do you not agree, Jenny?'

'Oh yes, this is just perfect—but the table was a lovely idea, Adam. I am sure Lady Dawlish and her friend are more comfortable there than they would be here.'

'I wanted them to enjoy the day,' he said, but his eyes were warm as he looked at her, as if it were she he had most wanted to please. 'Is the food to your taste, Jenny?'

'Lovely. I think I agree with Lucy's mama, everything tastes so much better in the open air—and these lobster tartlets are wonderful. I do not think I have tasted better.'

She hoped that her smile told him all…that it spoke of a future when they would have many similar days to entertain their friends and enjoy the good things of life.

Adam's eyes caressed her with a heat that set her tingling. She had never felt like this before, never wanted to touch someone as she wanted to touch him. She could almost wish that they were alone…

'I am glad you like them.' He left her to fetch a plate for himself, looking about him as he took a little of the various delights on offer. It was possible to see for some distance in all directions. He saw one of his men standing near the nearest tree, trying to look inconspicuous, and caught sight of another in the ruins. He instructed one of the servants to take a pasty and a glass of lemonade to both men, then returned to where the others were sitting.

Jenny was laughing at something Paul had said, as was Lucy. Hallam was sipping his wine, but like Adam his gaze moved constantly about the picnic site as if searching. Adam inclined his head and his cousin nodded. Everything was clear and it seemed that they need not have worried. Fontleroy was biding his time. After all, how could he have known what they had planned for today? Yet it was best to take precautions for Adam would never have forgiven himself had anything happened to one of his guests.

For the next hour or so everyone ate and drank, the servants moving from one to the other, filling wine glasses and replenishing plates. Jenny and Lucy tasted all the delights prepared for them and the ladies at the table did justice to a repast that Lady Dawlish afterwards declared fit for a king.

After she had declined to accept another morsel, an easy chair was set for her and another for her friend beneath the shade of the tree where the young ones lounged. While the servants cleared the table and loaded baskets of dirty dishes into the wagon, Adam and his guests chatted and laughed. Then Lucy stood up and looked at Jenny.

'I should like to walk to the ruins,' she said. 'Will you come with me?'

'Yes, of course. They are intriguing,' Jenny replied. 'I have been thinking I should like to explore them.'

'I shall escort you,' Adam said and stood up.

'No, no, we want to be private for a little while,' Lucy said. 'When we are ready for company we shall wave to you and you may join us…' Lucy looked at Paul and smiled invitingly.

Adam hesitated, but realised that perhaps Lucy wanted to find a private spot somewhere behind the abbey walls where she might relieve herself. It was the one awkwardness when one was on a picnic for there was nowhere the ladies could be comfortable at such moments.

'We shall wait for your signal,' he said and glanced at Hallam, who frowned and rose to his feet. He shook his head as his cousin's eyebrows arched. This was something they had not foreseen, but it could not be helped. Lucy must be given privacy and yet the ladies must be protected.

'I think I shall take a walk towards the copse,' Hallam said and set off. The stand of trees was at a right angle to the ruins and would not intrude on the ladies' privacy, but if anyone were waiting there for such an opportunity it would give Hallam a chance of preventing him from taking a shot at them.

'As you wish,' Adam replied. He watched the ladies walk towards the ruined abbey, his gaze moving from one tree to another lest Fontleroy should have somehow hidden himself behind one of them, but nothing happened.

Hallam walked to the copse and disappeared from sight for a few moments, then reappeared at the edge. He lifted his hand in salute and Adam knew he was signalling the all clear. Breathing a sigh of relief, he relaxed. He was too anxious. The ladies were perfectly safe. Fontleroy could not get close enough to them without being seen—and his men would stop him before he could draw a pistol and fire.

After a short interval, Lucy appeared at one of the openings of the ruins and waved. Paul stood up and he and Adam walked towards the abbey. At almost the same moment, Hallam began to walk towards them.

'Oh, do come and look,' Lucy called. 'We have

discovered a secret passage behind some creepers. I think it must lead to a tunnel or—'

Before she could finish there was a cry of alarm from behind her. She swung round, then threw out her arm and screamed.

'Jenny...he is trying to take Jenny...'

Adam began to run. His heart was pounding and his mouth was dry. How could Fontleroy have got into the ruins without anyone seeing him? Unless he had been hiding there all the time—in Lucy's secret chamber...

Lucy was frozen to the spot and screaming as Paul reached her, grabbing her and pulling her into his arms for a moment, before pushing her out of the ruins.

'Back to your mama at once. Leave this to us, Lucy.'

'But Jenny...it's the marquis...'

'Do as I tell you this instant!'

Lucy stared at him in dismay, tears welling in her eyes, and then she turned and ran.

Adam clambered over piles of fallen stone and a cross that had broken as it fell from one of the ruined walls. Now he could see the heavy creepers that must be hiding what Lucy thought was a secret passage and just a few inches away Fontleroy was struggling with Jenny and trying to compel her to go with him. She had clearly resisted with all her strength and the marquis had deep welts across his cheek where her nails had scored him.

'Vixen, I'll make you pay for this,' Fontleroy cried furiously and drew back his hand to slap her. 'I'll teach you to spit in my face.'

'Unhand me, sir,' Jenny said. 'I shall not—'

'Take your hands off her,' Adam cried, drawing his pistol. 'Stand away from her and face me like a man.'

'You are a cheat and a liar,' Fontleroy spat. 'I know how to treat men like you.'

'And I you,' Adam said. 'Let her go or I'll shoot you where you stand.'

'I'll kill her first,' the marquis said and grabbed Jenny by the throat, his powerful hands pressing hard. In that moment, Jenny brought her knee up sharply into his groin and he gave a howl of pain, letting go of her for one instant. She jerked away from him, stumbling out of his reach just as the shot rang out and falling to the ground in what looked to be a faint.

The ball hit Fontleroy square between his eyes and a look of astonishment came over his face as he pitched to his knees, stared at them for a few moments and then felt forwards to the ground. The next moment Adam was on his knees beside Jenny, lifting her into his arms. Tears trickled down his cheeks as he saw her pale face.

'Jenny, my love, my love,' Adam cried in an agonised tone. 'Please do not be dead… That devil… if he has killed you I shall not bear it…'

Her eyelids flickered, but she did not open her eyes. Paul bent over the man Adam had killed, turning him over with a grunt of satisfaction.

'He'll do no more damage,' he said. 'You finished him, Adam.'

'I fear he has done too much already. He has choked the life from her…' A moan from Jenny's lips gave the lie to his words. 'She lives yet. I must get her home and to a doctor.'

'I'll see to things here,' Hallam said. 'Leave the magistrates to me. Paul, take the ladies home and send one of the servants to fetch a doctor to Lady Dawlish's house. I'll send one of the men for the magistrates and see to this business. Don't give it another thought, Adam. I shall come and see you later.'

Adam nodded and turned away. He strode off in the direction of the carriages. Lucy had alerted her mother and cries of consternation greeted the sight of Adam carrying Jenny's limp body towards them.

Hallam looked down at the dead man and frowned. How had he discovered where they would be today? Had one of their servants betrayed them—or had he simply followed discreetly? Clearly Fontleroy had known something about the abbey they did not. He decided to investigate behind the curtain of creepers. If there was a secret tunnel perhaps the authorities should know about it.

Chapter Fourteen

Jenny stirred soon after Adam had placed her tenderly on the seat of his chaise, with her head lying on his lap. He'd taken off her bonnet and his hand stroked her brow. She coughed and cried out as her throat stung and he looked down at her anxiously.

'Are you in pain, dearest?'

'My throat…' Jenny rasped. 'It hurts…I should like some water…' She pushed herself up into a sitting position, glancing at him in an embarrassed manner. 'I am so sorry.'

'You have nothing to be sorry for,' Adam said in such a stern tone that it chilled her. Why was he so angry? 'I am at fault. I should have called off the picnic.'

Jenny shook her head. She wanted to tell him that no one blamed him and that the picnic had been a success, but her throat hurt—and she suspected that Lady Dawlish might indeed blame Adam for taking them on the picnic when the marquis was at large.

'Not your fault…' she managed. Adam had taken a little flask from his pocket and offered it to her. She drank some of the water, which was warm and tasted a little bitter.

'My servants have gone for the doctor,' Adam told her, his expression grim. 'He will give you something to ease your throat…and I can only beg you to forgive me for putting you at risk. I believed we had covered all possibilities, but I did not realise there was a secret way into the ruins.'

'Lucy found it…' Jenny managed and took another sip of the water. It was not pleasant, but better than coughing as she must without its soothing effect. Remembering some lozenges in her reticule, she looked for it and saw it on the floor at her feet. She picked it up, ignoring the slight dizziness it caused her to bend her head, untied the strings and took out the little box of sweets. Putting one of the lemon-flavoured lozenges into her mouth she sucked and felt it ease her throat. 'That is better…'

'You will be better soon,' Adam promised. 'I

shall never let anyone harm you again, Jenny. I am so very sorry.'

'Please, Adam. I do not blame you.' Jenny reached for his hand and held it. 'Do not distress yourself. No one could have known what he would do.'

'I did think he might attack one of us and ladies are always more vulnerable...'

'I do not think he found me particularly vulnerable.' Jenny smiled to reassure him. Her throat still hurt and she could feel a graze on her cheek where she'd fallen hard and her side was a little bruised, but she knew that she had escaped lightly. Had she not fought back and kneed the marquis where it hurt him, he could have killed her quite easily. 'But I am glad you were there. Is he dead this time?'

'Yes, I made certain of it. My pistol did not misfire, nor did I miss my mark. He will not trouble any of us again.'

'I am glad of it,' Jenny said and smiled at him. 'I do not wish harm to any, but I think he was an evil man—had he lived he would have killed again and again.'

'I wish he had tried to kill me rather than you.'

'He told me that he wanted me as his wife. It

was not his intention to murder me had I gone with him. He has always wanted me. I do not know why.' Unless it was because he knew she had a small fortune?

'You are very lovely, Jenny. I dare say quite a few men want you—including Sir James.'

'Sir James very kindly asked me to marry him. I declined because I did not love him.'

Adam looked at her for a moment in silence. 'Do you love me, Jenny—enough to marry me?'

'I think you know the answer,' she said shyly and smiled up at him. 'I should like to marry you very much Adam.'

'I cannot get down on my knees to ask you here,' he said, an odd smile in his eyes. He reached for her hand and kissed it. 'I shall be very honoured to make you my wife, Jenny Hastings.'

'Thank you. You are very kind, sir. I shall be very happy to be your wife.'

'You know that I cannot give you all the things you are entitled to expect...'

Jenny hesitated, knowing this was the time to speak. 'I do have some money of my own, Adam,' she murmured softly. 'I am not certain whether it is—'

Her confession was brought to an abrupt halt as

the chaise stopped outside Lady Dawlish's house and the door was opened, several anxious faces peering in at them from the pavement.

'Jenny, my sweet child,' Lady Dawlish cried. 'How are you? I feared you were dead when Adam carried you off. I have never felt so ill in my life. I swear my heart almost failed when Lucy told me what was happening. That wicked man—and you, sir. How dare you look me in the face? You knew that Fontleroy had escaped and yet still you took us on that picnic.'

'Please, ma'am,' Jenny croaked. Her throat felt sore now that the lozenge had gone and her head ached a little. 'You must not blame Adam. I shall be perfectly well in a an hour or so—if I could just lie down on my bed and be quiet.'

'You must have the doctor,' Adam insisted. He looked at Lady Dawlish awkwardly. 'I admit my fault, ma'am. I shall not easily forgive myself for what happened—but I hope to make it up to Jenny. She has generously forgiven me and accepted my offer of marriage.'

'Offer…' Lady Dawlish stared incredulously as Adam handed Jenny from the carriage. She seemed torn by indecision, shaking her head once. 'I am not sure…are you certain you can provide her with the kind of life she ought to have? I stand almost as a guardian to her, Adam. You should properly have consulted me before making Jenny an offer.'

'Jenny knows my circumstances and is prepared to accept me as I am,' Adam said and smiled at his intended.

'That is wonderful,' Lucy said and came forwards to take Jenny's arm. 'I am so happy for you, dearest.'

'Well, that is all very good,' Lady Dawlish floundered uncertainly, becoming aware that she was on the pavement and the subject of amused looks from passers-by. 'We cannot discuss this here, sir—but I shall ask you to step inside and be kind enough to explain yourself.'

She turned and stalked into the house, looking a picture of outrage. Paul raised his eyebrows at Lucy and she giggled, then shook her head, following her mama with Jenny leaning slightly on her arm.

Once inside, Lady Dawlish assumed command, giving Adam a regal look. 'Come into the parlour, sir. I wish for words with you. Lucy, you may take Jenny up to her room, for I am sure that she will wish to lie down and rest. Paul, please go into the garden or the back parlour. I wish to be private with Adam for a time.'

'Of course, ma'am,' Adam said and frowned.

'No,' Jenny said. 'I shall not be sent to my room, though it is what I dearly wish for. Much as I love you, dear Lady Dawlish, I shall not allow you to question Adam without me. He has made me a proposal of marriage, which I have accepted— and nothing you can say will change that.'

Lady Dawlish looked uncertain. She, Jenny and Adam were now in the parlour, Lucy and Paul having taken themselves off elsewhere.

'You know your uncle would not approve of an imprudent marriage, Jenny.'

'I care nothing for my uncle's approval. He would have seen me married to Fontleroy and thought it a good match.' Jenny sighed and pushed the hair back from her eyes. 'If you are concerned that Adam has little money and must find the wherewithal to meet his grandfather's debts, I know all of the story, ma'am. It does not matter. I would happily live in a cottage with Adam—'

'I think it need not be quite that bad, my love,' Adam said, but there was a gleam of appreciation in his eyes. What a revelation and a delight she was. He folded his arms and watched as she prepared to do battle.

'I am certain it need not,' Jenny said and sent him an uncertain look. 'Please do not be angry with me, Adam. I know that I should have told you before—and I did not mean to deceive you, but I did tell you I had some money…'

The smile left his eyes and his brow furrowed. 'I thought you meant a thousand or so.'

'It is considerably more,' Jenny said. Her throat ached and the last thing she wanted to do was to explain with Lady Dawlish watching, but she could not stop now. 'My father lost some of his money and everyone assumed there was nothing left—but that was not the case. My lawyer told me before I left London that I was something of an heiress…and now I have his accounts…' She faltered uncomfortably.

'Go on…' Adam's mouth had set hard.

'My uncle sold the house and land, which amounts to…' Jenny swallowed hard. 'I think the letter said a little over ten thousand pounds.'

'Ten thousand pounds!' Both Lady Dawlish and Adam stared at her, with varying degrees of astonishment.

'I did tell you, ma'am, though not how much…'

Jenny faltered, her heart sinking as she saw Adam's grim look. 'And then there is whatever comes from my father's investments in industry… which my lawyer is selling for me presently.'

'And how much is that likely to be?' Adam asked coldly.

'I do not know. I did not ask.' Jenny's hands trembled. She was more afraid of Adam's disgust than the marquis even when he'd had his hands about her throat. 'Forgive me, Adam. I knew… I heard you say that you disliked having to look for an heiress and—'

'So you decided to play me for a fool,' he said bitterly. 'You allowed me to think you almost penniless. Did it amuse you when I told you of my difficulties?'

'No, of course not. How could you think…?' Tears started to Jenny's eyes. 'You must know I did not. I did not intend to deceive you, Adam. Please believe me…'

'This alters things.'

'Certainly it does,' Lady Dawlish said, beaming at them. 'You can afford Adam now, Jenny. He will be able to clear most of his debts and I have no doubt that he will soon bring the estate about and keep you in the style that you are entitled to expect. Had I known you were a considerable heiress I should have had no objections to the match.'

'I, on the other hand, have several,' Adam said and caused Jenny to look at him in distress. 'You have been through an unfortunate ordeal and I shall not keep you further. Please go and rest, Jenny. I shall speak to you another day.'

'Adam, please don't go like this.' Jenny caught at his hands. 'You know I love you.'

'Do I?' He looked at her coldly. 'Excuse me, I must have time to think. We shall discuss the future in private at another time.'

Brushing off her hold, he strode from the room and the sound of the door closing hard behind him made Jenny jump.

'Well, I am surprised at him,' Lady Dawlish said. 'Whatever can be the matter?'

'Adam's pride has been hurt,' Jenny said softly and blinked back her tears. 'Please excuse me, ma'am. I must lie down.'

'I shall have a maid bring you some honey and lemon,' Lady Dawlish said kindly. 'Do not worry, Jenny. Adam is a sensible man. He will realise how fortunate he is and then he will beg your pardon.'

Jenny shook her head. The tears were very close. She did not wish Adam to beg her pardon, nor to think himself lucky because she had a fortune at his disposal. She wanted him to smile at her as he had in the carriage on the way home and tell her he loved her.

Walking from the room, she hurried upstairs and threw herself down on the bed as the tears shook her body. For some minutes she was held by a storm of weeping, but then they subsided and she began to think more sensibly.

Adam had asked her to marry him. He was too much of a gentleman to go back on his word— but would he ever forgive her for deceiving him?

Adam walked swiftly through the streets, having dismissed his chaise. He was in no mood to be driven home. Too restless to speak to either Hal or Paul, he needed to walk. He needed time to think, because his mind was in a whirl.

Why had Jenny lied to him? Not just for a few days, but for weeks—months. How could she listen to his explanations of why he must marry an heiress and not tell him the truth? Why had she not told him? She must have made the decision to keep her secret—but what was her motive?

She knew of his reluctance to marry an heiress. He'd unburdened his soul to her—even in the carriage on the way to the picnic she had not spoken. No, she had mentioned that she had some money, but he'd assumed she meant pin money, enough to perhaps buy her own clothes—but ten thousand pounds...

With just a part of that Adam could buy time from the bank. If they were no longer breathing down his grandfather's neck, it would give Adam time to find a way of making enough money to restore the estate. The income from his own estate would enable him to set up his breeding stables. Hal had suggested importing wine—and there were other investments he might make with the rest of Jenny's money. Investments that would bring them in an excellent income...

He stopped walking, almost causing a man following to walk into him, and apologised. No, he couldn't use Jenny's money—it would be as if she'd bought him...something he knew he would hate. His pride would not let him accept her money...yet it would solve all his problems.

Adam felt as if he were on the rack, pulled this way and that. How could he expect her to share the privations of life on a tight budget when she

was a considerable heiress? He would be a fool
to ignore his wife's money when it could provide
the key to the lifestyle they both preferred.

His pride wanted to reject it out of hand, but
that might hurt her for he knew instinctively that
she would want him to do what he needed to do
for the sake of the estate.

It was a damned coil! He knew that common
sense decreed that he should use the money, even
if he paid every penny back as soon as he could.
The thought of using Jenny's money at all left a
nasty taste in his mouth, though he knew it would
be sensible. He would tell her that it would be
paid back, even though it would in law become
his when they married. Had he not been in such
dire need, he would have secured her fortune to
her and her children in the marriage contract—
but he could not in all honesty afford to do it.

Suddenly, Adam laughed and his frown cleared.
He realised that despite his anger at being deceived and his dislike of being forced to accept
that her money could solve his problems, he had
not once thought of drawing back.

Now why was that? As a gentleman he could
have offered her the chance to reject him, but
Jenny would not have taken it—and so he could

not in all honour withdraw his offer. The amaz-ing thing was that he did not wish to. Indeed, he had suddenly discovered that it was the last thing he would want—the very worst outcome.

Because he was in love with her. When had that happened? Adam smiled as he reviewed his rela-tionship with Jenny and realised that it must have begun almost from the first time they met...when she'd sat beside him as they drove to Ravenscar. He'd been aware of lust, which he'd acknowledged even then to be unusual when in the presence of an innocent young lady. He'd begun to respect and like her when she acted so calmly in the face of unspeakable tragedy, and his feelings had inten-sified over the weeks. Knowing that she'd come to him at some considerable risk to her reputation had made him realise how much he liked and re-spected her. Yet he had not known how much she meant to him until he saw her struggling with Fontleroy.

His rage had mixed with fear, making him un-able to think clearly as he ordered the marquis to let her go. Jenny's own quick thinking and brav-ery had provided him with the opportunity and he'd shot the moment she was out of range. After that he'd been overcome with anxiety for her—

and then relief in the carriage that she was not badly hurt, followed by euphoria when she accepted his proposal.

Adam had not had a moment to understand his feelings before he was being attacked by Lady Dawlish for a reckless proposal—which he admitted it was, for had Jenny had no money of her own it would have been a struggle to maintain a wife and save the estate.

Adam found to his horror that his cheeks were wet. He was crying in the street! He had not cried since his parents died—even for the comrades that had died fighting the French. That was too bitter a wound to weep for and Mark's death had been too hard to bear.

Suddenly, tears, which were also partially tears of happiness, had released his grief for his cousin. What a fool he'd been to agonise over Jenny's fortune. He was a man, not a mouse. He would use the money to save his grandfather and to build up the estate—and then he would repay Jenny every penny, which she could spend as she pleased or keep for their children. He would find ways to make them both rich and when he did he would shower his beautiful wife with jewels and fancy clothes—though in his heart, he knew that all

Jenny wanted or needed was to be loved. Yet he would give them to her all the same.

Adam laughed out loud, then turned his steps and began to make his way back to Lady Dawlish's house. He must explain to Jenny—tell her how he felt.

He had been walking only for a few moments when he stopped once more and shook his head. Much as he wanted to tell her of his love and his decision, he knew she had been through enough that day. He must allow her to rest and recover. He would send her a note and call to see her in the morning.

'Jenny—are you awake?' Lucy asked, coming tentatively towards the bed. 'Mama said not to disturb you—but there is a letter for you and I wanted to talk to you. Are you feeling better now?'

'Much,' Jenny said and sat up. 'I did not truly need the doctor because the drink your mama sent up made my throat much easier.'

'That terrible man!' Lucy cried and sat on the edge of the bed, reaching for her hand. 'I am so glad Adam shot him. Paul said he would have done so, but you were in his line of fire.'

'It is all over now,' Jenny said. 'Did you say there was a letter for me?'

'Yes. It is from Adam. I think he wants to apologise for going off like that…' Lucy gave her the note and Jenny ripped it open. She read the few lines and nodded at her cousin, unable to keep from smiling. 'Oh, I am glad, because I know you love him.'

'Yes, I do. He was just shocked and upset because he felt I had not told him the truth. He wishes to know why I felt the need to keep it a secret, but he has forgiven me and says he loves me very much.'

'That is all right then,' Lucy said and smiled. 'Paul did not tell me he loved me—but he asked me to forgive him for being such a bear of late. He apologised for shouting at me at the ruins—and of course I have forgiven him.'

'Did you tell him how you feel?'

Lucy shook her head. 'No, I could not. We are friends again, as you suggested, Jenny. I think that is all we should be for a while. I do not think that either of us would feel right if we…we could not marry or be engaged for months, Jenny. I do not mind now that I know he doesn't hate me.' She laughed. 'He thought I blamed him, but of course

I never did—it was just all so horrid that I did not know what to think.'

'I am glad you have settled it between you,' Jenny said and reached for her hand. 'I am sure that in time you will reach an understanding.'

'Yes, perhaps.' Lucy sighed. 'It is such an odd feeling, Jenny. Mark is still there between us. We are both aware of him—and neither of us knows how to act. I think it will take some time before we could think of falling in love with each other—even though it is very hard not to wish for it.'

'I think you are being very sensible, Lucy. Your mama wishes to take you abroad for the winter. You should go with her, dearest. The time spent travelling will help to clear your mind. When you see Paul again you will know how you truly feel.'

'Yes, I know you are right,' Lucy said. 'I was desperate for him to tell me he loved me—but now we are friends and it no longer seems to matter. I am content to wait and see what happens. It would be terrible if I made a mistake again.'

'I am sure you will not,' Jenny said. 'Are you going out with your mama this evening? I do not think I wish to come. I should rather stay here and rest, if you do not mind?'

'Mama has sent her apologies to Mrs Morton, with whom we were engaged. We shall dine quietly here—and if you do not feel like coming down I shall have a tray up here with you.'

'You must dine with your mama,' Jenny said, settling against the softness of fresh linen pillows delicately edged with lace. 'I want only some soup and bread and butter—and another drink of honey and lemon. If you would like to sit and talk after you dine, bring a book of poems and you can read to me for a while. I should be glad of your company, but I shall not get up this evening.'

'Yes, of course I will come.' Lucy bent to kiss her cheek. 'I am so glad you were here with me for this difficult time—and I am pleased that everything is as you would wish it with Adam.'

'I have still to explain to him,' Jenny said with a tremulous smile. 'But I hope he will understand…'

Jenny was sitting alone in the parlour when Adam arrived the next morning. She was wearing a morning gown of jonquil silk that floated and rustled as she moved and had dressed her hair in soft waves back from her face and swirled loosely in a knot at her nape. Around her throat, she wore a row of tiny seed pearls that had been her mother's and matching pins were scattered through her hair. As Adam was shown into the room, she rose to her feet shyly and greeted him with outstretched hands.

'Adam, I am glad to see you. Thank you for forgiving me—you must know that I never meant to hurt or lie to you. It was a misunderstanding at the start that I did not know how to correct. I knew that you despised heiresses and I did not want you to despise me.'

'Despised heiresses…?' Adam frowned, then remembered. 'Did you overhear something that night in London?' He smote his forehead with the palm of his hand as she nodded. 'What a coxcomb you must have thought me! I was jesting with friends—but it was a protest because I felt that I was being pushed towards making a match that I could not stomach and not meant personally against any particular young lady. It was my situation I disliked, not the unfortunate heiresses.'

'I have since realised that,' Jenny said and laughed. 'When I saw you at Ravenscar—your caring and your strength—I knew I had been wrong to think you arrogant. You were so kind to me even though in terrible distress over your cousin. I believe I fell in love with you instantly. After that it became impossible to explain.'

'Yes, of course I see.' He took her hands and held them, looking down at her, a flicker of amusement in his eyes. 'I have been in such a fret, Jenny. I knew that I ought to marry money for Grandfather's sake, but I could not bring myself to do it—and I also knew that you were the woman I wanted above all others, though…' his hands held hers tightly '…I did not realise how much I loved and needed you until I thought Fontleroy might kill you.'

'Oh, Adam…' She moved towards him, lifting her face for his kiss and then she was in his arms. 'I do love you so very much. I was afraid that if you knew I had a little money you would not—' Her words were lost beneath a passionate kiss that left her breathless. His tongue demanded and she opened to him, allowing his teasing entry, such a deep, intimate kiss that when at last they drew apart she was well aware of the effect it had had on his body and her own. His need was so apparent that she had felt his heat and the hardness of his arousal as he held her pressed against him. 'I see I was foolish to worry…' She laughed up at him, confident now that he wanted and loved her as much as she loved and desired him.

Adam's fingers moved down her cheek, stroking her white throat above the pretty neckline of her gown and then he bent to kiss the tiny hollow at the base of her throat. Jenny gasped, her head going back as she felt herself surrender to the growing need inside her. He trailed his fingers across her throat and kissed the V above her swelling breasts, of which a glimpse was possible beneath the dip of her gown.

'I adore you,' Adam muttered huskily. 'Never doubt it, my darling. I cannot wait to have you as my wife and, if you will consent, shall post up to town and arrange a special licence. We can be married anywhere we choose then—here or from your uncle's home in London.'

'My uncle and aunt are my only true relatives,' Jenny said. 'Although I would never wish to live with them again, I think I owe them the courtesy of being married from their home. I hope that Lucy and Lady Dawlish will come up for the wedding—but perhaps we could arrange a little dinner here before we leave and invite the friends I have made in Bath?'

'It will take me five days to purchase the licence, arrange the wedding and speak to your uncle,' Adam said. 'I should return by the evening of the last day and we could hold a small dinner and informal dance six days from now—if that would suit you? I know Hallam will see to things here while I arrange the wedding in town for... say, three weeks? Does that give you enough time to gather a trousseau, my love?'

'I have several new gowns and perhaps we may purchase more in Paris. I shall need a gown for my wedding day, but—'

Adam placed a finger to her lips. 'That will be my gift to you. Give me your measurements and the name of the seamstress you would favour and I shall see to it.'

'Thank you.' Jenny smiled shyly. 'Please do not be offended, Adam—but I should consider it a favour if you would call on Mr Nodgrass while you are in town. He had the intention of selling all Papa's investments—and, if it would not trouble you too much, I should like you to discover what he has done and to decide if it would be better to keep some of them. It has occurred to me that you might manage them and do better than the five per cents, which is where he intended to invest the money.'

'You would like me to be your agent?' Adam frowned and her heart caught. Would he be angry again? 'I think that is a wise decision, Jenny. Much as it pains me to speak of money at such a moment, I think I should tell you that I shall with your permission use a little of your capital to secure the earl's estate. It will be repaid when I am able and I intend that the marriage contract will secure the rest of your fortune for your use and that of our children...' He smiled and touched a finger to her lips. 'Yes, I know you would willingly give me every penny, but, though I am prepared to borrow a portion of it, and to manage your assets for you, I shall not take all your money. I have various ideas and I believe the bank will be happy to frank me once it is known I have married an heiress. It is an odd thing, but when one has money banks are only too happy to lend one more.'

'Oh, Adam...' Jenny giggled. 'It sounds so strange to hear you say that when I had accustomed myself to thinking I had very little.'

'Your fortune is substantial and we shall use it for the benefit of our family, dearest. The earl's estate is a fine property and it would be a pity to lose it when with the proper management we could save it for our sons.'

'Yes, it would,' Jenny said and looked up at him lovingly. 'I am looking forward to seeing the earl's estate—but may we forget business now? I should really like to be kissed again.'

'And I am very happy to oblige you, my love,' Adam said and drew her close. 'So very, very happy to oblige…'

Chapter Fifteen

'Are you looking forward to this evening?' Lucy asked, coming into Jenny's bedchamber wearing a gown of the palest-lilac silk edged with silver lace. She wore a diamond pendant set in silver and suspended on a silver chain and her hair was dressed high on her head and curled in little ringlets. Her eyes were bright with excitement as she looked at Jenny. 'Mama has said that I may dance three times this evening, providing that I behave with decorum and choose only family members— which means I may dance with Hallam and Paul and Adam—if you will spare him to me for one dance?'

'Yes, of course I shall.' Jenny laughed at her pleasure in the evening. 'I do not think anyone could fault you for dancing with family, dearest. Besides, Adam and Paul have both decided that they will wear only token mourning for the celebrations. It is our wedding dance after all, and though we have invited only our closest friends and relatives, it is meant to be a joyous occasion.'

'Yes, I know.' Lucy handed her a small box. 'This is a little gift from Mama and me—just something for this evening, dearest Jenny, because we are both so very fond of you.'

'Thank you so much…' Jenny opened the velvet box and saw a pretty diamond-and-pearl pin in the shape of a bird. It was small and exactly the kind of thing she liked, not at all ostentatious. 'It will pin to the shoulder of my gown. I love it, Lucy. I shall always treasure it.'

'Mama will give you silver for your wedding gift and I have a surprise for you, but we wanted you to have this. I know you have family jewels in Mr Nodgrass's safe, but this is yours and never worn before.'

Jenny pinned the little pin to the shoulder of her gown. Her dress was yellow silk and trimmed with soft tulle at the bodice and the flounce to her skirt. Her hair was waved back from her face and piled high into little curls and ringlets, with one swathe of shining hair left to fall over her right shoulder. As yet she had no engagement ring, but knew that Adam was bringing it with him that evening.

Her heart was racing with excitement. Adam had travelled hard to reach town and return in time for their dance, wasting no time on the journey, yet the five days they had spent apart had seemed for ever. It was almost six days now and she'd wondered if he would call during the day, but he'd merely sent her a posy of flowers with his love.

Jenny felt as if she were walking on air as she went down the stairs with Lucy. Soon she would be with Adam again, and then she would return to her uncle's home for a few days before their wedding.

Jenny's heart caught as she saw Adam was waiting for her. He had been as impatient as she and arrived some fifteen minutes before they were due to leave. He came towards her, his eyes seeming to devour her as they moved over her hungrily, absorbing every line of her face and figure.

'So lovely…' he breathed. 'I have been on fire to see you, dearest. You had my note? Your aunt is delighted with the match and your uncle claims the privilege of giving you away. I think he feared you would not invite him and is pleased that you have forgiven him for his stupidity. He understands the error of his ways now.'

'What do you mean?'

'Much as I hate to mention business at such a moment I must.' Adam frowned. 'Suffice it to say that your papa was an astute businessman. I was in time to stop the sale of your assets, which are worth several times the sum your uncle achieved for your father's estate. The income they generate each year is alone enough to solve any problems I might have had developing the mine had the bank been unwilling to advance me what I need, which they are not. Not surprisingly in the circumstances, they could not do enough for me. We shall hardly need to touch your capital and we shall certainly not sell your assets. You see, Grandfather uses the same bank as your father and they knew more of his assets than I had dreamed… I am given to understand that he may be almost, if not quite, a millionaire, on paper at least.'

Jenny stared at him, hardly comprehending what he was telling her. 'Are we so rich?'

'Yes, my love, and like to become more so,' Adam told her and laughed. 'I have been told that a rich seam of tin has been found in the old mine and, if we go deeper in the newer mine, there is copper also. It seems that fortune has decided to favour us, Jenny.'

She shook her head in wonder. 'Oh dear, I had no idea that Papa was so wealthy. I am glad that you will have the bother of it all and not me.'

Adam laughed. 'That is what a husband is for, my love. I shall make more money for us in time and you may spend it as you wish.'

'Oh, I can do that well enough,' she said, giving him a teasing look. 'Papa was, it seems, something of an entrepreneur—shall you be the same, Adam?'

'You know, I think I might. Mr Hastings's example has inspired me and all I needed was the capital to set up the ventures I had in mind— but enough of this, Jenny. Tonight was meant for pleasure—and I must give you this…' He took a box from inside his coat and opened it. 'Your left hand, please, my love.'

Jenny held out her hand and he slipped a lovely solitaire-diamond ring on to the third finger. The shoulders were silver to set off the stones supporting the large perfect diamond in the centre and suited her finger to perfection.

'I was not sure of your favourite stones,' Adam said. 'But there are several rings amongst the earl's family heirlooms and other trinkets, besides those that belonged to my mother—and your own mother's jewellery, of course. I have a surprise for your wedding gift, but I thought it best to let you decide which of the various family jewels you would like remodelled for your use.'

'This is lovely,' Jenny said, holding her hand up to admire her ring. 'Thank you so much, dearest Adam. I shall treasure it. I think I like pearls as much as any jewel, but in time I may wish to wear others from Mama's box—or your family's heirlooms. There is plenty of time to decide.'

'You look charming as you are,' Adam said. 'I have noticed that you do not care for ostentation, which is why I chose as I did—but, as I said, the other jewels will be at your disposal. I wrote to Grandfather and told him the good news and I know he will make an effort to be at our wedding. He will be delighted to meet you, Jenny.'

Jenny smiled and was about to reply when a tap at the door heralded the arrival of Lady Dawlish. She beamed at them and reminded them it was time to leave.

'We must leave now or our guests will begin to arrive before we are there...'

'Yes, of course,' Jenny said and held out her hand. 'Adam has given me my ring.'

'Beautiful, as you deserve,' Lady Dawlish said. 'Well, it is all as I hoped from the start. I am happy to have been of service to you, my love, and congratulate myself on having helped to bring about such a wonderful match for you—and you, too, Adam.'

Adam glanced at Jenny. Seeing the roguish look in his eyes, she was hard put to it not to laugh. If her kind friend had any idea of the fortune Adam had just told her was at her disposal, she would go into hysterics. However, she was well meaning and sincere in her wishes—and, indeed, had Jenny not been travelling to stay with her that fateful day none of this would have come about.

'I know how much I owe you, my dear Lady Dawlish,' Jenny said. 'I am so happy I think I must look foolish...'

'Oh, no, she looks beautiful, does she not, Adam?' her hostess said coyly.

'Jenny knows exactly what I think of her,' Adam said and reached for her hand. 'Come, my love.

Lady Dawlish is right. We must not keep our guests waiting.'

'And I cannot wait to dance with you,' Jenny said. 'Though you must ask Lucy to dance with you once, Adam. She will only dance with family this evening—so you must ask her, please.'

'I shall be delighted to dance with Lucy,' Adam said and looked down at her. 'As long as I can spend the rest of the evening with you.'

'So you are to marry the heir to Earl Benedict,' Aunt Martha said and then kissed Jenny's cheek. 'I am glad you have come home to be married—I thought you might not after what your uncle did.'

'You and my uncle meant to be kind,' Jenny said. 'Had I not gone to stay with Lady Dawlish I might never have met Adam—and so all is well that ends well.'

'Yes, I dare say,' her aunt replied and looked a little sheepish. 'I could have died when I heard what terrible things that man…Fontleroy…had done. I had no idea of… Believe me, I should never have condoned his courtship of you had I known.'

'From what Adam has discovered he was living on borrowed time and deeply in debt. Adam thinks he must have known about Papa's secret investments and that is why he was so determined to marry me.'

'Yes, I dare say.' Her aunt looked outraged. 'How dare he deceive us all! The man was a positive rogue. Please forgive me...'

'How could you have known?' Jenny smiled at her. 'It is all forgotten, Aunt. All I want now is for you to help me prepare for my wedding—and for us all to be friends.'

'Well, that is generous of you, Jenny, and I shall accept your offer. Your uncle is determined to make amends and he wants to give you something you would really like as your wedding gift, but he does not know what it ought to be.'

'Anything my uncle wishes to give me will be perfectly acceptable.' Jenny was thoughtful for a moment, then, 'However, I think I should like a small carriage dog—and perhaps a phaeton and pair of my own. He must consult Adam about the horses because he is a good judge of quality. Adam has promised to teach me to drive when we go down to his grandfather's estate. We are to spend a few nights there before travelling to Paris and then through France. However, we shall not take the grand tour for Adam is eager to oversee events at his mine.'

'Will you be living at the earl's estate?'

'Adam says the choice is mine. If I do not dislike it, we may make our own apartments there, though he has his own estate and we shall spend some time there.'

'I hope you will come to London sometimes?'

Her aunt sounded wistful and Jenny smiled. 'You will be very welcome to come and stay wherever we live, Aunt—and my uncle, too.'

Aunt Martha dabbed at her eyes. 'How kind you are, my dear—and I must say you look delightful in that yellow colour.'

Jenny's wedding gown was of warm ivory silk, swathed across the bodice with layers of tulle and trimmed with Brussels lace at the edge of the elbow-length sleeves. She wore a bonnet of the same shade decorated with deep-yellow silk primroses and tied with yellow-satin ribbons at the side. Her stole was of heavy deep-yellow silk and trimmed with a small ivory fringe and tiny diamonds; her shoes had flared heels and were of soft ivory leather embroidered with yellow daises and centred with diamonds. Around her throat, she wore Adam's wedding gift—a double row of large creamy pearls with a deep topaz drop in the shape of a teardrop.

'You look wonderful,' Lucy said when she brought Jenny's bouquet of yellow roses with sprays of scented white freesias. 'I think I have never seen you look as lovely, dearest.'

'It is because I am happy and because of the lovely gown Adam chose for me,' she said. 'He wanted to arrange it all for me, though he has not seen it finished, of course—but he told the seamstress that he wanted a gown fit for a princess, which I believe it is.'

'Yes, it is lovely and suits you to perfection,' Lucy said and kissed her cheek. 'I love the pearls Adam sent you; they are gorgeous.'

'Beautiful,' Jenny agreed and kissed her back. 'I owe you so much, Lucy. Had you not invited me to stay with you I might never have met Adam.'

'Do you not think it was meant to be?'

'Perhaps…' Jenny paused as she heard her aunt calling to them. 'We must go down, Lucy. My uncle is waiting to take us to the church.'

Jenny's heart raced as she saw Adam waiting for her in front of the altar. The sun shone on the silver cross and candlesticks, shedding a variety of colours on to the old stone floor. Adam was so very handsome, dressed in a dark-blue coat, pristine white linen and pale-buff breeches with long boots, he stood out from the crowd. Jenny's heart filled with love for him, her breath catching in her throat. She had thought once that this day would never happen and she could scarce believe how lucky she was that he loved her, as she loved him.

He turned his head and smiled as she walked towards him, the look in his eyes sending little thrills of pleasure winging through her body. She knew that he thought her lovely, and, by the fire in his eyes, sensed that his thoughts were of later when they could be alone together. She longed for that too, but for the moment they must think of their guests and make sure that everyone enjoyed themselves—though for Jenny all that mattered was the smile in Adam's eyes as he greeted her.

'You are beautiful, my darling,' he murmured softly. 'I am so fortunate to have found you.'

Jenny half-shook her head, her eyes conveying that she believed she was the lucky one as he reached for her hand and held it and the vicar began the wedding ceremony.

'Dearly Beloved, we are gathered here this day

to join this man and this woman together in Holy Matrimony…'

Jenny's heart filled with joy as she heard the murmur of the congregation, the vicar's voice and outside the high tuneful song of a thrush. This was her perfect day and she would remember it all her life.

'I am delighted to meet you,' Earl Benedict said, taking her hand to kiss it. 'You are as lovely as my grandson told me and I believe he has been very fortunate in his choice of a bride. It is my fervent hope that I shall live long enough to see your son born.'

'Grandfather!' Adam protested.

'No, Adam, the earl means no harm. I shall do my best to oblige you, sir. I hope that we shall have at least two sons and a daughter—but I cannot promise it.'

'Damn me, but the girl has spirit,' the earl said and looked amused. 'I am certain that if you wish for such a family you will achieve it. I thought you lovely, but I did not know you had so much sense. Adam has chosen even better than I expected.'

'Grandfather is to stay in London for a few

days,' Adam said, 'which means we may stay at his house until we embark for France.'

'How lovely,' Jenny said. 'I was hoping to see your home very soon, sir, and that is a lovely surprise.'

'You have given me more than I had ever hoped for,' the earl told her. 'You must tell me what you wish for and if it is at all possible I shall grant your wish.'

Jenny laughed and shook her head, turning to look up at Adam. 'I already have everything I could ever want,' she said and held out her hand. She smiled as he took it and then bent his head to kiss it. 'But I shall enjoy seeing your home, sir.'

'Tonight I shall tell you what to expect,' Adam promised and the look in his eyes promised so much more.

They spent the night at a house provided by one of Adam's friends. It was a small country house staffed only by a few servants, who had been very discreet, leaving a tasty cold collation for them in the sitting room of the master suite in case they were hungry and then disappearing.

'Alone at last,' Adam said, reaching for his

lovely bride. 'Have you sensed how impatient I was to be alone with you, dearest?'

'No more impatient than I,' Jenny assured him. She looked up at him, anticipating his kiss. Her body was on fire with longing and a deep need that she hardly understood but knew was the need to be one with him—to be his wife in every way. 'Much as I enjoy the company of our friends— and I loved your grandpapa, Adam—but I too longed for this moment.'

'My sweet darling,' he said, stroking her cheek and down the line of her throat. His hand moved across her breast, which was soft beneath the thin muslin of her gown. 'Are you hungry? I believe they have done us proud if you care for something before we retire.'

'I told your grandfather that you are all I want. It was true then and it is true now, Adam. Please, take me to bed now. Make me your own, my dearest love. I have dreamed of this moment and I am ready...'

She needed to say no more for Adam's mouth was on hers, his kiss making her moan with pleasure and melt into him. Her nipples pouted and strained beneath her delicate gown, aching for his touch. He bent down to catch her behind the knees and carry her to the bed, sitting her down on the edge.

'I should have called for your maid,' he said, looking at her ruefully. 'I shall ruin your gown.'

'Unhook me,' Jenny invited and turned her back so that he could unfasten the tiny hooks at the back of her travelling gown. Once they were done, she shrugged it off her shoulders and together they tugged the skirt down. Their mutual impatience made Jenny giggle and she wriggled to help him free her of the silken gown. Now just in her delicate chemise, she looked at him, waiting for him to slip the straps down. 'Is it all right?' she asked as he hesitated. 'You are not disappointed?'

'Disappointed?' He looked incredulous. 'I was just enjoying the moment, Jenny. You are so lovely…' He slipped the delicate undergarment down, revealing her shapely breasts, and then bent his head to tease the pink nipples with the tip of his tongue. Jenny sighed and her body arched, her head going back as a ribbon of fire ran through her. She was burning up, losing control, as she gave herself up to voluptuous pleasure. 'My sweet precious darling…so beautiful…'

Adam eased the chemise from her so that she

was now naked. His eyes devoured her for some moments, then he bent his head and kissed both breasts before pushing her back into the soft pillows. Removing his clothes by ripping off his shirt and impatiently pulling off his breeches, he revealed just how impatient he was to claim his bride, his manhood leaping with anticipation as he lay down beside her and began to kiss her lips.

Stroking and kissing her, Adam brought Jenny gently along the path to passion, his mouth, tongue and hands playing her like a delicate instrument. As he sought out her inner citadel, he found her warm and wet with her own moisture. Her body moved beneath his hands, rising to his touch and beginning to writhe as the pleasure mounted.

'You are ready, my love?' he breathed against her ear.

'Oh, yes, yes,' she cried, moaning as he moved across her, the smooth hardness of his manhood pushing against her. His urgency was obvious as he parted her legs wider and moved across her, seeking entry and finding her wet and willing. She cried out as he entered and he stilled, but her fingers dug into his shoulders, the nails pressing into his skin, and he pressed further into her.

Then he began the slow rhythm of love that had been played out since a man first loved a woman. 'Yes…that is so lovely…'

Adam drew her on, their bodies slicked with sweat as they strained and eased and then strained again, searching for that place…and then as Jenny seemed to melt and fall into little pieces, Adam fell against her and spent himself inside her. A spasm of pleasure so intense it was almost pain shook her several times and she moaned in his arms, his lips against the hollow in her throat.

'Jenny, my darling…' Adam looked down at her in wonder, wiping the tears from her cheeks with his fingers. 'I did not hurt you?'

'No, how could you think it?' she said and buried her face in his shoulder, which tasted salty. 'Everything you did pleased me so much. I have never been so happy. I did not know that loving could be so perfect.'

'Nor did I, my love,' he said and laughed. 'No woman has ever made me feel that way—nor come close to meaning what you mean to me. You are all the things I ever admired or thought becoming in a woman and more.'

'Do you truly feel that?' she asked and sat up,

pushing him down into the pillows and gazing down at him. 'I know there must have been others...'

'If there were, there will not be again,' he vowed and kissed her, pulling her down on top of him and running his hands down the smooth arch of her back. 'You are all the woman I shall ever want, my sweet precious Jenny.'

Jenny laughed and reached up to kiss him, then, a teasing look in her eyes, she said. 'How long before we can do that again?'

'My greedy little cat,' Adam said and laughed. 'I think we shall have a glass of wine to refresh us... and then I shall see what I can do to please you.'

'Oh, Adam...' Jenny was breathless with excitement as she saw the house for the first time. 'I thought you said it was a bleak place? I have never seen anything as lovely. I adore it!'

'Truly?' He looked at her in surprise and took her hand. 'You are not just saying it to please me?'

'No, it is just a perfect house for us—if your grandfather would allow us to share it.'

'It would please him very much. I suppose you could refurbish it to your liking.'

The house had been built centuries earlier, its

walls of yellowish-buff stone warm in the sunshine. The windows were many and criss-crossed with lead so that the little panes looked like jewels in the sunlight, the roof sloping and tiled with slate that looked blue beneath an azure sky. Although in need of some repairs here and there to the stonework, it was a graceful house of classical lines. Set back at the end of a long drive of ancient oak trees, it had wide sweeping lawns, a sunken garden and a sundial, besides roses growing over the verandas. As the carriage stopped and Adam helped Jenny down, she looked about her with excitement.

'Papa's house was nice, but it was so modern—this is wonderful,' she cried. 'I have always wished to live in an old house like this. Tell me, is there a priest hole or a secret passage? Are there flagstones and steps—and can you wander from room to room, always discovering some new secret?'

'Yes to all your questions,' Adam said and laughed as her excitement bubbled over. 'I suppose I liked the house when I was younger, but in recent years I had grown used to seeing it only as a monster that guzzled money and always needing repairs that could not be afforded.'

'We can afford them now, can we not? I should

love to restore it, to make it beautiful for another hundred years—could we do that?'

'Yes, if you wish it,' Adam said. He reached for her hands. 'How did I become so fortunate, Jenny? Tell me how I may deserve you, if you please, for I can hardly believe how lucky I am.'

'Oh, I dare say I may think of something to-night,' she teased, a wicked look in her eyes. She laughed up at him. 'Are you going to carry me over the threshold of our new home, Adam?'

'Naturally,' he said and swept her into his arms. He looked down at her with love as they approached the line of smiling servants. 'Good morning, Harris. My wife will greet you all in a moment. I believe we should be down in half an hour, but she wishes to see her apartments…'

Leaving them smiling and whispering behind their backs, Adam carried her up the stairs to the apartments he had chosen. Once they were inside he kicked the door shut behind them.

It was at least an hour later that he summoned some very happy-looking servants to the great hall to tell them that their new mistress was ready to meet them—and that she had decided to make her home here amongst them.

His announcement was greeted with cheers of approval and relief—and then he ordered champagne for everyone.

* * * * *

Discover more romance at

www.millsandboon.co.uk

- ❤ WIN great prizes in our exclusive competitions
- ❤ BUY new titles before they hit the shops
- ❤ BROWSE new books and REVIEW your favourites
- ❤ SAVE on new books with the Mills & Boon® Bookclub™
- ❤ DISCOVER new authors

PLUS, to chat about your favourite reads, get the latest news and find special offers:

- f Find us on facebook.com/millsandboon
- 🐦 Follow us on twitter.com/millsandboonuk
- ❤ Sign up to our newsletter at millsandboon.co.uk